St[...]
Painting

Also by Cheryl Hollon

Webb's Glass Shop Mystery Series
Pane and Suffering
Shards of Murder
Cracked to Death
Etched in Tears
Shattered at Sea
Down in Flames

Paint & Shine Mystery Series
Still Knife Painting

Published by Kensington Publishing Corp.

Still Knife Painting

Cheryl Hollon

KENSINGTON BOOKS
www.kensingtonbooks.com

KENSINGTON BOOKS are published by

Kensington Publishing Corp.
119 West 40th Street
New York, NY 10018

All Kensington titles, imprints, and distributed lines are available at special quantity discounts for bulk purchases for sales promotion, premiums, fund-raising, and educational or institutional use.

Special book excerpts or customized printings can also be created to fit specific needs. For details, write or phone the office of the Kensington Sales Manager: Kensington Publishing Corp., 119 West 40th Street, New York, NY 10018. Attn. Sales Department. Phone: 1-800-221-2647.

Kensington and the K logo Reg. U.S. Pat. & TM Off.

ISBN-13: 978-1-4967-2524-0
ISBN-10: 1-4967-2524-7
First Kensington Books Mass-Market Printing: July 2020

ISBN-13: 978-1-4967-2525-7 (eBook)
ISBN-10: 1-4967-2525-5 (eBook)
First Kensington Books Electronic Edition: July 2020

10 9 8 7 6 5 4 3 2 1

Printed in the United States of America

Dedicated to my late grandparents
Della Mae and Howard Courtney Buchanan

Acknowledgments

This first book in a brand-new series has been a lovely trip down memory lane. My parents are both from the area where this story is set, Wolfe County, Kentucky. I've spent most of my summers running barefoot in the soft grass, gazing up at the Milky Way in the evenings, and hiking the hundreds of trails in the Daniel Boone National Forest. Although I'm a good cook, I'll never reach the standard of biscuit perfection that my grandmother baked every single morning. I can still taste them. I hope I have done justice to a complicated part of my upbringing.

I have so many people to thank for getting this book out of my head and onto the page. It's always a long journey and sometimes the path disappears or wanders away. Luckily, I have a tribe of supporters.

I thank my parents for a wildly original raising. Mom and Dad thought that children should be shown how to live, not lectured into it. My mom taught her two girls and two boys how to cook, clean, knit, sew, paint, draw, and not be afraid to tackle anything new. She praised the trying—not the result. My dad is gone now but he taught us all to hunt, fish, camp, track, shoot, garden, and how to use power tools. They both instilled in me a work ethic that I still appreciate.

My mother's parents let me run loose on their little truck farm most summers. I loved the smell of barns, gardens, and wildflowers. I treasured the freedom to paddle in the creek, climb the big hill, pet the cow, torment the chickens, and generally make a huge nuisance of myself. They're buried in a peaceful cemetery overlooking the tiny bend in the road village of Trent, Kentucky.

My mother's parents were hardworking, generous, kind, and clever back-country folk. My Grandma Buchanan was the best biscuit maker in Wolfe County. That was an important skill in those days. She made at least an iron skillet full every morning from knee-high until way into her eighties.

My mother's middle brother, Harold Gene Buchanan, inspired the Uncle Gene character in this series. He left us too early but managed to leave behind an inspirational and scientific legacy to his family and friends. He was a big personality full of boundless energy, curiosity, and drive. He showed me, by example, that your background doesn't limit your ability to achieve your dreams.

Ramona DeFelice Long is an amazing award-winning writer, editor extraordinaire, and refined woman with deep roots in the southern heart of Louisiana. She knows what makes a good story and can tell me in a way that doesn't scare the ever-loving bejesus out of me. Thank you from the bottom of my heart.

First readers are important and I have a powerful one. We exchange pages every month and meet to discuss them. Sam Falco, you're my hero.

I'm crushed to report that my wonderful agent, Beth Campbell, has left BookEnds Literary Agency to pursue the next stage in her publishing career. She has inspired me to write better and try harder to produce the best writing I can. I wish her the very best. I know we'll hear about her soon.

My new agent is James McGowan, the latest member of the cast of rock stars that make up the fabulous staff that Jessica Faust of BookEnds Literary Agency has gathered. He's enthusiastic about this new series and my new projects. I'm counting on him to be my champion in negotiating the twisty passages of modern publishing.

My extraordinary editor at Kensington Publishing Corporation, Elizabeth Trout, has managed to take my jumbled plot threads and wibbly-wobbly emotional crises and unfailingly guide me to a much better story. Larissa Ackerman has been devoted to this series by consulting with me to brainstorm new promotional and marketing themes with creative and fresh ideas. I finally met Michelle Addo, who rocks Kensington's new CozyClub Mini-Cons held all over the country. When I appeared with the other cozy writers at Poisoned Pen Bookstore in Scottsdale, Arizona, it was a bucket list event for me.

I wouldn't be published at all if not for the Sisters in Crime organization and their online chapter, the Guppies. The fishy name comes from the following: The Great Unpublished. The chapter started out as a collection of unpublished writers sharing information about the confounding world of publishing. The secret to its success is that after reaching that revered status of published, the members stay in the group and reach back to help others. Out of more than 860 members, the split is now about 50/50 published to unpublished. If you have any inclination to follow the writer's journey, you need to sign up right now. Here's the link for the national group: https://www.sistersincrime.org

I am grateful for the dedication of booksellers everywhere who love readers and are kind to writers. My local bookstore in downtown St. Petersburg, Florida, is Haslam's Book Store at 2025 Central Avenue. The owners have welcomed me with unstinting support and I've even been honored to meet all four of the bookstore cats: Beowulf, Teacup, Clancy, and Emily Dickinson.

My next favorite local bookstore is owned and managed by the irrepressible Nancy Alloy of Books at Park Place. She has moved to a new location in nearby Pasadena Shopping Center near our beautiful beaches. I enjoy talking all things books with her and her dog, the very skeptical Watson, who greets me with subtle and rare affection.

Finally, I'm delighted to announce the new gun in town, Tombolo Books. Owner Alsace Walentine makes it her personal mission to get to know the people in her community so that she can provide a succinctly curated bookstore. I am so lucky to live in the Tampa Bay area.

In today's online world, book bloggers influence who discovers your books. I met my first real live book advocate at Malice Domestic, Dru Ann Love, who runs https://drusbookmusing.com, posts reviews, cover reveals, new releases, and interviews. Her main feature is "A Day in the Life" essays in the voice of the character of a new mystery. Thanks, Dru—I'll hug you in the hotel lobby at the next mystery conference.

My muse of many years, Joye Barnes, is completely responsible for my lack of writer's block. Every time I get a little stuck, I mentally look her in the eyes and ask, "What would you be thrilled to have happen next?"

Many writers struggle through their writing process hideously alone without the support of their families. I'm not one of those. I have the devoted encouragement of my sons, daughters-in-love, grandchildren, parents, brothers, sisters, and a large extended family.

I am so grateful to you, the readers. There is no greater reward than to hear that one of my books helped someone get through a difficult time by providing a few hours of distraction. That's one of the reasons I write. Other than the fact that I'm completely addicted to writing, of course.

George is my constant cheerleader, relentless taskmaster, overall handyman, and ever ready book bag carrier in support of my writing dream. He has earned the title of trophy husband for his role in this adventure.

Chapter 1

Miranda Trent felt the color drain from her face as she stared at the blood on her kitchen floor. Of the many nightmares she had experienced over the last few weeks, none held a candle to the living reality of death at her feet.

The brilliant fall morning had started with such promise.

Her rescued puppy, Sandy, had slept through the night for the first time.

She perfected her morning cup of coffee by simply using a filter to purify the tap water and adding organic half and half.

Her Kentucky farmhouse smelled pine fresh and lemony clean after yesterday's manic efforts to get it spic-and-span ready for her clients.

Every detail was as perfect as she could make this first day of a new venture.

Promises were destined to be broken.

But she didn't expect so many at one time.

Chapter 2

Saturday Morning, Hemlock Lodge

Miranda paced like a soldier, her fists clenched, her heart beating fast, as she chanted under her breath, "Please don't let me die. Don't let me die of embarrassment." Weeks of planning, permitting, construction, advertising, practicing, and loss of sleep had brought her to this point of excited anticipation. Her business was a real enterprise.

The thick treads of her hiking boots echoed on the oak wood floor, and her threadbare black corduroys swooshed with every step. Her path crossed in front of the two-story stone fireplace, the focal point inside the lobby of Hemlock Lodge.

It was built in the typical architecture of the 1960s. Perched upon a dramatic ledge, it offered stunning views from the wraparound balconies that overlooked the Red River far below. Deep in the Daniel Boone National Forest in the highlands of eastern Kentucky, it supplied the best accommodations nearest the hiking trails. It was the quiet time of the morning, right after the lodge guests ate a massive breakfast and headed out for the day's adventure hikes.

Miranda glanced at the wall near the entry door to make sure her flyer was still pinned onto the bulletin board. She had replaced it three times in the past week. Someone was removing them and she thought it might be the receptionist. An entire stack from the brochure stand had disappeared as well.

She considered it a positive sign that six clients had managed to overcome the miserable internet access to find her website and sign up for her cultural adventure tour. Miranda pulled a loose thread from the small red logo embroidered over the front pocket of her special-ordered khaki shirt. It was designed to be untucked to give her a wide range of movement. The logo branded her new business, Paint & Shine.

She scanned the wide-angle view of the valley below through the floor-to-ceiling windows. The trees sparkled with the excitement of change that fall colors brought to the rugged cliffs of eastern Kentucky. For the first time, the beauty of the trees didn't calm her.

Sleepless nights didn't help her mood. Her worries thrived and multiplied in her restless mind—a creative mind that kept coming up with more and more ways for her business to fail. Statistics revealed that four out of five new businesses failed within the first year.

She fiddled with the six pin-on badges in her hands, one for each client who had paid for a three-

hour cultural adventure. It combined a group
painting at a scenic overlook with a traditional
Southern dinner at her farmhouse, and finally a
moonshine lecture with samples presented by the
owner of a distillery. Six backpacks sat beside the
fireplace loaded with the supplies her clients would
need to complete a painting of the overlook at
Lover's Leap.

Group painting classes were popular in New
York City, where last month she had been eking
out a scant living as a classical portrait artist. Typically, each client would bring a bottle of wine or
growler of craft beer, paint along with an instructor, and take home a finished painting and memories of a great night out. Her business was a new
concept for this area of outstanding natural
beauty. The nearest competitor was in downtown
Lexington, Kentucky—more than an hour's drive
away.

Her mother had questioned her choice. "You, a
teacher? You're too quiet!" That had stung, but
Miranda felt strongly about sharing the simple joy
of painting a beautiful view in the great outdoors
on a mountain trail—no screens, no music, only
nature. *This is important; I'll deal with my introver-
sion.*

"Are you waiting for someone, honey?" The white-
haired, sharp-eyed, plump woman behind the registration counter looked over her red half-moon
reading glasses at the still pacing Miranda.

"Yes, ma'am. I'm waiting for my class to arrive."
Miranda walked over to the counter. "My name is
Miranda Trent. I'm the art instructor for today's

outdoor painting class. It's the notice that's pinned up over there." She pointed to the bulletin board.

"Trent? Are you one of those Trents out by Laurel Valley? You have their look about you."

Miranda nodded. "My grandparents used to run the post office and general store over in Laurel. Well, actually, Grandma ran the post office while Grandpa ran the store. It was mostly a gathering place. In summer, Grandpa sat out on the porch swapping knives and whittling wood sticks with the other old men. In winter, they moved indoors to sit around the wood stove beating each other at checkers."

"I declare, now that I look at you, there's a faint resemblance to your mother all right. You're lucky to get the wavy black hair and green eyes." The woman leaned forward and smiled. "It looks like you skipped out on inheriting the broad Trent nose. How's your momma faring?"

"Very well, ma'am. She says she'll come down from Dayton to visit me every other weekend." Miranda nervously shifted her weight like a schoolgirl. She stopped when she noticed it. "I think she's a bit homesick."

"Along with half the folks in Ohio and Indiana. We went to high school together many, many years past. Well, you tell your momma that Doris Ann Norris says hi and that I still miss her wonderful Peanut Butter Potato Pinwheels."

"I'll mention that the next time she calls." Miranda twisted her lip sideways, uncertain of Doris Ann's feelings towards her. "And since I moved here, she calls several times a day." Without thinking she pulled her cell from her back pocket and checked for messages. There weren't any, yet.

"She must be worried," said Doris Ann.

Miranda tucked away the phone. "Maybe. When I moved to New York City, it was once a week at best. As soon as I move back to her hometown, she's like a mama bear with a truant cub."

The front door opened, and Miranda snapped her head to look at an old couple with their arms hooked together and using canes on their opposite sides. Definitely not her clients.

"Did I hear right?" continued Doris. "That you moved back into your late Uncle Gene's farmhouse up on Pine Ridge?"

"He left it to me in his will. I wasn't expecting it. He was always interested in my paintings—he even bought a few—but I thought he was just trying to give me some cash for art supplies. I was shocked to be the sole beneficiary."

"He was a good upstanding man, your uncle. He had a big heart."

"My mom sent me to stay with him most summers. I keep expecting him to come into the house with a stomping of dusty boots on the porch and a slamming of the screen door." She pressed her hand to cover her mouth for a moment.

"I wonder why I didn't see you those summers. Most youngsters are up here climbing all through the trails in these woods."

"I mostly helped Uncle Gene with his big garden. After chores, I sketched outdoors and then after supper, I read books in my room. The neighbors barely knew I was there." She looked at her watch—only ten minutes yet to go.

"Are you getting settled in?"

"I moved in last month, but I still feel like a fish out of water." The farmhouse was located about midway between Hemlock Lodge and Campton, the nearest town.

I also had a lot in common with my Uncle Gene. We shared the problems of coping with our introverted personalities in an ever more social world. I loved my summers of peace and quiet.

Doris Ann suddenly stood up with a great heave, and came around to smother Miranda in a hug that lasted a full minute, ending with a backrub. "Honey, hearing that your Uncle Gene passed away was such sorry news."

Miranda felt the enormous pain of losing her favorite uncle wash over her—again.

She wanted to run and hide. Hugging was another serious challenge for her. As a child, she had been able to squirm out and run away, but not as an adult. She marveled at the unstinting compassion that was second nature in her large collection of Kentucky cousins.

They were all huggers.

Doris Ann released her and held Miranda out at arm's length. "Your uncle was a gentle soul. He kept that little farm going all by himself longer than he should have with his bad heart. The turnout for his funeral was the largest that Wolfe County has seen in a mighty long time. I don't remember seeing you there. Did I miss you in the crowd?"

Miranda carefully escaped Doris Ann's hold. "No, I didn't make it to his funeral. I had a Midtown gallery opening that day. I had worked on the portraits for months. He would have understood, but I still regret not being at the graveside. I heard it was a lovely service and he's buried right down the road from the farmhouse in the old Adams Cemetery." Miranda coughed to clear a catch in her throat. "That's a comfort. I sort of feel like he's watching over me."

Doris Ann pointed to the Paint & Shine flyer on the bulletin board in the hallway. "I didn't know that was you. You must have spoken to the manager on one of my days off." She tilted her head back and frowned. "He give you any trouble?"

Miranda thought about it. "No, he seemed a little stiff, but not negative."

"Well, he's not from around here. The flyer just says the name of the business—not that you're the owner or that you're a local. Anyway, bring your next flyer straight to me. I'll put it up, no fuss. So, this is a new business?"

"Yes. This is the first event and I need to get enough clients before the end of the year to pay for the farm's property taxes. I'm trying to get employment in the school system as a temporary art teacher, but that's going to take some time," said Miranda. Miranda tugged at the bottom of her shirt, a nervous tic she first displayed in kindergarten. *This is awful. I'm gabbling. Why did I tell her all that?*

"Well, bless your heart, dearest. Folks 'round here don't really hold much stock in artists and their freewheeling ways." Doris Ann shook a stubby finger. "It just doesn't seem like a proper way to make a livin'. How's this deal work?"

"I know this is unusual for the area, but there

are lots of tourists who are looking for a cultural experience and something to take home as a souvenir. I provide all the painting supplies and step-by-step instruction. No art experience needed. Then, after the class, we go to the farmhouse for a home-cooked meal paired with moonshine cocktails from the Keystone Branch Distillery."

"Well, I don't hold with spirits," huffed Doris Ann. "You've certainly put a lot thought into this. I hope it works out."

She noticed the pleasant tone in Doris Ann's voice turn cold enough to freeze a river.

Her head held high and her spine stiff, Doris Ann returned to sit behind the reception desk. She reached for a stack of papers and began to straighten them into a tidy pile.

Miranda's chest tightened and her insides quivered. Her mother had warned her that Doris Ann might disapprove of the moonshine component of her cultural adventure. An alcoholic brother had caused Doris Ann to take on a near evangelical opposition to drink. Since it was in a state park, the Hemlock Lodge served no alcoholic beverages. It was the perfect place of employment for Doris Ann.

Miranda nodded a goodbye and resumed pacing in front of the fireplace, peering at everyone who walked into Hemlock Lodge. Mentally, she reviewed the various ways her business could fail. Like a threatening storm, the worries returned to plague her. One of them was the situation she faced right now—no one would show up.

The door swished open to admit a family of five with two toddlers and an infant in a stroller so large that it looked like it could comfortably hold a baby elephant.

This is absolutely horrible. No one will show up on the first day. I'm a failure.

Finally, at five minutes past the official start of 9:30 a.m., a well-groomed, tall, almond-skinned man walked over with his hand stretched out. "Hi, you must be the painting instructor. I'm Joe Creech from Dothan, Alabama," he said in a soft Southern tone. He drew his hand through close-cropped jet-black curls with a distinctive white patch of hair over his right eye.

"Welcome, Joe." Miranda shook his hand too hard and with too many pumps. "Here's your badge and a backpack with everything you'll need out on the trail over to our lookout at Lover's Leap. You're a long way from home. If you don't mind my asking, what brings you here?"

Really? Try to stop chattering.

"I've received an exploratory grant from my university to support my doctoral research. Mainly, I'm going to look through the town hall records to gather income and population data." Joe pinned the badge to the front of his green plaid flannel shirt. "I'll be here for a couple of weeks."

"You know the trail is classified as challenging?"

Joe tilted his head back and laughed easily. "Yes, I read that on your website." He patted his round belly. "I'm actually in pretty good shape. I'm not decrepit, yet. I have quite a few more years to go before retirement. I'll be fine." Then he wandered over to the huge windows to watch the bird feeding stations installed along the sidewalk on the cliff side of the lodge.

Popping in from around the corner by the elevators, a young couple holding hands nearly walked into the low bentwood coffee table before looking away from each other. The slim, fair-haired young woman put a hand over her mouth. "Oops, excuse me, I wasn't paying attention. Are you the instructor for the painting class?"

"Yes, I'm your group leader, Miranda Trent." She shuffled through the badges in her hand and drew out two. "You must be Mr. and Mrs. Hoffman, the newlyweds."

The petite bride looked at her equally blond husband. "That's the first time we've been called that." She clapped her hands together. "Mr. and Mrs. Hoffman. I love the sound of that. It's so romantic."

The young man flushed to his ears, looked away from his bride, and turned to Miranda. "Call us Laura and Brian, please. We're from Akron, Ohio."

Brian smiled weakly and took the badges from Miranda. He pinned a badge to Laura's neon pink sweatshirt. She followed that by rising up on her tiptoes with a leg kicked up and giving him a quick kiss on the cheek. He blushed a deeper rose and pinned the badge onto his own sweatshirt. Oblivious, Laura dragged her new husband over to the loveseat, where she plopped down and pulled him beside her. She grabbed his hand in both of hers.

"Is this the painting class?" said a fortyish woman in designer jeans accompanied by another plump woman in similar jeans. Both wore red Converse shoes.

"Welcome to the Daniel Boone National Forest,"

said Miranda. "You must be Kelly Davis and Linda Sanders—all the way from New York City."

Kelly took both badges. "That's us."

Miranda looked down the short corridor to the entry door and didn't see anyone else. She had one more client in the class. The sequencing of the events meant that her schedule was tight, and any delays could cascade into a timetable disaster. She needed to leave the lodge right now and get out on the trail to keep from using up all her slack time.

If he doesn't show, I'll have to refund his money and there goes any profit. With only five clients, I'll barely break even. First lesson learned—allow a lot more time for gathering everyone together before the hike.

Looking at her watch to confirm that it was more than fifteen minutes past the class start time, Miranda stepped over to the reception desk. "Doris Ann, I'm expecting one more client. He hasn't arrived, but we need to get out there on the trail. Could you do me a big favor and give him his badge along with a backpack? Just tell him to follow the markers for the Original Trail and then follow the number nine Laurel's Ridge Trail out to Lover's Leap."

"Sure, I can do that. I'll mark up a map and send him on his way."

Miranda felt a sense of pride. The one thing you could count on from country folk is that they are eternally helpful, the good ones anyway.

Her jaw clenched, Miranda picked up her backpack and motioned to her class. Five clients would be a break-even day for her business—not a horrible start. "We've got to get on the trail. Follow me."

Chapter 3

Saturday Morning, View of Lover's Leap

If those towering cliffs could speak, Miranda thought they would have told her to take her clumsy, noisy, clueless clients back down to Hemlock Lodge, instantly refund their Paint & Shine cultural adventure fee, and direct them to move back to the city at once. Luckily for her, cliffs don't speak—they merely hint at danger through silent looming menace.

The clients stood as mute as statues at the trail's end. It was common to be awestruck by the beauty of the deadly view. Miranda gazed at Lover's Leap and for the millionth time lost herself in the stacked rocks and whispering pines. The group managed the steep climb up to Natural Bridge and stood at the end of the sandstone arch. The main trail continued to a stunning overlook.

Joe was barely out of breath. Only Linda seemed to struggle a bit. But after quickly crossing the flat arch over the valley, she gulped down half her water and recovered her breath in good time. "Why didn't you warn me we would be so high? I'm afraid of heights."

"I'm so sorry. I'll add that to the flyer for the future."

After taking yet another unnecessary head count, Miranda turned to face her little class. She felt a bubbling gurgle in her gut.

Goodness, I'm way more nervous than I thought I would be. Teaching is not going to be a piece of cake, but I've got to do this if I want to make this business a success.

Miranda took a long deep breath and cleared her throat.

"I scouted out this large clearing just a few steps over here to the right of the view. It's roomy enough for all of us to paint." Miranda walked along the cliff trail a few yards and slipped the backpack off her shoulders and placed it in a leaf-littered space about ten feet from the cliff's edge. "This is where we'll paint our landscapes. I'm going to set up right over here. So, each of you choose a spot behind me where you can see my canvas and still have a view of Lover's Leap."

"This is so beautiful," said Joe Creech. "It looks a little bit like the Ozark Mountains. I feel right at home."

Miranda pulled two folded easels from her backpack. "Oh, I almost forgot. Don't block the trail. This is one of the more popular hikes." She unfolded and stood up two easels. She placed a blank canvas on one and a finished painting of Lover's Leap on the other. "I always stand while I paint, but if you want, you can sit on your canvas bag. The easels will adjust to either height."

"Sweetie," whispered Laura to Brian loud enough for Miranda to hear. "Let's put our bags close together and sit in the back away from the others." She took her groom by the hand and they fashioned themselves a little nest area.

Now that they were about to paint, Miranda smiled with confidence. "We're using a quick-dry acrylic paint. I'll squirt puddles of the colors we're going to use onto your paper pallets. Use the mason jar for washing out your brushes. Put the jar on the ground and put your three brushes inside it. For any of you experienced artists, don't worry about damaging your brushes by keeping them in the water. These are student grade acrylic brushes. Definitely not the kind Rembrandt would use. We're only going to be out here for about an hour. Trust me, your water cup is the safest and cleanest place for them."

Each of her clients finally claimed a painting spot in the clearing. There was a good deal of friendly chatter as they juggled and jostled on the narrow path. It was a good sign. A happy class was easy to teach. She noticed that Joe looked a little lost.

After they settled and placed a blank canvas on the shelf of their easels, Miranda took a large bottle of water and poured two inches into each mason jar. "Just for fun but mostly for clarity, I've named your brushes Papa Bear, Mama Bear, and Baby Bear. Can you guess which one is which?"

There were giggles and groans through the group.

"Let's get up in the front," said Kelly to Linda. "I love the colors of the trees, especially the bright yellow and vivid red. It's breathtaking and I want to be closer."

Miranda grabbed her six-pack of paint bottles nestled in a cardboard soda carrier. Each color was held in a large ketchup-type bottle about the size of a one-quart milk container. She squirted a generous glob of each color onto everyone's palettes.

"First, we'll lay in the sky on the top third of our canvas. You'll notice that I put your paint colors on the edge of your palettes. That's so we can use the center for mixing colors. Now, don't fuss about that too much. We're all going to paint in the French Impressionist style, which means we are seeking to create a general impression of a scene, not a photographic likeness.

"Okay, so the deal here is that I go first to show you what needs to happen and then you paint." Miranda picked up her largest brush and held it in the air. "Use Papa Bear to gather up a generous glop of blue. Then, still using Papa Bear, gather up about half that much white and mix them like this." Miranda tilted her palette and showed everyone. "Now, it isn't necessary to mix the colors completely. You want a little interest and texture in your brush strokes."

Miranda noticed that her brush was trembling. She put her hand down by her side for a moment and inhaled a slow deep breath.

Just keep calm—you can do this.

Then she raised her brush and laid down a nice blue sky using a twisting motion to add texture to the quickly drying paint. She stepped back from the canvas and looked around at the class. "That's another thing you want to do. Step back and look at your work from a distance. Now it's your turn. Go for it."

Timidly, slowly, one by one, each client began working on the sky of their painting. At each canvas, she made small suggestions to encourage them to brush more freely. "It's normal to feel a little stiff at first. Just try to loosen up."

She walked among the clients. Joe had finished and was staring out at the view. "Isn't it fascinating?"

He returned from his thoughts and smiled. "It seems so ageless. Time must mean very little to those rocks."

Miranda agreed.

She waited until everyone had completed the sky before she went back to her canvas. "Now, clean off your brush by swishing it in the mason jar of water, then wipe it dry on your paint rag."

"Yuck!" said Laura. "My water is all blue now. Won't that mess up the rest of the colors?"

"Good question. The answer is no. Don't worry about the color of your rinse water. That doesn't affect the brush, the color, or the painting. I know it seems like it should, but the color is so diluted that it doesn't."

Miranda picked up her brush. "Now, take your clean brush—"

"Aha!" echoed loudly on the trail behind Miranda. She jumped a foot and bumped her easel. She grabbed the edge of the wet painting and saved it from tumbling into the dirt and leaves along with the easel.

"What the—" she sputtered. She turned.

"I found you!" A large heavyset young man appeared at the outcrop of the view. "I am so doggone sorry. I got up in plenty of time, but somehow, I just didn't get a-goin' fast enough to meet you at the lodge." He was black haired with ice-blue eyes and wore an all-black ensemble of jeans, cowboy boots, and a classic Rockabilly Western shirt decorated with snap buttons. His accent tagged him as local. "And then, a course, my truck balked at starting up so early."

Miranda smiled. "I'm happy to see you." She poked her brush into the mason jar and scrambled over to shake his hand. "Find yourself a nice spot where you can see the view as well as see my painting. I'll get you caught up to the rest of us in two shakes. You couldn't have arrived at a more perfect time. I see that Doris Ann gave you your badge."

"Thanks, ma'am. I'm mighty sorry to cause you so much trouble."

"I'm glad that nothing serious delayed you. So, you're Shefton Adams." Miranda handed him his materials. "We may be related on my dad's side. His mother was an Adams from over on Pine Ridge."

"Then we are surely related. I live right down there across the road from the old Adams homestead in Gene Buchanan's farmhouse." He embraced her in a huge bear hug that lifted her feet off the ground. She stiffened and wanted to push him away but smiled brightly to cover an aversion to public displays of affection.

The newlyweds giggled.

I keep forgetting that bear hugging is like shaking hands here. My New York City ways are not helping me.

After he planted her back on the ground, she raised her voice. "Everyone, this is Shefton Adams. He's a local and apparently, we're cousins. If you'd just sound off with your name and where you're from."

Each client welcomed Shefton with an introduction. Miranda waited until everyone had returned their attention to her before continuing. "Now, back to painting. We're going to work on our painting, moving down the canvas from the background to the foreground." She noticed the frown on Kelly's brow. "That means from the top of the canvas to the bottom of the canvas." She used her brush as a pointer on the finished painting.

"This is the best time of year for painting this view. The fall colors are gorgeous. What we want to do is make varying sized blobs of the colors. First, we want to make the background colors a little muted to give them the illusion of distance."

She took a shallow breath and swallowed to clear her voice. It always took her a little bit of time to get comfortable with speaking to a class. She could tell by the scratchiness in her voice. She also knew to trust that it would go away.

Miranda used green, yellow ocher, and orange to demonstrate the distant view of the fall foliage. "I'm making these color blobs fairly small towards the top of the canvas and then making them brighter and larger towards the bottom. That gives it a perspective." She walked around to their canvases. "You guys are doing incredible."

"Help! I've got too much orange." Joe stepped

back from his canvas. "I didn't realize it until just now."

"Let me look." Miranda stood at his canvas. "Yes, too many orange blobs make the leaves look like a neon bar sign. Let this section dry and go back over the orange bits with some ocher to tone them down. You don't have to cover them all. We do have some years where the trees turn mostly orange, but this year seems to be a yellow one."

Miranda showed them how to mix ocher, white, and a touch of black. Then she laid in the next block of color that would become the tall cliff of the rugged chimney stacks of Lover's Leap.

Shefton hadn't yet completed setting up his easel. He was trying to get it level in the uneven scrub just beside the trail. Miranda noticed his struggles and pushed one of the easel legs into a bit of soft ground. He grinned. "Thanks."

Linda and Kelly were not only keeping pace with Miranda, but they were finishing their painting steps in minimum time. She figured that being from New York City gave them an understanding of art just by living there. That was certainly her experience with the Big Apple. They appeared to be confident and relaxed.

In about forty-five minutes, when they reached the final stages of painting, a lean young man in a dark green uniform appeared on the trail. He walked over to the group with his thumbs in his belt and a broad smile across his weathered face. "Your group has definitely captured the fall colors, Miss Trent." He rocked back on his heels. "Doris Ann sent me down here to give you a little history

about our famous view up here at Lover's Leap.
That is, of course, if you want to know."

Miranda sighed in relief. She had been expecting him but had not been able to confirm that he
would be able to give one of the rangers' cele-
brated talks out on the trail instead of in front of
the fireplace at Hemlock Lodge. "I would very
much appreciate that."

She hoped that adding a speech on local history
to her class would make the group feel more connected to the area—and set the mood for some authentic cuisine and moonshine. She beamed her
gratitude at him. "Thank you." Then she turned to
the class. "Clean off your brushes and stick them
in your water jar. We have a surprise speaker." She
signaled for the ranger to come up to where she
was standing.

He walked over by Miranda, turned and faced
the clients with his arms folded across his chest.
"Good morning, I'm Austin Morgan, your local
forest ranger here in the Daniel Boone National
Forest. The view you're painting is our most famous, Lover's Leap. The area you're exploring by
trail is reckoned to have the most natural sandstone arches east of the Mississippi River. Please in-
terrupt me at any time. I don't really have a
memorized talk, so your questions actually guide
my remarks."

He waited for a couple of seconds. "This park
was established in nineteen twenty-six but tourists
have been coming through here since eighteen
eighty-nine. Natural Bridge is a sandstone arch
that is seventy-eight feet long, sixty-five feet high,

twelve feet thick, and twenty feet wide. Some geologists believe that the arch is at least a million years old. Now that you've been on the trail, what do you think?"

"What's the legend behind Lover's Leap?" asked Kelly.

"Ah, of course. There are several variations of the story and nothing has ever been proven. The valley below here is only accessible by dedicated trail buffs and expert rock climbers—too rugged for most. But that's not the only reason this area is shunned by the locals. They're convinced that the chimney of rocks over there is cursed."

"Cursed? Oh no!" The New Yorker girlfriends pretended to be scared by waving their hands in the air, then giggled.

Miranda rolled her eyes and shrugged an apology to the ranger.

"The most popular legend behind the Lover's Leap name is about a Native American princess, Winona, the daughter of a Cherokee chief. She chose to leap rather than marry a cruel suitor she did not love. Her spirit is rumored to appear on this very trail on the night of the new moon. That's when the forest is the darkest." He paused for effect. "I personally think she just likes to show up better."

He grinned, then pointed down the trail. "Right about there, just by that crooked pine at the last bend in the trail."

Everyone turned and looked.

Ranger Morgan paused until all of them stared at the trail. "Everyone who has ever claimed to see

Winona has described her as wearing white buck-skin."

"Have you ever seen her?" asked Kelly.

He pressed his lips together. "I'm not sure. Like most locals, I'm not out in the woods after dark for good reason. I've had several unsettling experiences along this trail, but I can't claim to have seen her."

Kelly shrugged her shoulders. "Too bad. That would make a great ghost story."

Ranger Morgan waited for the group to settle. "Another tale is that the brothers of a ruined maid threw her lover to his death. There was a strong moral code in the beliefs of the original European settlers, the Scotch Irish. They brought their clannish ways to these highlands along with their music. They kept to themselves and handled their troubles without the aid of the law.

"After the maid left the baby with the father's family, she also came out here and threw herself to her death.

"Finally, it is rumored that during the height of the infamous family feud, a Hatfield girl and a McCoy boy ran away to get married, but were cornered. They embraced and threw themselves over so that they could be together in eternity."

"Shoot! I've dropped my paintbrush," said Shefton. "I'm almighty sorry, miss."

"Don't worry. I have plenty of extras." Miranda handed over a fresh brush to Shefton. "Sorry for interrupting; please continue."

Ranger Morgan smiled and hooked his thumbs through his belt loops. "No problem, Miss Trent.

I'm finished." He scanned the group. "Any more questions?"

Linda waved her hand. "Where did Daniel Boone live?"

Scratching at the back of his neck, Ranger Morgan laughed out loud. "I was wondering who would ask that one. I get that one the most. Anyway, the short answer is that he founded the village of Boonesborough, one of the first settlements west of the Appalachians.

"Boonesborough is a small unincorporated community in Madison County, about forty-five miles from here. It's smack dab in the central part of the state along the Kentucky River and is the site of Fort Boonesborough State Park."

He glanced at everyone. "As a final point, I want to remind everyone to keep to the trails, don't litter, leave footprints, and take memories." He tipped his hat and everyone clapped. Then he turned back down the trail and with his long strides reached the bend in the trail in seconds.

Miranda put down her brushes and ran like a deer to catch up with the fast retreating ranger. "Hold up a second, Ranger Morgan."

He turned with a broad grin. "Please, just Austin. We've been neighbors forever."

Miranda moaned. "Okay, Austin it is, but in front of customers, you're Ranger Morgan."

"Sure, that will work out fine, Miss Trent."

"Please." She smiled wide. "Just Miranda. Our families have lived down the road from each other for generations. It seems strange that we've both come to own the family homesteads this year. I'm sorry I didn't make it down to your mom's burial. My condolences."

"Thank you. It's comforting that our relations are all together again in the Adamses' cemetery barely a quarter of a mile from their homes."

"That is comforting. Thank you for saying that. Anyway, I'd like to invite you over to the farmhouse for the food-tasting event."

"I'm not fishing for an invitation. You have clients to satisfy."

"I've got Mrs. Childers and Mrs. Hobb doing the cooking back at the farmhouse. There will be tons of food and it shouldn't go to waste. I also want your opinion on the quality of the moonshine."

He again tipped his hat. "I'm not sure about this; I can't really be seen supporting a commercial enterprise. But we are neighbors. Okay, I'd be delighted to stop by if I can. My work hours vary a lot."

Miranda watched for a moment as he turned quickly and headed down the trail. She hadn't thought about a conflict of interest. He was right; she'd have to be careful about that.

She returned to her demonstration easel and taught the last few painting touches to the class. As usual, those final small flourishes had the biggest impact. She heard surprised comments all around.

Miranda flushed with pride. *Maybe this will work.*

The last step in the painting lesson was to sign their art. Miranda lined everyone up to pose with their finished works in front of the view of Lover's Leap. As she snapped a photo, she smiled, satisfied with how happy everyone seemed.

"We're going to take trail number one, the Original Trail, on our way back down to Hemlock Lodge. It descends the staircase to get below Natural Bridge and we'll pass through Fat Man's Squeeze."

The famous feature was a pinch point in the rock formation also locally known as Fat Man's Misery. There was some good-natured chattering about the narrow channel and that it should probably be renamed Super Model's Dash.

Miranda took the narrow channel first, demonstrating how to hold the painting in front and grab the backpack by its top handle and carry it behind. It felt a little awkward, but it worked.

They were several minutes down the trail before Miranda looked back and counted the clients again. There were only five. Shefton wasn't with the group. "Where's Shefton?"

Kelly yelled over her shoulder back at Miranda. "He was behind me before we tackled the Fat Man's Squeeze." She whispered to Linda, "Teacher's pet."

"Tell everyone to continue on down and meet up in the lobby of Hemlock Lodge. I'm going to chase him down." Miranda stalked up the trail, irritated with herself that she hadn't been more observant earlier.

"Really?" Kelly shrugged and tapped Linda's shoulder. "Tell everyone we have to wait while teacher finds her lost pet."

Linda frowned at her friend, then whispered, "What's wrong with you? Why are you being so nasty?"

Kelly turned sharply to Linda and mouthed, "You know."

Linda widened her eyes and uttered, "No I don't."

Miranda waited until she heard the message travel from client to client over the bickering between Linda and Kelly. Then she scrambled back uphill to the pinch point in the rock formations.

She didn't meet anyone else coming down the trail. This was not a good situation. What if there was an accident? A sinking sickness hit her gut.

Good grief, if he's gotten caught in Fat Man's Squeeze, he'll have to be rescued. It will hit the local papers and he'll never forgive me for that. There's the alternative path, but I forgot to say anything about it. But then, he probably wouldn't have wanted to call attention to himself. This tour leader stuff is tricky. I didn't consider that I might have to think like a life coach.

She came face to face with a young couple with two small children who had obviously made it through the narrow slit. That meant that he wasn't blocking up the pass, but then if not, where was he?

"Hi there!" she called to the family. "Have you seen a young man in a black cowboy shirt along here?" They all said no.

She hustled back down the trail to where the alternative path joined up and was barely in time to meet a red-faced Shefton. He was looking down, desperately trying to rub out the red cliff dirt stains from his fancy shirt. His fierce look told her to ask no questions.

"I'm fine, Miss Miranda. Just fine."

Miranda formed a smile but thought that Shefton was not at all fine.

In a few more minutes of totally silent hiking, they joined the rest of the group gathered back in Hemlock Lodge's lobby.

"Y'all look like you've had a grand old time." Doris Ann greeted them from behind the registration desk. She admired everyone's canvas one by one as they gathered in the lobby and made use of the facilities. "You sure did all right by the view at Lover's Leap. Miranda, I think this little business of yours might be something you can be mighty proud of."

"Thanks, Doris Ann." She leaned in close to Doris Ann's ear and whispered. "Now, for the tricky part—the traditional Southern meal accompanied by a moonshine tasting."

"Little lady, you know I'm still not happy that you're serving shine, don't you? I'm glad you can't do that here in the park. You do know better than that at least?"

"Yes, ma'am. I do. The owner himself will be bringing samples from his distillery in Lexington. We'll be on my private property—nowhere near the park."

Doris Ann nodded with tightly pursed lips. "Well, that's at least legal, then." She turned back to her computer. "Bye now."

Miranda considered the situation pragmatically. *There might be others who will react negatively to the moonshine. I'll have to be a good bit more diplomatic with how I promote that part of the tour experience. Is this a bad promotional choice? I hope not.* She stared into the fire looking for an answer.

The fire just crackled.

Chapter 4

After freshening up at the Hemlock Lodge bathroom facilities, the clients piled into Miranda's rented eight-passenger van. During the thirty-minute drive to her farmhouse, Miranda pointed out unique rock formations, named the crops growing in the fields, and identified roadside wildflowers. She also described the birds and butterflies that migrated through the area.

"Stop!" shouted Shefton.

Miranda hit the brakes and yelled "Hold on!"

There were grunts, shrieks, and the sound of tumbling possessions from the back.

She stopped inches away from a common box turtle about the size of a large grapefruit. She looked over to Shefton. "Good eye. I didn't see him at all. I would have been upset if I had run over him."

He smiled weakly from a pale face. "I would have thrown up in your brand-new van."

"It's a long-term rental, thank goodness. You better get behind the van and stop the traffic. The leaf peepers are out in full force." Shefton leapt out of the passenger seat and ran around behind the van. He began waving his arms like a windmill to divert the path of the oncoming drivers.

Miranda put the van in park and switched on her hazard lights. Out in front, she carefully lifted the turtle and placed him down in a bit of dirt off the shoulder away from the road. She stood there until he started moving in the direction away from the road.

"He's fine now," she bellowed over the noise of the traffic. "Let's go." They got back in the van and drove away in an uneasy silence.

In a few minutes, Shefton cleared his throat. "I know they're not endangered or anything. I just like them."

Miranda was continually amazed at these Appalachian quirks. The locals would shoot a groundhog on sight and yet save a turtle from getting hit on a busy road. She wondered just how many more oddities she had missed about her relatives during her long summer vacations, but drove on. "I like them, too. Thank you."

Finally, she pulled off onto a newly paved road that climbed at a fairly steep grade. In about a mile, it led to a sparsely graveled dirt road that led to the farmhouse. It was an original Sears & Roebuck Catalog house that had been ordered and built by her grandfather in 1929.

So strange to think that it was common to order a house kit from a Sears catalog and have it shipped by rail and truck to your site. Sears mail-order catalogs were in millions of homes, so large numbers of landowners were able to open a catalog, see different house designs, visualize their new home, and then purchase it directly from Sears.

The house faced the road showing a wide porch that stretched along the entire width with a wooden swing at one end. Her grandfather's handmade slatted benches were placed at the other end. Miranda's uncle hadn't painted the farmhouse for at least a decade, and the bright colors had faded to pleasing pastels. The house looked a bit shabby but nicely rustic against the bright yellow leaves of the silver maple tree in the front yard.

"Go on in," said Miranda after she had parked. "We're eating at the big round table in the dining room, which is just beyond the front room." She looked at the New Yorkers. "For the out-of-towners, that means the living room. There's a small bathroom just through the kitchen, which is at the back of the house. I'll check with our cooks, but I think we might have at least twenty to thirty minutes before we eat."

Her clients piled out of the van and began to wander off in all directions. Before she could say anything else, she heard toenails scrabbling on the wooden porch and looked over to see a goldish streak of desperate puppy. He tumbled down the steps and squatted in the nearest clump of grass. After he finished, he ran over and began to chew on Miranda's bootlaces.

"Sandy! How did you get out of my bedroom? Did the church ladies let you out?" She would have to remind her cooks that Sandy needed to be kept inside, ideally in his crate. Most locals let their dogs run loose. Miranda was still operating on her New York City view of dogs, which was on leash at all times if they were out of the apartment. Goodness, how long was it going to take to acquire the local culture norms?

Connecting with the congregation of a local church to prepare home-cooked food for her business as a fundraiser had been her mother's idea. Miranda was skeptical but the price was right—less than she would spend on ingredients.

She picked up the blond fluffy terrier mix puppy and had to rear back her head to dodge his puppy-breath kisses. "Sandikins! You need to get back to your safe place right now." She tucked his wriggling little body under her arm.

Looking around the property with the critical eyes of a stranger, Miranda's heart sank as she took in the general shabbiness of the old farmhouse. She frowned at the overall seediness of the scraggly lawn, the missing boards in the outbuildings, and the badly needed load of gravel for the driveway. The soft yellow house paint was serviceable but all the trim colors desperately needed a freshening up.

The outbuildings had never been painted, but some of them needed to be knocked down. She still needed to use the back shed for storing wood and coal until she could afford to install central heat and air next spring.

The sturdy shed near the barn was in the middle of construction to turn it into a safe chicken coop with room for a dozen traditional laying hens. When she had a little more cash, she would order her first chicks. She would also need to get expert local advice. Her uncle had kept about a dozen free-range hens. She wished she had paid more attention to the practical side of running the farm. The only thing she knew about chickens was that she wanted them.

The same neighbor who had helped her uncle with chores had driven up to the farmhouse and offered his services as a handyman. Jerry Rose was an absolute wonder and had been a lifesaver in updating the kitchen. He reminded her of the character George Utley, the handyman from her mother's favorite sitcom, *Newhart*. Miranda could walk into her mother's house on any afternoon and she would be watching an episode.

Then there were the stacked cinder blocks that had served as porch steps for the last twenty years. Miranda was embarrassed. This kind of thing was common here in the back country and a reluctance to replace rigged-up items that worked perfectly was engrained in her sense of economy, too. The phrase "If it ain't broke, don't fix it" came to mind.

However, she could be in real trouble for bringing tourists to a business that had no accommodation for clients with mobility issues. A simple wooden handrail worked fine for family and friends, but not for a business. That added to the pile of reasons to worry about the growing list of improvements vital to installing a distillery in the barn.

Last month, when she had been notified by her Uncle Gene's executor about the farmhouse bequest, she had been dumbfounded. For the first time, her dream of running a distillery appeared possible. Her desire to create a fine moonshine was only exceeded by her deep love of painting.

Equipment financing would be tricky since she was nearly flat broke. Her first financial hurdle to secure her ownership of the farm was to pay the taxes. Her Paint & Shine business idea certainly seemed like the quickest way to bring in revenue and spread the word about her plans.

She watched the newlyweds clasp hands and head off behind the house towards the weathered barn. Miranda raised her voice. "Be careful in there. That's the site of my new distillery and there's a few survey holes that were dug to check the foundations." They waved an okay and continued up the dirt double track.

Joe stood in the front yard and stared across the deep valley that ran parallel to the road in front of the property. He was looking down at a two-story Queen Anne nestled in a small overgrown clearing. The abandoned house was large with a wide covered porch on three sides. The white paint had flaked off decades ago and the house stood bare naked in weathered gray pine boards.

Joe turned to Miranda. "How long has that house been empty?"

"The Adams's mansion?" Miranda turned her head to look across the valley. "My goodness. It's been like that as long as I can remember. I think my uncle said that it was built in the late 1800s. The Adams matriarch lived there until she died in about 1970. She was the last one of that particular family line."

"It was probably a unique sight in its day with all that gingerbread trim. Do you know who owns it now?"

"I think it belongs to the Kash family now. They're my closest neighbors. We passed their house on our way here. They use the old thing for storing lumber for building projects. They're all distantly related to Shefton's family. Is it part of your research?"

"No, it's nothing. I was just curious." He stuffed his hands in his pockets. "Research is my passion but also an obsession. I'm not always able to resist asking questions."

"Mrs. Childers might know something about the mansion. She's our head cook today. Her family has been here since this county was first settled. She knows everything. In fact, that reminds me, I'd better put Sandy back in his crate, and see if Mrs. Childers needs anything." Miranda opened the screen door and went into the house.

Sandy seized that moment of distraction to plant a quick lick right on Miranda's open mouth. Miranda sputtered and held Sandy out of licking range.

The front room was small but cozy, with a free-standing cast-iron stove on the right side as you entered from the porch. A long couch was on the other wall facing the fire and two comfy rocking chairs sat on both sides of a little table just inside the front door. An assortment of straight-backed chairs squeezed in wherever there was a bit of room.

A colorful rag rug took up the entire center of the room. Vintage family photographs and several of Miranda's original oil paintings of the Red River Gorge hung on the walls. Not the Ritz, she thought, but not a pigsty either.

"Such a cozy room," said Linda. She pointed to the floor. "That rug is handmade, isn't it?"

Miranda felt the warmth of pride spread in her chest. It had taken weeks of begging to convince her mother to let her have the rug. "Yes, my grandma made it donkey's years ago. It's created out of strips of wool cloth she ripped up from the family's worn-out winter clothes. Back then recycling wasn't a fad; it was a way to conserve fabric and make use of every scrap."

"It's fabulous. That's exactly what I've been trying to find in the country stores out here. It's perfect for our new apartment. What are you asking for it?"

Miranda covered her shock at such a rude question by adjusting the blooms in a fresh-cut wildflower arrangement. She had picked them at first light and arranged them in a white ceramic vase. They looked perfect on the small wooden table framed by the large front window.

She recovered. "I'm so sorry. The furnishings here are family heirlooms—very sentimental. Nothing is for sale in here except for this small selection of my paintings." Miranda waved a hand at the landscapes depicting scenes in the nearby forests. "I still have most of them boxed up from my move from New York. They're stacked up in the barn. If you're interested, the prices are written on stickers attached to the frames."

"Are the frames included in the price?"

Miranda sighed. She should have anticipated

that one based on her experience in submitting work to art galleries. "No, but if you add fifty dollars, that will cover it."

She opened a heavy wooden door to the right of the front door, which led to her bedroom. More to the point, it held Sandy's crate. She tucked the little wiggle worm into his blanket and started the Snuggle Puppy windup toy that she had bought. Apparently, the soft ticking reminded Sandy of his mom's heartbeat so that he would feel calm and settle. At least that's what the fancy pet shop owner in Lexington had told her. Sandy wriggled his way deep into the blanket and quieted down with his chin on the toy. *That should keep him quiet until everyone's gone—maybe.*

She went back out through the front room and into the dining room. It was dominated by a large round mahogany dining table with a matching buffet. She was proud of her mother's hand-embroidered tablecloth stitched in seasonal colors combining laurel leaves and Scottish thistle. The low centerpiece picked up the colors with bright autumn leaves and more wildflowers.

Well-worn ladderback chairs were positioned in front of eight place settings. A napkin that contained the silverware was placed on white china plates with a laurel leaf pattern on the border. The water goblets were from her grandmother's large collection of cranberry Depression glass. The room looked just like she remembered from the holiday celebrations she attended here as a child.

Linda had followed her. "Wow, I love the look of the table."

"I love it, too. I have learned to appreciate the

time and skill required to produce a large inventory of embroidered linens. That buffet is stuffed full." She didn't add that some of them were still musty and needed hours of work to be washed, starched, and ironed. "I must say, it adds the perfect country cottage touch to our meal."

Miranda went on into the kitchen, the last room at the end of the shotgun-style farmhouse. She had been surprised to discover that her uncle had begun to upgrade his kitchen. It was completely out of character for this man who loved to keep things exactly as they had always been. She suspected that he had been preparing for her eventual ownership, but he ran out of time.

He had purchased a stainless-steel refrigerator and installed a matching dishwasher, but the original primitive cupboards were still hanging along the back wall. The original porcelain farmhouse sink had been upgraded with a fancy new faucet and a garbage disposal. The sink looked out onto the barn by a large double-hung window along the back outside wall.

Her only major purchase had been the six-burner professional gas stove. It replaced a four-burner apartment-sized version that had replaced the original cast-iron wood-burning cook stove. If getting wood every day hadn't become too much effort, Miranda was positive that the wood stove would still be standing.

"Goodness, Mrs. Childers. The table setting looks wonderful and the smell of your cooking is driving me mad. Is everything about ready?"

"Hi, sweetie." Mrs. Childers tucked a stray wisp of wiry gray hair back into a small bun at the nape of her neck. She automatically wiped her hands on a gold floral apron trimmed in red rickrack. Her plump shape disguised strong muscles built as a result of handling huge pots when she served as head cook in the now-closed Wolfe County High School cafeteria. She folded Miranda into a smothering hug and heaved a deep sigh. "I think everything is as good as it's going to get."

Miranda surfaced from the second smothering hug in as many hours. *I know this is normal here, but will I ever get used to this? Maybe not.*

Mrs. Childers kept up her running patter. "This is some chance you're taking inviting all these strangers into your uncle's home like this. I've told you before that I don't hold with all this hard liquor business. These young folks might get rowdy. There's no tellin' what kind of bad trouble can come from this."

Miranda escaped from Mrs. Childers's clasp. "Yes, ma'am. We've had this discussion many times, now. A little bit of chaos and excitement is perfectly normal for a tourist adventure. That's what they expect."

Miranda tried to identify the contents bubbling in the aluminum pots and steaming away in the cast-iron skillets. The food on the stove didn't look right.

"You've prepared the whole menu just like we discussed. Right?"

"Well, sweetie—not exactly. We're starting with a light salad of locally picked greens topped with fresh fried green tomatoes. Then I've got a hearty venison stew where I added potatoes, carrots, and onions straight from my kitchen garden."

"But—" said Miranda.

"Now just you wait," continued Mrs. Childers. "For sides, I've got steamed green beans with bacon. I grilled corn on the cob on this fancy new stove. Plus, even though I had already decided to serve up spicy corn bread, I'm famous for my biscuits, so I had to make both. They turned out perfect in the new oven."

"But—" Miranda tried again.

"I really have to say that I am delighted that you took care of dessert. I've got your Dutch apple cobbler warming in the oven to be served with some of my hand-churned vanilla ice cream that I had put by in my freezer."

Miranda rubbed at the rising pain originating at a point between her shoulder blades and ending at the base of her skull. "That's not what we discussed. You said you were going to have chicken with dumplings. Chicken doesn't compare well to venison. They have two completely different taste profiles."

Mrs. Childers looked at Miranda as if she were speaking in foreign tongues. Miranda rubbed the back of her neck harder. "Dan is going to be furious. I hope he packed up a wide selection of moonshine. It's too late to tell him. In fact, he should be here by now."

"Who is this Dan?"

"Dan Keystone. I've told you about him, again, more than once. He's the owner of Keystone Distillery just outside Lexington. It's part of the event. It's the moonshine pairing that he's creating for each course that these folks are paying good money to enjoy."

Mrs. Childers flapped her hands like she was shooing flies. "I don't want to know anything at all about that."

Miranda narrowed her eyes. Mrs. Childers was being especially prickly, but why? "Oh, I almost forgot, I invited Austin to our dinner, so he'll bring the total number of diners up to nine." She could come up with last-minute changes as well.

"There's always room at the table for a neighbor." Mrs. Childers planted one hand on her hip and shook a finger at Miranda. "I'm not at all happy with this moonshine nonsense. Lord a mercy, it will bring you nothing but grief."

Miranda felt her shoulders droop. "But you knew that was part of the package. I explained it very carefully when we agreed that you and Mrs. Hobb would cook. How else would you be able to donate so much money to your church's roof fund drive?"

"I know that." Mrs. Childers spoke like she was talking to a little child. "But you know I don't approve of drink. I naturally thought that you would respect your elders' wishes and cancel that part of the tour."

"Unfortunately for you, the tourists today seem extremely interested in authentic Kentucky moonshine. I've had quite a few phone calls to ask if a distillery tour was included in our package."

"That's as it may be, but I'm going to do everything in my power to convince the town council to deny your permit to start a distillery in the barn. I have powerful friends who will listen to me." She stooped to open the oven door and transfer the sheet pan of fresh biscuits to the worktable. The aroma made the whole kitchen smell like a buttery heaven.

Mrs. Childers inhaled a deep sniff. "Oh, I do love this wonderful kitchen."

This is my kitchen. Not the cook's kitchen. My kitchen.

Miranda swallowed, then relaxed her stiff shoulders. She unclenched her jaw. "I know you don't like it, but this is the way it's going to be. It's my business!" Miranda realized she had yelled. She lowered her voice immediately and quickly patted Mrs. Childers on the shoulder. "I'm so, so sorry. I didn't mean to raise my voice. I'm under a great deal of pressure right now and it has shortened my temper. Everything will be fine, I promise."

Mrs. Childers shut the oven door with a bang and threw Miranda a fierce look. "You mark my words. You will regret this."

She's the best cook in the county, but she's going to drive me mad. I need her support in order to be successful in this part of the county. I need that permit as well and Mrs. Childers is the quickest way to round up support in getting the permit approved.

Miranda looked around the room, through the kitchen door, and out the back porch. "Where's Mrs. Hobb?"

"She'll be right back. I sent her up the road to borrow some home-churned butter from Elsie. Store-bought butter just isn't good enough for my prized biscuits."

"But I—never mind." Miranda's swirling thoughts were interrupted by a sharp yipping from her bedroom. She scurried to the front to discover Sandy fiercely barking towards the window that faced out onto the side yard. Miranda opened the crate, restarted Sandy's heartbeat toy, and the dog circled and settled down to nap. She backed out of the room and quietly shut the door. She returned to the kitchen.

"Have you seen Dan?" Mrs. Childers shook her head no. "He should be here by now. I want to get everyone seated so he can introduce the first pairing."

Mrs. Childers looked at her but said nothing.

Miranda noted the cold shoulder treatment. "Fine. If you would, please wait five more minutes before you fry up the green tomatoes, and put the appetizer plates at each setting. I need to tell Dan about the menu changes before he gets into the house."

She left through the back door and walked around to the side yard. Miranda stood by the well near the back of the house to see if she could see him coming down the dirt road. She put her hands on her hips and began figuring out how she would play this if he didn't show up.

She could refund some of the money. Ugh, bad idea. She couldn't really afford to do that on her very first tour. She could bring up some real moonshine from her secret stash down in the root cellar under the kitchen. Her pairing might not work as well as Dan's, but she would at least deliver the promised experience.

She decided that she needed to check her stash just in case it was needed. She went back into the kitchen and opened up the cellar door. It was a small handmade opening tucked underneath the stairwell that went up to the attic. Her grandfather had used every trick up his sleeve to conserve building materials. She carefully lowered herself down the rough stepladder to a hard-packed dirt cellar and brought up one of the mason jars of moonshine that her uncle had left.

She popped back up into the kitchen and quickly shoved it into the refrigerator.

Mrs. Childers gave her a scathing look but still wasn't speaking to her. She was placing the fried green tomatoes on top of the salad plates that were arranged on a large tray. She said, "These are ready to serve as the first course."

"Could you please hang back just two more minutes? I'm going to check the road one last time for Dan."

Racing through the house out to the front porch, she saw a puff of dust in the distance that meant a vehicle was speeding down the road.

That better be him and he better have a good excuse.

Dan parked his logo-decorated panel truck and yelled out to Miranda, "Sorry, I'm late." Dan was tall, with thick dark hair. He flashed his pearly white teeth at her.

He trotted around to the back of the truck, opened the double doors, put a zippered carryall bag over his shoulder, and hefted a wooden crate filled with mason jars of distilled moonshine. "There was a jackknife accident on I-75 just north of the I-64 junction. A semi slipped off the road and blocked both turnoff lanes." He followed Miranda into the kitchen. "Do you have the Ale-8 soda pop? I need that for the first concoction."

"Of course, it's in the refrigerator."

"Fantastic, I have everything else with me. How's it going?"

Miranda groaned. "Normal for a first day on the job. Things are a little chaotic. A client showed up late and we had to start the hike without him. The cooks let my puppy outside as if he were a country dog, but he is not. And then you were late, but now you're here."

"Sorry."

"Thank goodness you're here now. We're more than ready to start the 'Shine' part of the Paint & Shine experience. If you can get things set up in the dining room, that would be great. I've cleared a spot for your stuff on the sideboard. You can mix your cocktails there in front of the group. They'll love that. It's better if you stay out of the kitchen. The cook doesn't hold with hard liquor."

"No problem, I'm used to that."

"I'll gather everyone up. They've been wandering everywhere. When you've got the first cocktail mixed, call us to the dining room."

"Fantastic," said Dan. They started off towards the house.

"Oh shoot," she said. "Dan. I'm sorry, I almost forgot to tell you. Mrs. Childers changed the main course to venison stew."

Dan's eyes went wide. "Not chicken?"

"Nope. Welcome to the confusion."

Turning away before he could respond, Miranda stood at the edge of the porch and cupped her hands around her mouth. "Dinner's ready! Come and get it!" She went back into the dining room in time to see Mrs. Childers placing the first course at each of the nine place settings. She looked calmer but still didn't look at Miranda.

Clients arrived from all directions to claim seats

and chatter with each other across the large table. The mood was excited and filled with anticipation.

The newlyweds sat next to each other holding hands and looking only at each other. In contrast with the rest of the group, neither of them smiled. Instead, they looked pensive and serious.

Beside them, Kelly and Linda sat down and immediately began to critique the plating of the salad greens and fried green tomatoes, and sniff the water in the goblets.

That's natural, Miranda thought. Criticizing the meal was a principal form of entertainment in New York City. She had done her share when she lived there. They've probably never cooked an entire meal for company in their lives. She could be wrong—people in New York do cook, but these two didn't seem at all interested.

"That's Highbridge Springs water in your glasses. It's bottled in a family-owned business just a little southwest of Lexington. I love the taste and they've been big into recycling since the eighties."

Dan finished creating the first cocktail. He placed nine small mason jars filled with ice and a yellowish liquid on a tray. In each jar he had placed a lollipop in the shape of an artist's paint pallet to act as the stirrer. He seemed genuinely excited to share his knowledge of Kentucky moonshine lore.

Dan pointedly looked at the empty chairs then sat the tray back on the sideboard. He was clearly disappointed that his whole audience wasn't yet in place. He threw a frown at Miranda. "How many are we missing?"

Miranda ticked off her fingers. "Shefton Adams, Joe Creech, and I invited Ranger Morgan, although he might have to work."

At that moment, Shefton rushed in from the front room and sat next to Linda. "Sorry to be late, I was down by the barn. Wow! That's an authentic tobacco barn. There are piles and piles of tobacco stakes in there still fit to use."

"Tobacco hasn't been raised here for over a decade," said Miranda. "My uncle just couldn't bring himself to empty the barn of all the equipment. Most folks around here have made the switch to growing organic vegetables. It took a long time to establish a market with the big cities—like Lexington, Louisville, and Cincinnati, but they are gaining ground. I'm going against the grain by wanting to start a distillery."

"Grain?" said Dan. "That's an awful pun."

Miranda chuckled. "Exactly, but legal moonshine around here doesn't make sense to the locals. They still see it as bootlegging. I don't have a choice."

"What do you mean?"

"I didn't tell you?" Miranda frowned and lowered her voice. "Part of the deal for inheriting this farmhouse is that I have to have a working distillery within the first ninety days."

"That's not good news. We'll be competitors."

"Not really. I'm only going to produce small batch, limited runs. Don't worry, I only intend to make enough for my tour clients." She looked at the two still empty seats. She was beginning to get irritated. "Anyone seen Joe lately?"

Linda spoke up. "I saw him in the living room over by the fireplace right after we got here, but I haven't seen him since."

Miranda walked out into the front room. It was empty. She opened the front door and went out onto the porch. She cupped both hands around her mouth and yelled, "Joe! Joe, lunch is ready."

No answer.

"Will I do, instead?" said Austin as he came up the driveway and on up the steps. "Who are you hollering for? I didn't see anyone on the walk from my house."

"One of my clients has wandered off. I'm going to need to be clearer about what is off-limits, I guess."

They went back into the dining room and there was Joe, seated at the table. "I'm sorry, I didn't hear the call. I was trespassing in your front bedroom in order to comfort your puppy. There was some kind of noise that frightened him. I heard him whimpering and couldn't resist his charms. He's back to sleep now."

"Thanks. That's sweet of you." She didn't recall a noise. Miranda rubbed her hands together. "Okay, we're all here. Let me start with an introduction to your guide for all things related to moonshine. This is Dan Keystone, owner of the Keystone Branch Distillery over in Lexington. He's turned a family tradition into a legal business using family recipes and trade secrets handed down the generations. It's rumored, but only a rumor, definitely not confirmed, that his great-grandfather became friends with Al Capone during a brief stay in the big house."

"That's never been proved," said Dan.

"Right," said Miranda. "The truth is that his father and my uncle were great friends and jostled for the title of best moonshiner in Kentucky. It's all legal now, of course, and Dan's moonshine is among the best."

She nodded her head towards him and he cleared his throat. "Good afternoon. I'm glad to be here to introduce you to the traditional spirit of the backwoods. It has been called mountain dew, hooch, white lightning, and corn whiskey. The most common description is moonshine, which harkens back to the most popular way it was made—distilling by the light of the moon."

He handed one of the little four-ounce jars to each of the clients from his drinks tray. "Now, this here is a great little aperitif to get our experience started. I've poured a jigger of Keystone green apple moonshine over ice and topped it up with Miranda's favorite soda pop, Ale-8."

Miranda rolled her eyes. "Thanks."

The group began to reach for their little mason jars. "I've added a twist of lime and a strip of candied ginger.

Dan reached out a hand. "Oh, I almost forgot, those little lollipop stirrer things are edible. Not only are they pretty, but tasty, too."

Dan raised his sample. "Enjoy your taste of Kentucky."

The guests began to sample the drink.

Laura and Brian clinked their mason jars, removed the lollipops, and knocked back the entire portion. Then their eyebrows shot up and they both produced that distinctive cough that informed all that they weren't used to drinking strong spirits.

Joe sipped the liquid solemnly and nodded. "I would never have thought to cut the shine with Ale-8, but this is refreshing."

Shefton piped in. "It's certainly not something I'm comfortable with. I was raised to stay away from drink, but I have to admit, I like the taste."

Kelly drank as tiny a sip as was humanly possible and then frowned. Her eyes went wide and she gulped quickly from her water glass. She didn't utter a single word. She looked a bit sour, as if she regretted coming along.

"This is so luscious," said Linda. "The tartness of the green apple is a great complement to the ginger in the soda. This is a wonderful drink." She sat back in her chair. "I'm looking forward to the rest of our tasting."

Dan glanced over to Miranda. She frowned, as Mrs. Childers had been hovering in the doorway antsy to serve the first course and now seemed to be ignoring them. "I'll tell Mrs. Childers that we're done with the appetizers. She's been concerned that we might get the timing wrong for her main course. There's nothing worse than dry, over-cooked venison."

She went through the doorway to the kitchen and saw Mrs. Hobb standing in front of the back porch door with a dish of butter in her hand. Mrs. Hobb stared at the floor then opened her mouth to an ear-splitting scream.

Miranda followed Mrs. Hobb's gaze and there was Mrs. Childers lying face up in front of the stove with a large kitchen knife protruding from her bloody chest. She was surrounded by a scattering of cutlery, broken dishes, and a spilled pan of biscuits. Miranda felt the image sear itself into her mind's eye as if she was going to paint it as a masterpiece.

Mrs. Hobb abruptly fell silent, then crossed the kitchen floor to stand over her lifetime friend. Her mouth opened to say something, but nothing came from her lips. Instead she grabbed her chest, bent over, shrieked in pain, then fainted in a heap at her dear friend's lifeless feet.

Chapter 5

Saturday Noon

Miranda stood rigid with her mouth open. Her brow wrinkled in confusion as she tried to make sense of what was happening.

The excited hubbub behind her prodded her into action. She turned around to the crush of her clients trying to look around her into the kitchen. She threw her arms wide and yelled out, "Stay back. Does anyone have a cell phone with a signal? We need to call 911."

Silence followed like a stalled video.

Dan pulled out his phone from his top shirt pocket and looked at the screen. "No signal."

Then everyone came to life at once. There was a rustling as some had their phones within handy reach and some scrabbled into backpacks and others fumbled through their handbags for cell phones.

A high voice: "What's happening? What's wrong?"

A deep voice: "Nope, no signal."

Another man: "No bars for me."

A woman said, "My battery has gone dead."

Austin's calm voice lifted above the din. "I've got about half a bar—that won't be good enough for voice, but I am texting now."

Miranda palmed her forehead. "I'm being dense, there is rarely a decent signal up here. Sometimes I can't even text. but my neighbors have an old-school land line. Mine isn't installed yet. The phone company disconnected my uncle's old rotary phone after he died." She pointed to the nearest person in the dining room. "Brian. Quick. I need you to drive down the hill to the little cottage on the left side of the road and tell them to call for an ambulance. Oh, and call whoever serves as the local police."

Shefton put his useless cell back in his front pants pocket. "Yep, that's Roy and Elsie's house." He looked at Brian. "They're real friendly."

"Of course, you would know that." Miranda took another calming breath. "They've lived down there since forever. Brian, here are my keys. Take my van and use their phone. Just be careful to keep our dirt road unblocked at Roy and Elsie's. Their house is right at the edge of the road because it overlooks a steep ridge."

"I'm going with him," said Laura, not even looking at Miranda in case she said no.

"Fine, but you have to go now. Run!" Brian and Laura disappeared.

Austin peeked past Miranda into the kitchen and gently pressed Miranda's shoulder. "Let me by. I'm a trained first responder. I can help."

He stood just inside the threshold and glanced

down at Mrs. Childers. Then he stepped around her to put two fingers on Mrs. Hobb's throat. He spoke over his shoulder. "Mrs. Hobb is alive, but her pulse is erratic. I think she's just fainted." He repeated the check on Mrs. Childers. His shoulders slumped and he blew out a fast breath. "Mrs. Childers is gone. She's past help."

Miranda continued to stand directly in the doorway, blocking anyone else from entering the kitchen.

Austin looked at the back door of the kitchen, tiptoed over, and locked it. He walked back to the stove and turned off all the burners and the oven, too. He returned to stand in front of Miranda.

"We'll bar the kitchen door after we get Mrs. Hobb out of there. I haven't had to use any of my crime scene training up to now. It was only a two-hour class, but the first priority is always to the living. At this point, all I can do to help the police is to limit the number of people who go into the kitchen."

"What about the EMTs? Shouldn't they take care of Mrs. Hobb?"

"It will take at least fifteen minutes for them to get way out here. More likely closer to thirty. We're on our own for a bit. That's the major downside of a rural life."

Shefton peered around Miranda at the kitchen threshold. He scanned the destruction and involuntarily took a step back. "What in the . . . Are they dead?"

Austin replied in his professional ranger voice, "One is dead and one has either had a heart attack

or fainted. Come on in and help me get Mrs.
Hobb turned over to this side away from the body.
Then I think we need to try to bring her to."

Shefton's head bobbled agreement.

Miranda turned around to the clients pushing
through one another to see through the kitchen
door. She waved her hands like shooing chickens.
"Everyone out. Go on into the front room. They
need space to work on Mrs. Hobb to get her out of
there."

Austin edged around the still body of Mrs. Childers and gently turned Mrs. Hobb over. He quickly
ran his hands over Mrs. Hobb's arms and legs
searching for broken bones or dislocations. "Nothing broken. She seems sound." He signaled for
Shefton to take Mrs. Hobb's feet while he slipped
his hands under her arms.

Both of them avoided looking at the knife. In a
quiet voice, Austin told Shefton, "Slide her over
there by the sink. Let's keep it slow."

Miranda glanced at Mrs. Childers and her stomach turned sour. She thought she might throw up.
She closed her eyes and took a long, slow breath
until the feeling faded away.

She recognized the eerie stillness that surrounds
a person who is no longer breathing. It was rein-
forced by the dusty gray tone of her flesh, indicat-
ing that blood no longer flowed through the body.
She recalled that drain of color in the moment her
dad died in hospice. It was many years ago, but
that image was crystal clear. Mrs. Childers was the
same shade. She was truly gone.

They managed to turn Mrs. Hobb over gently.

But then Shefton made a retching noise, clamped a hand over his mouth, and dashed into the bathroom, slamming the door behind him.

Austin waved for Miranda to come in and he pointed to some kitchen towels that were piled up on the worktable just out of his reach. Miranda handed them over. Austin bunched them into a roll and placed them under the lolling head of the cook. He sat back on his haunches.

Miranda looked at Austin. "Now what?"

"Do you have smelling salts?"

She raised her eyebrows. "Uh, no. My first aid kit only treats cuts and scrapes. You know, hiking trail stuff."

"What about cold water?"

"Yes." She turned, opened the refrigerator and pulled out a plastic gallon of spring water.

"Pour some on a cloth. We'll give that a try to bring her around."

Miranda opened a drawer, pulled out another kitchen towel, and poured water on it until it was damp. She passed it to Austin. "Thanks. Do another one for her wrists."

He folded the wet towel into a compact oblong and began dabbing it on Mrs. Hobb's forehead and temples.

Miranda soaked another cloth and bent down to take Mrs. Hobb's hand. She pressed the wet cloth directly on the pulse point on the inside of her blue-veined wrist.

Mrs. Hobb groaned like a drunk coming to from a three-day binge. Her droopy eyelids fluttered and opened for a moment before she squinted them shut. She groaned again, followed by a low, long whimper of pain.

Miranda turned the cloth over to the cooler side and pressed it back against her wrist.

Mrs. Hobb jerked her hand away and her eyes flew open with the white showing all around. "What's happening?"

Austin removed the cloth from her forehead and took her other hand. He held it firmly. "You've had a terrible shock and you fainted."

Miranda bent over and added, "Mrs. Hobb, do you have a heart condition? Do you carry any medication for angina or asthma? Does anything hurt?"

Mrs. Hobb struggled to sit up. Austin pressed her back down to the floor with a firm hand on her shoulder. "No, not yet. We don't want you to get up too quickly. We're waiting on an ambulance to take you to the hospital."

"I can't go to the hospital! That's clear into Lexington. Who will take care of my house? I don't want anyone in my house."

Miranda leaned over. "Now, Mrs. Hobb, you've passed out from shock and there may be other complications. You may have had a heart attack or a stroke. You simply have to get checked out by a doctor."

Shefton came out of the bathroom looking a bit pale, but in control of himself. He quickly assessed the situation and stepped in to bend down and artfully block Mrs. Hobb's view of her friend's body. "What do you think? Should we give her a wee dram for the shock? Should I get some from Dan?"

Both Miranda and Austin nodded yes. Shefton grabbed a small jelly jar out of one of the open kitchen shelves and dashed into the front room. He returned in a moment with about an ounce of shine. "Try this. It's the smoothest variety Dan brought."

He bent down and held the jar to the cook's lips. She took a tentative sip. Her eyes widened, and she signaled for another taste.

"Thank you, that's very kind. I do take a nip now and again, and this brew is mighty fine, mighty fine, indeed."

The moonshine appeared to calm Mrs. Hobb until she glanced across the kitchen and moved her head around to see her friend's motionless body. She sat up before any of them could stop her and began to cry. "Oh, dear, oh dear, oh dear. She's gone to be with our Lord, hasn't she?"

Miranda dropped the wet cloth on the floor and squeezed Mrs. Cobb's hand in both of hers. "Yes. I'm afraid she's passed away. We've called the police."

Another cry escaped from her pale lips and she began struggling to get up but stopped. "Who killed her?" She looked about fervently. "Are they still here?" Then she clutched at her chest. "Oh, my heart, my heart."

Miranda looked over to Austin and Shefton. "Let's get her out of the kitchen, then somebody should take a look around the property. The killer could still be here. That thought might be affecting her heart. Strange that she doesn't think it was an accident." She paused. "We also don't want her in the way when the officials arrive, if they ever arrive."

Austin and Shefton managed to pull their substantially heavy patient up from the floor. By supporting her one on each side, they walked her from the kitchen through the crowd of clients in the dining room to the couch in the front room.

Miranda ran ahead into her bedroom and grabbed two pillows and a soft blanket. "Sorry, folks, shift yourselves out of the way. We're going to put Mrs. Hobb here." She spread the blanket on the couch just before Shefton and Austin helped the cook sit down.

Miranda plumped the pillows and put them behind Mrs. Hobb's head as they eased her back. As an attempt to stave off shock, she ran back into her bedroom and snatched a quilt from the foot of her bed, then unfolded it and tucked the quilt in around the groaning cook's reclining figure.

After they had made her as comfortable as they could, Miranda leaned over the pale woman. "How are you feeling now, Mrs. Hobb?"

She looked into Miranda's eyes and motioned for her to bend down.

When Miranda put her ear close to Mrs. Hobb's lips, she whispered, "My heart is doing flip-flops like a dying chicken. It hurts like the dickens." Mrs. Hobb pressed her hand to her chest.

Miranda straightened up and turned to Dan. "How long since Brian and Laura left to call for the police?"

"It's only been ten minutes, but it seems much longer," said Dan.

"Hmmm." Miranda tugged at the bottom of her shirt. "It would take him about two minutes to start knocking on the door and another five minutes for Elsie to get out of bed, calm the dog, then answer the door."

Dan raised his eyebrows.

"She raises chickens and goats." Miranda confirmed her opinion of him as a big city boy.

He looked at her with a crinkled brow.

She huffed her impatience. "They have to be milked and fed at dawn, so she gets up early then takes a nap right after lunch."

He stared at her.

"I mean a serious, take off your clothes, get back in bed, serious nap. Also, Roy might be out of town so she would make doubly sure she knew who it was. Brian would have had to explain it through a crack in the front door. It will help that he has Laura with him. Elsie is also a very old-fashioned country lady. She wouldn't let them in the house without being properly decent. That means getting back into her clothes, lipstick, and running a comb through her hair."

"Still, they should have called and be on the way back by now."

"I wish I had a phone that worked." Irritated, Miranda looked over to the kitchen door. The New York clients were standing in the doorway to the kitchen. "Hey! You guys can't be messing around in there." She grabbed up a chair on her way through the dining room. "Get back! You might be used to hearing about this stuff every day on the news in the city, but this is rare out here. Now go on and sit in the front room, or better yet, out on the porch."

She placed one of the dining room chairs in the threshold to block the way to the kitchen. She sat down in it with her arms tightly crossed and one leg swung over the other. Her foot wriggled in extreme annoyance.

Brian and Laura finally returned. They lurched into the house, glanced at Mrs. Hobb, Austin, and the others, then Brian stood wheezing in front of Miranda.

"What in heaven's name took you so long?"

"The van wouldn't start back up so we had Roy look at it. He fixed a loose battery cable, and then gave us a jump so we could get back here. I called everyone I could think of," he gasped. "Ambulance, Fire, Sheriff, Highway Patrol. They should all be on their way pretty quick." He glanced at Miranda. Another great gasp. "According to your neighbor, until you arrived, nothing like this ever happened here."

Miranda cringed. *So, of course, it must happen now—at my new home.*

Chapter 6

Saturday Afternoon

"What on earth are you guys doing?" Miranda asked the group hovering in the doorway to the kitchen. "Get on back into the front room." She picked out Dan. "We need to keep everyone of the way. Otherwise, we'll never get out of here. Do you have more samples that could maybe distract them?"

"Definitely." Dan pointed to his sample box on the sideboard, then raised his voice. "Would y'all like to continue sampling my wares?"

Like the chorus in a musical, they all nodded their readiness to taste more of Dan's moonshine cocktails. Dan grabbed his box of distillery samples, the carryall bag, then he led everyone out onto the porch. They settled on the swing, the benches, and in the various rockers and chairs. They appeared very pleased to be distracted.

Miranda considered their readiness to be entertained to be a bit indifferent, but then they didn't know Mrs. Childers.

The emergency vehicle from the Wolfe County Volunteer Fire Department arrived first and pulled up to stop in front of the farmhouse. The volunteers traveled from their fire station on Main Street in Campton, Kentucky, the nearest town of any size at all in the area. The vintage ambulance took up the entire width of the gravel road that ran by Miranda's farmhouse. Because the driveway was already packed, one of the volunteers got out and guided the vehicle onto a small level turnout at the side of the road next to Miranda's abandoned outhouse.

Another burly, fresh-faced, uniformed fireman hopped out of the vehicle and they trotted up to the porch, each lugging a large black case. The tall one spoke in a calm but commanding voice. "Did you call the fire department for an emergency, miss?"

Miranda stepped out onto the porch. "Yes. Mrs. Childers has been stabbed to death and Mrs. Hobb appears to be having a heart attack, but she might have just fainted. Do you have paramedic training? Not all fire responders do. Can you help?"

"I would say so, miss. Most of us are ex-military," said the second fireman, who sported a deep farmer's tan. "Let's see what we can do."

Miranda led them into the front room, where a wide-eyed and pale Mrs. Hobb stared at them from the couch. Her hand was pressed to her chest, and her breath was deep and quick beneath the quilt. Austin knelt on the floor holding her hand but let go to stand back and give the firemen room to take care of her.

Miranda followed them into the front room. They

greeted Mrs. Hobb warmly—like long-lost boys addressing a beloved grandmother.

"Howdy there, Mrs. Hobb. Are you having your palpitations again?" said the tall fireman as he bent over to look into her face. "It's me, Little Jimmy, from down by Buchanan Fork."

"Oh yes, sweetie pie, I'm sufferin' something terrible." She looked beyond Little Jimmy. "Hi Mac, it's so good of you to come and take care of me. I'm so glad they sent you." She tilted her head and smiled sweetly.

Little Jimmy turned back to Miranda. "You said there was another situation?"

"Yes, in the kitchen. I don't think you can help there."

"We'll just make sure. Come on, Mac." They moved the straight-backed chair, crossed the threshold, and returned in less than a minute.

Little Jimmy nodded quietly to Miranda. "She's definitely beyond our help." Then he bent down to Mrs. Hobb. "How do you feel?"

"This has been so awful. It's especially nice to see you two again."

"Why's that, Mrs. Hobb?" said Little Jimmy.

She grabbed his arm in a surprisingly strong grip that turned his skin white. "I don't want to go to that big hospital way over in Lexington again," she pleaded, as fat tears began to roll down her pale cheeks. "It's such a lot of trouble for everyone. They'll only keep me long enough to run those horrible scans. Then my granddaughters will have to come and get me. They drive me everywhere. They're so sweet, but it's so much trouble."

"We'll try to do that, but—"

"Can't you give me one of those wonderful pills that young Doctor Watson gives me so that my heart will settle and the pain will go away?"

"We'll see. Let's just check out your little ol' ticker, first." Little Jimmy took a knee by the sofa and grabbed a stethoscope from his black case. He pressed it to her chest in several places, listened to her heart carefully, hung the stethoscope around his neck, and then took her hand in both of his. "Mrs. Hobb, you know we can't give you those special pills. They have to come from your doctor over in Campton."

Austin pointed to Shefton and Dan and motioned for them to go out the front door. "We're going to take a quick look around the farm just to make sure no one is still around who shouldn't be here."

Mrs. Hobb looked up at the two firemen and her eyes reminded Miranda of a begging kitten. "Can you good fellows just take me over to his office? It's much closer than Lexington. You know he's the only one who can treat my palpitations. I don't want to go to Lexington. Young Doctor Watson will fix me up all nice and proper." She looked from Little Jimmy to Mac and then back to Little Jimmy. Another fat tear coursed down her cheek. "Please?"

Mac's gaze searched out Miranda. He took her gently by the elbow and led her over to the corner of the room speaking low. "I know Mrs. Hobb has had a shock, but her pulse is steady as a rock. This is a grab for attention. I think we'll take her over to Campton and call up the young Doctor Watson. He'll give her a sedative." His voice dropped even lower. "That's what Doc's magic pills are. He dispenses maximum strength melatonin for her nervous condition. It's quick and nonaddictive. Works a treat."

"I think that's exactly what you should do. From her reaction, taking her to Lexington might actually give her a real heart attack."

Mac and Little Jimmy began preparing Mrs. Hobb for transportation. Mac went out to the ambulance, and brought the gurney into the tiny front room. He lowered it down to the floor to be level with the couch. They each grabbed the edge of the blanket that Mrs. Cobb was lying on and expertly transferred her without the tiniest peep from their patient.

Little Jimmy deftly substituted a general issue medical blanket in place of Miranda's quilt. He tossed the quilt to Miranda. "We'll have your blanket down at the station whenever you want to pick it up."

"My purse!" screeched Mrs. Hobb. "You need to get my purse! It's in the kitchen."

Miranda used a no-nonsense voice. "I'll bring it out to you as soon as I can. I'm not going to move anything in that kitchen."

"But I need my identification," wailed Mrs. Hobb.

Little Jimmy chuckled as he started rolling the gurney out to the porch. "Don't worry, Mrs. Hobb. Everyone knows you."

Just then, they heard the wail of an emergency siren making its way up the gravel road. Miranda stepped out onto the porch. The vehicle was travelling at a fast-enough speed to leave a dust plume hanging in the air like a posse in a cowboy movie.

Little Jimmy turned to Miranda. "You called the sheriff's office, too?"

"This is a remote area. I told Brian to call everyone." She stood with her hands on her hips as the patrol car sped up the road—all lights still flashing. The driver didn't turn off the siren until the vehicle slid to a stop at the precise point in the road to block absolutely everyone, including the ambulance, from both the driveway and the public road.

Miranda frowned, hoping against hope that this responder wasn't a Barney Fife.

The siren whined off and driver's side door opened. A tall, slim deputy wearing a traditional khaki uniform yelled over the roof of the patrol car. "Did you call in a murder?" His face was flushed, and he yelled in a tinny high-pitched voice.

Oh, lordy, lordy. He IS Barney Fife!

"Yes, we reported a death about a half an hour ago." She pressed her lips together to avoid adding a comment about what took him so long.

The color drained from his flushed face like pulling the plug out of a bathtub. He swallowed. "Okay, ma'am. I was really hoping it was just a prank call." He looked at her. Then he looked down the road where the dust he had disturbed still hung above the road. "I guess I need to look at the body."

"I would think so." Miranda turned and held open the screen door.

The deputy made his way up the steps, took off his hat, and stood before Miranda. "My name is Deputy Gary Spenser, ma'am. I'm real new to this job and I just want you to know that if I faint—not that I will—just in case I do—it's not because I don't care about doing a good job. I've just never had good nerves. Being stricken with nerves runs in my family." He put his hat back on and went through the door to the front room.

Miranda followed and almost bumped into him when he stopped in front of Mrs. Hobb lying on the gurney.

Deputy Spenser turned back around to Miranda. "She's not dead," he said in an accusing voice. "She hasn't been murdered at all." He puffed out his chest. "This is a serious offense. You have falsely reported a murder."

Little Jimmy turned from checking the straps securing Mrs. Hobb to the gurney. "This isn't the victim. Mrs. Hobb is suffering from a possible heart attack after discovering the body of her friend, Mrs. Childers. The body is that way." He pointed his long arm towards the kitchen.

Deputy Spenser turned an even paler shade of pasty white. His gaze followed Little Jimmy's pointed arm. Then he hitched up his utility belt and marched into the kitchen like a condemned man going to his execution. He stopped sharp at the threshold of the kitchen. He propped his hands on his hips in a superman pose.

"Oh lordy, lordy, Mrs. Childers has been murdered," said Deputy Spenser in an even higher voice yet. He turned around to say something to Miranda, but the words never made it to his lips.

Miranda watched as his face went completely slack-jawed and he swayed back out of the kitchen. He knocked into the doorjamb and then slid down the wooden molding. He landed on his bottom and fell back onto the floor in a dead faint, with one long leg splayed in the kitchen and the rest of him in the dining room.

Miranda dropped her chin to her chest. *This is worse than Barney Fife. How on earth did he get a job as a deputy? Who is he related to?*

"Mac, can you look after the deputy?" said Miranda. "I'm going out to use his patrol car radio to get some real help." She patted Mrs. Hobb on her shoulder. "I'll be as quick as I can. Try to stay calm while we get this cleared up. The patrol car is blocking the ambulance."

"Fainted, did he?" Mac looked at the downed deputy. "Not surprising. Can't believe they sent him out here. In fact, I'll bet the sheriff doesn't know anything, yet. Deputy Spenser must have answered the emergency call and like an idiot decided to tackle this alone. Silly, but not surprising, as he's been like that his whole life."

Mac opened his medical case and took out a small capsule. He stooped down next to the indisposed Deputy Spenser and snapped the container of smelling salts, then waved several passes under the deputy's nose.

Deputy Spenser's head jerked back and wacked the side of the kitchen doorway with a loud thud. "What—"

Mac waved the capsule under Deputy Spenser's nose again and frowned when the deputy grabbed his hand. "Hey, stop it. You fainted."

"I'm so sorry. I absolutely swore to myself that I wouldn't faint. I must have also hit my head."

Miranda left them to wrestle with their pride and went out to the patrol car blocking the road. She opened the door, feeling like this was a bad dream, and sat in the driver's seat. She picked up the mic and pressed the push-to-talk button with her index finger. "Hello. Hello. Can anyone hear me?" She released the button.

Silence.

She waited a long moment and tried again. "Hello, hello. This is Miranda Trent up on Pine Ridge. I need help."

When she released the button this time, there was a rush of static, followed by a feminine drawl. "Who's on this frequency? This is an official police channel."

"Yes, ma'am. I know that. I'm trying to get help."

"Where's Deputy Spenser? He's the only one that's allowed to use this channel."

"He is here, ma'am. But he's passed out in the kitchen and I thought you guys should send more help."

"He what? What's he doing out there? I don't have a record of an emergency."

"I was afraid of that. It looks like he answered the call without telling anyone. I desperately need help."

"Oh, of course. What's the emergency?"

"Deputy Spenser came to investigate a death up here at my place. It's the old Buchanan Farmhouse out on the top of the hill at Pine Ridge. He took one look at the body of the cook and dropped into a dead faint. She's been stabbed in the chest with her own butcher knife. Also, my second cook appears to be having a heart attack, but the fire rescue guys are taking care of her. Can you send someone else out right away?"

"I'm so sorry, Miss Trent. That's a sore trial for sure," said the dispatcher. "I'll tell the sheriff to

come out there right away. Just hang on a second."
The radio fell quiet.

Miranda reckoned that the dispatcher was speaking to the sheriff on another channel.

The static returned. "Miss Trent, you say someone has been killed. Who?"

"Mrs. Childers, my cook."

"Which one?"

That caused Miranda to pause. The dispatcher was right—there had to be dozens of women with the last name Childers in this area. It was a common family name.

"Naomi. Mrs. Naomi Childers. She has been stabbed to death in my kitchen."

"Was it an accident?"

"I don't think so."

"Who stabbed her?"

Miranda drew in a deep breath. "I don't know. No one has been seen driving away, so if she was killed, the murderer is likely either nearby or still at my farmhouse."

After saying those words, Miranda leaned back and let the tears flow down her cheeks. Although they were never close, she had known Naomi Childers all her life. Widowed early, but part of a large clan of family members, Naomi had thrown her prodigious energies into volunteering both in her church and in the community. Her only close relative was an estranged niece who lived in Winchester.

The dispatcher spoke once more. "Murderer? I'll tell the sheriff to step on it."

Chapter 7

Saturday Afternoon

Miranda looked towards the porch and saw the firemen take Mrs. Hobb around to the back of the ambulance. One of them yelled out to her.

"Can you have somebody move the patrol car? We can't get the gurney around it."

Miranda raced into the house and found Deputy Spenser lying on the couch where Mrs. Hobb had just been. He was still pale, his eyes were closed, and the back of his hand lay across his forehead, covering his eyes, the mirror image of Mrs. Hobb only a few moments before.

"Deputy, where are your keys? I need to move your car so the ambulance can leave."

Deputy Spenser unclipped a bunch of keys from his utility belt without disturbing the hand over his eyes. He held them straight out.

Miranda grabbed them and ran back out to the road. She got in the patrol car, feeling like a teenager sneaking a stolen ride. She started it, put it in gear, then drove it about twenty-five yards down the gravel road. Then she waited for the ambulance to back out, turn onto the road, and make its way out toward Doctor Watson's office in Campton. Little Jimmy waved his thanks to Miranda as they left.

Miranda pulled the patrol car into the parking spot that the ambulance had just freed up, shut off the engine, took the keys, and walked back up onto the porch. Just as she was about to open the screen door, another patrol car arrived and drove beyond the already crowded driveway and parked in front of the outhouse. This car displayed "Wolfe County Sheriff" on the doors and the top of the trunk.

Miranda hopped forward, then looked around when she was bumped in the back by the screen door. Kelly pushed herself out to stand at the edge of the porch. Of course, she let the screen door slam.

Do these people have no mothers?

"Who's this now? Talk about activity. Grand Central Station is nothing compared to the commotion at this little farmhouse."

Another bang of the screen door announced her friend Linda. "What's going on now? You're up to your neck in officials, Miranda. Did you call this one, too?"

Miranda folded her arms and pulled back her shoulders to stand as tall as she could. "We're calling in the proper emergency services for an awful event. Could you both go back to sit in the front room please? I know everyone is anxious, but it would help the situation if you could try to stay put."

The women looked at each other and gave a "who cares" shrug before they went back inside. Miranda caught the edge of the screen door before it could slam again.

The sheriff walked at a deliberate pace up the narrow dirt path to Miranda's front porch steps. He was tall and lean with a trim salt-and-pepper mustache. He had put on his hat and rested his hand on the Colt .45 revolver in its holster at his hip. He was followed by a petite, dark-haired woman wearing black work trousers and a white oxford shirt and carrying a large black case. Both wore worried looks.

When they reached the bottom porch step, he tipped his hat. "Good afternoon, Miss Trent. I'm Wolfe County Sheriff Richard Larson and this is my wife, our county coroner, Felicia Larson. I hear that you have a situation."

Miranda shook hands with them. "Yes, sir. Hello, ma'am. I'm relieved that you're here. We have a horrible situation—no, a tragic situation, a terrible accident. Follow me." She led them into the front room, where Deputy Spenser was throwing up into a dusty galvanized bucket.

Miranda was thankful that someone had taken the trouble to fetch it from the coal shed. She was upset enough without having to deal with a terrible mess on her grandmother's rag rug.

"Dagnabbit, Gary. What do you mean taking this call without letting me know?"

Gary looked up without lifting his head very far out of the bucket. He started to speak but instead retched into the bucket again.

Sheriff Larson huffed in frustration. "You're not helping, Gary. You've seen worse on the highways. Get out of here into the fresh air as soon as you can stop puking." The sheriff turned back to Miranda. "Sorry 'bout this, Miss Trent. Gary's only supposed to work traffic. We get a lot of reckless speeding and drunk driving on our roads and we simply have to have someone do it. He's the only one who showed up when I asked for applicants to take the position. I might have to rethink my options."

Miranda raised her eyebrows and led them through the dining room among the quiet and pale clients sitting or standing around the table, still sampling Dan's moonshine. She elbowed her way through with the officials close behind her. Then she stopped at the doorway into the kitchen to let them go first.

Chapter 8

Saturday Afternoon

Sheriff Larson took one step into the kitchen and stopped abruptly, causing his wife to bump into his back. "Oh shoot, honey. It is Naomi Childers, just like we were told." He turned to his wife and squeezed her hand for a second.

"The poor dear." Coroner Larson stepped in front of her husband and placed her case on the floor over by the kitchen counters, as far away from the stricken cook as she should get. She opened the case and put on plastic gloves and grabbed a high-intensity flashlight. She knelt beside the dead woman on the floor and pressed two fingers to her flabby throat. She glanced at her watch. "I'm declaring Naomi Childers to be deceased at one twenty-five p.m."

Coroner Larson looked up at her husband. "Rich, we've got to call Lexington."

"Why? This is an accident. It looks like a kitchen accident."

She stood up. "I wish I could be that certain, but I'm not. I don't see how such an experienced cook could accidently fall like this. I can see why you would wish that it was an accident, because investigating our neighbors and friends as murderers is not what I want to do either."

"Is there any chance?"

"That it was an accident? Right off, no. I think it was deliberate." She stooped beside Mrs. Childers and shined the flashlight on the area where the knife entered the chest. "A kitchen accident wouldn't involve such a deep wound. The stab location is also suspect—right in the middle of the chest. Most kitchen knife fatalities involve an accidental slice to an artery or a dismemberment. This is—at first glance mind you—a deep plunge into bone and muscle."

"I can see that."

She stared her husband square in the eyes. "You have to treat this like a crime, because we can't afford to get this wrong. We need help with this. We don't have the crime scene resources that they have in Lexington. We're country. We're limited."

"But—" said Sheriff Larson.

"No buts." She lowered her voice to a sharp whisper. "What if this is a serial killer? What if this is the start of a killing spree?"

"Really, honey!"

"I know. That's an exaggeration, of course, but sweetie, there are lives and reputations at stake. You saw the crowd out there. How many of them have been in and out of this kitchen? Probably all of them."

"But—" tried Sheriff Larson again.

"I know you want to keep what happens in Wolfe County private to ourselves. That's how we were raised, but this needs everything that Lexington has to offer. You have to put your personal feelings aside. Do you want to be responsible for letting a killer go free?"

"You know better than to ask me that. I'll call them all right. Their forensic experts are the best, but you need to rein yourself in a bit. I know you would like to solve a serial murder case for some completely unexplainable reason, but this is not going to be that case." Sheriff Larson pulled out his cell phone. "Right. No signal. I'll go out and use the radio to get in touch with the Homicide Unit. They'll be irritated, but it's better if we ask nicely." He turned back to his wife. "I'm sure you'll be the acting coroner, no matter which organization gets the case."

With both hands propped on her hips, she turned to face the body of Mrs. Childers. "I know. I'll be extra, extra careful."

The sheriff returned to the dining room.

"Miss Trent, I think you heard that we're calling Lexington in on this." He glanced at the wide-eyed clients around the room. "Everyone, relax. I'll be right back." He skimmed over each client one by one. "I'm sorry to disrupt your schedules, but I'm sure you're all willing to help us in any way you can. You're all witnesses and I'll begin taking statements shortly."

He hustled out of the house to use the radio in his vehicle.

Chapter 9

Miranda closed her eyes and rubbed them until they stopped itching. Lack of sleep wasn't helping the situation at all. She had been worried about how this cultural experience venture would turn out. The reality was far worse than her wildest nightmares.

She took a deep breath. "Attention, please. May I have your attention?" Austin and Dan appeared in the front room doorway and leaned in. "We're going to be stuck here for quite some time."

"But, why? We didn't do anything!"

"That's ridiculous. We don't even know these people."

"I'm hungry."

"I'm thirsty."

"How about more shine?"

Miranda held up both her hands. "Hold on! Let's try to help instead of getting in the way. Dan, could you give everyone another sample of your strongest brew for a pick-me-up? Oh, I have an idea. Shefton, could you run down to Miguel's and get half a dozen pizzas? Split them up any way you like as long as two of them are vegetarian."

"But the sheriff told us not to leave."

"I know—but he's keeping us out of the kitchen and he knows I have tourists here. Besides, I don't think he wants to talk to a bunch of starved witnesses. It's been a long time since breakfast. Oh, get some sodas, too. I can't get into the refrigerator. Wait a sec." She pulled three twenties from her billfold. "You'll need some cash. They don't take credit cards down there."

Shefton took the cash. "I've got you covered, cuz. I'll tell the sheriff where I'm going." He smirked. "Wouldn't want to be accused of trying to leave before they complete their investigation." He started to leave, then questioned the room. "Wait, whose car can I take?"

Dan dug his keys out of his front pocket and tossed them to Shefton.

"Thanks, I'll call in the order as soon as I get some signal. I should be back in about thirty minutes." Shefton sped out the door.

"Right," said Miranda. "That's food on the way. Austin, you know how to draw water from our well, don't you?"

"Born here, remember? Oh, I get it. We can't get any running water from the kitchen sink. Good idea. I'll get some drinking water from your old well. Everyone already has a water glass." He left by the front door and headed for the still-working well in the side yard near the back of the farmhouse.

With everyone's immediate needs taken care of, Miranda walked into the front room and saw Deputy Spenser get up from the couch. Apparently, Dan had rustled up a washcloth and he held that to his mouth for a last swipe. "Excuse me, Miss Trent. I'll just take myself off and go talk to the sheriff." He tried to hand her the cloth.

"Keep it, Deputy. I have plenty."

Deputy Spenser rolled his eyes but had no strength to speak as he trudged out to the sheriff's car.

"Could we at least get out of this room?" asked Linda.

"Yeah, I've got to go the bathroom," said Kelly, her expression pained. "Really bad."

"I do too," said Linda.

Miranda shook her head no. "The kitchen is being investigated by the sheriff and the coroner. They don't know that they're blocking the only way to get to the bathroom."

"But they can't keep us from the bathroom," said Brian.

"That's too cruel," said Laura.

"They don't mean to be cruel, but that's not what they're thinking about. There are several old-fashioned solutions." Miranda tried her best to keep her voice cheerful, but that seemed to alert her clients that something was in the works that might not be fun.

"What are you talking about?" Laura looked dubious.

Miranda paused. Her mother had predicted that her business would go wrong. Well, it can't go more wrong than this, she thought. It was going to fail in a spectacular way. However, that was not the fault of these nice tourists. They deserved her best efforts.

"Please, I've got to go!" said Kelly.

Miranda pointed outside. "Out behind the barn for the men and boys."

"Great," said Brian as he rushed outside. He grinned. "I'll be back in a whizz."

"And for the women and girls?"

"I'm so, so sorry. We are out in the country where in the past folks took care of things themselves. So, this morning I cleaned it."

"Cleaned what?" said Kelly.

"The outhouse. The outhouse still works."

Miranda hadn't seen a haughty look like that since she'd left New York City. It was typical to witness that look several times a day on every day she lived there.

Definitely whenever she mentioned her address. She had subleased a tiny three-room apartment in Queens that had provided her with an obnoxious roommate. Her salvation was the one south-facing room that flooded with light. It was her painting loft. She made ends almost meet by working at the Museum of Fine Art in Manhattan. She slept on a cot in a corner of the loft and stored her sparse wardrobe using a few hooks on the wall.

She got snooty looks when she appeared for art events. She owned one little black dress that she wore with black ballet flats. It also served as her work uniform. She had a collection of scarves that she used to change up her look. Since everyone in New York City wore black, she hoped it wasn't noticed, but occasionally it was. Then she got the haughty look.

Even though she never felt like she fit in, she knew her art had grown by leaps and bounds in both depth and maturity from the experience of living there.

Sheriff Larson returned and stepped into the kitchen. He turned his head down towards the coroner. "Just to let you know, the Lexington Chief of Police is sending a homicide investigation team. He says they'll be here in about two hours." He left.

The coroner was right behind him. She glanced back at the kitchen. "I've done all I can do here. Lexington will have to decide where they want the autopsy performed. I would expect them to take her to their morgue, but you never know, they might be swamped."

"Sure. Why don't you drive Gary's patrol car back to the station? He can help me here with keeping tabs on everyone. He should be feeling okay by now. I'll let the dispatcher give you a call when they decide what they're going to do with Mrs. Childers. Meanwhile, I'll begin taking statements. I want their first impressions documented in the case file. In two hours, they'll forget details."

He turned to Miranda and looked around the tiny farmhouse. "I'm going to need a private interview space. Any suggestions?"

Miranda stepped back. "I've only just moved in so my bedroom is packed full of boxes. I haven't touched anything in my uncle's bedroom. It's right over here." She opened a wooden door that was tucked into the right-hand wall of the dining room at the bottom of the stairs. "I can move a couple of chairs in there for you."

Sheriff Larson walked into the bedroom that was sparsely furnished with a single bed and a small table holding an alarm clock. At the opposite wall was a wooden wardrobe. The wall that adjoined the dining room supported a row of pegs on the wall. Every peg held sporting gear of some sort: fishing rods, a fly-fishing vest, a bow and a quiver of arrows, heavy jackets, waders, two holsters containing guns, and hats of every type.

In the far corner was a worn, overstuffed, comfortable reading chair with a foot stool and a side table stacked with books that Uncle Gene hadn't gotten around to reading. Miranda looked at the stack and saw the bookmark tucked midway into a copy of *Cyber Attack* by Tim Washburn. *I didn't know he liked these kinds of books.*

"My late Uncle Gene loved hunting and fishing." Miranda felt her voice rise in pitch and speed.

Ugh! I'm babbling again. It wasn't necessary to explain the stuff in the room—he's a clever man and will figure it out for himself.

"This is fine." He stood with his hands on his hips. "Not ideal—but better than in the barn. I'll get Deputy Spenser to bring in a dining room chair."

"I can do that."

"Good. Why don't we start with you?"

"Sure." Miranda could feel her heart pounding against her chest. Surely, her nervousness was plainly visible and would indicate to Sheriff Larson that she should be arrested immediately for the murder of the best biscuit baker in Wolfe County.

But no, he didn't arrest her.

While Sheriff Larson explained to the still-pale deputy about the importance of keeping control of the potential witnesses, Miranda snagged the nearest dining room chair and placed it in her uncle's bedroom next to the reading table. It looked like a stage setting in a play. She imagined the billing lit up on the theater marque:

MURDER AT THE FARMHOUSE
STARRING JANET LEIGH

She shook her head to clear her thoughts. *I need to settle down and concentrate.* Finally, Sheriff Larson turned his attention her way.

"Now, Miss Trent, let's get to the bottom of this." He reached into his top shirt pocket and took out an official-looking notebook with a badge insignia on the cover. He settled it on his knee. Then he pulled out a pen from the same shirt pocket and clicked it to start writing.

"First, give me the names of everyone who is here. Start please by separating the staff from the tourists who came for your event, and then also I need to know who the locals are."

"But surely, you know who is local?"

"I need to hear it from you. People lie. That's important information."

"Sure, first the tourists are Joe Creech from Dothan, Alabama. Laura and Brian Hoffman are the newlyweds from Akron, Kelly Davis and Linda

Sanders are from New York City. Of course, you already know our only local tourist. That's Shefton Adams." She took a deep breath.

Sheriff Larson had been taking notes. He peered into Miranda's strained face. "You're doing fine. Keep going on."

"The distillery representative is Dan Keystone from Lexington. The other locals are Ranger Austin Morgan, Viola Hobb and, of course, the late Naomi Childers." Miranda expelled a pent-up breath and folded her hands in her lap.

"That was great—you have an organized mind. Artists often have a completely different way of looking at things. That helps quite a bit." He scribbled for a few minutes, then raised his eyes. "Now, rumors running around town are saying that you and Mrs. Childers had words about your new business. Some pretty loud arguments, in fact. Is that right?"

"Yes. Doris Ann wasn't the only opponent against my serving moonshine on the tour. Mrs. Childers strongly objected to serving the moonshine with the cultural meal. But I increased my donation to her pet project, the church roofing fund. She still wasn't happy, but at least she stopped complaining about it. I should have offered her more money sooner."

"Did you kill her?"

"What?" Miranda stood straight up out of the chair. "What a horrible thing to ask! I can't believe you asked that." Miranda sat back in the chair and clapped a hand over her mouth.

Sheriff Larson leaned in close and whispered, "But that's what I need to know."

Chapter 10

Miranda sat in her late uncle's bedroom on a dining chair that she had brought into the room with her. She found it hard to believe she was being interviewed by Sheriff Larson for her possible involvement in the death of her cook.

He had just asked her if she had killed Mrs. Childers.

She just stared at him. She opened her mouth to speak and felt her jaw drop but no words came. She couldn't answer.

The sheriff leaned forward and lowered his voice. "Miss Trent, I understand that you're shocked by what has happened. Mrs. Childers is dead. The investigation will be intense and personal. It will disrupt everything in your life. It's what you must expect if justice is to be done."

He stared into her eyes, making doubly sure his message was received. "Are you ready now to give your statement?"

"Do I need a lawyer?"

"Do you think you need one?"

Miranda gulped, sat forward, and straightened her shoulders. "No, sir, I do not. I am innocent. What do you want to know?"

"Let's start with telling me how you decided to hire Mrs. Childers. She doesn't usually work for anyone but the church. Mrs. Hobb, now, she is always looking for extra money, but I was surprised to hear that Mrs. Childers would be your cook."

Miranda tightly folded her hands together to keep from digging at her nails. "It was my mother's idea. She knows everyone who's anybody in Wolfe County. She and Dad grew up here and Mrs. Childers is—was—the best traditional Southern cook. So her meal recipes and presentation would be completely authentic."

"That's important to your tour?"

"Yes, tourists can always sniff out a scam and then they love to spread the word on social media like a house afire. The more real culture I provide, the better for my business. She also has a reputation for her influence with the city council, so I was counting on her spreading the good word about my business. I really needed her help."

"And what about Mrs. Hobb?"

"That came about after I told Mrs. Childers how many people could be in each group. I can handle up to ten for the painting session. She said it was too much work for just one cook." She paused recalling Mrs. Childers's sharp, insistent tone.

Sheriff Larson looked up. "Go on."

"When I saw how much preparation is needed

for these meals, I was staggered. I've never cooked for a large group. Anyway, she recommended Mrs. Hobb. She also appeared to need an audience, and they were best friends from all the way back to first grade. I think another reason was that it also gave her someone to order about."

The sheriff had a coughing fit after that last remark. He leaned back in the easy chair and let the fit progress to an out-loud laugh. "That's perceptive. I had noticed the same behavior myself." After noting down something, he leaned forward again. "Now let's start going over the activities of your event from the first thing until now."

Miranda took in a long, slow breath, and then just let the words spill out as they wanted to. She heard them tumbling over each other in no particular order and in no particular logic that she could see.

After she finally stopped talking, Miranda folded her hands tightly. Her index finger was bleeding at the nail. She didn't remember biting it. She pressed her thumb to the wound to stop the bleeding.

She must have made some sense because when she stopped, the sheriff didn't seem annoyed with her account.

The sheriff continued to write in his notebook for what seemed like a century.

Finally, he looked up. "Thank you, Miss Trent. That's a big help with the general situation. I have a better understanding of your business and how things were meant to go."

"Is that all?"

"From me? Yes. If I have time before the Lexington gang get here, I may have a few more questions after I talk to everyone else that I can squeeze in."

She stood and was surprised that her legs were shaky. "What happens now?"

Sheriff Larson stood as well. "I'm going to continue taking statements. I'm sure the Lexington officers will want statements as well."

"What can I do to help? I could round up folks."

"That's generous, but I think that Deputy Spenser is capable of shuffling everyone in here for their interviews. But I would appreciate it if you could tell him to send in Ranger Morgan."

Miranda didn't see Deputy Spenser, but found Austin and told him that he was next to be interviewed. He raised his eyebrows. "This ought to be interesting." He quietly opened the bedroom door and slipped inside, closing the door behind him with a sharp click.

Miranda looked at the kitchen doorway and a shudder ran down her spine. How long would poor Mrs. Childers have to lie there? It seemed so callous. She hoped that the Lexington officials would hurry. The weather was cool, but . . . Miranda shuddered again.

Your thoughts are getting ghoulish, girl. Stop it.

She was desperate to get a bandage for her finger, but she couldn't get to the bathroom. She went into her backpack in the dining room and got the first aid kit, and used a handy wipe to clean her hands. Then she wrapped her finger in one of those stretchy bandage strips. That would stop her from tormenting that finger, but she knew she would begin picking at the bandage, so she slipped another one into her pocket.

Everyone was hanging around in both the front room and the dining room with the condemned atmosphere of a dentist's waiting room. Deputy Spenser was standing next to the front door.

In the dining room, the pizza boxes had been cleared away and a single box containing the leftovers remained with its lid open. Miranda was surprised to feel hungry. She opened one of the Ale-8 bottles and grabbed the last meat slice. She ate it where she stood and downed the lemon-lime soda in one long swig. She put the empty bottle in the returnable carton on the table and began to make her way to the front door.

Deputy Spenser stepped into her path. "The sheriff said to keep everyone close by."

Miranda was about to speak when she heard a pitiful whimper from her bedroom. "Oh shoot, it's Sandy!" She opened her bedroom door and rushed over to the crate. "Sweetie! I'm so sorry. I forgot all about you. I'm a miserable puppy mommy." She opened the crate and Sandy bounced into her arms, whimpering and giving her puppy licks at double speed.

She kissed the top of his head, went out into the front room, and headed for the door. Deputy Spenser stepped in front of her. "No one can leave."

Miranda held the wriggling puppy within an inch of his face. "Do you want to clean up after him? He's about to poop everywhere."

"Um, uh—" Deputy Spenser stepped back, retched, and slapped a hand over his mouth.

"Absolutely, I'll be right outside. That's close enough for you to keep an eye out just by standing here in the front room."

He opened his mouth to speak.

"I live here, remember. This is my house. Just where do you think I'll go?"

"Yes, ma'am."

Sandy did his business as soon as Miranda set him on the grass. *He's such a good puppy.* That was a long time to be crated. While Miranda cleaned up, Sandy found a small stick under the big maple tree and brought it back to her for their usual game of fetch-a-stick. It was part of Sandy's potty-training routine. Miranda was happy to be outside in the fresh autumn air. It was good to be away from the gloom inside.

After playing a good deal longer than usual, she picked Sandy up and they collapsed into the porch swing and snuggled into the quilt that permanently lived there. It was the first quiet moment since she had left the farmhouse that morning for Hemlock Lodge. It seemed like a million years ago. In less than a minute, Sandy was napping in her lap.

The screen door opened and Austin joined her on the swing, taking care not to wake Sandy.

"How was it?" she asked him.

"I've known Sheriff Larson since I was a kid. He's a great guy. That's why he keeps getting re-elected for Sheriff. He's fair, but I'm as likely a suspect as anyone else."

"I wish I felt the same, but this is the first time I've met him. I am getting a horrible feeling that I'm an outsider, a flatlander for heaven's sake. My family has been in this area for generations. This 'you're not from here' treatment must be what tourists experience when they visit. That's what I want to change. It's awful."

"That's unfair. The sheriff is trying to protect everyone here from the Lexington Police Department. Past events have taught Wolfe County folk to be wary. That group is going to be the real outsiders."

"Who's in there now?"

"The newlyweds. They insisted that they were going to have to get back to Lexington to catch some sort of event that they had already paid for."

"That worked?"

"Sure, it's not really the sheriff's case, is it? The Lexington officials have already alienated everyone here and they haven't even arrived to be horrible in person."

Miranda and Austin let the silence between them rest easy. It was such a beautiful day to swing in the fresh air with nothing but falling leaves, hummingbirds, squirrels, and fluffy clouds to watch.

"This is not going to end well, is it?" asked Miranda.

"What do you mean?" Austin stopped the swing from moving with his boot.

Sandy whimpered and began to fidget. Austin released his foot to resume the gentle swinging. Sandy nuzzled further into the quilt and puffed a great sigh.

Miranda patted his little bottom. "With the two organizations both working on the same case, there's bound to be some territorial competition. No, that's not right. Sheriff Larson won't work

against them, but they won't use his local expertise. I've heard the same thing happens in differ-
ing precincts in New York City. This case is going
to take a back seat to crime in Lexington, isn't it?"

Austin nodded. "That's unkind, but unfortunately, I think you're right on target."

"But do you think this is a real possibility, not
just coming from my imagination? I have an intense and sometimes overactive imagination."

"Yes. I can see that," he chuckled, then looked
at her frown. "I think it's a good thing."

"Everyone in these parts knew that Mrs. Childers disapproved of my plan to serve moonshine
at my events. She knew about the clause in the will
that called out for me to start a distillery in the
barn. She threatened to speak to the town council
about denying my planning permit."

"You don't know that for certain. It's possible
that she wouldn't have been able to sway the council. She didn't have complete control."

Miranda frowned. "She is, I mean was, a right-
eous force of nature. My mom claims that she was
a powerful influence in this area for decades. Mrs.
Childers had arranged for members of her church
to go out talking to their neighbors and making
sure that everyone would be on her side of the
issue. I was definitely in danger of having that permit denied."

Austin opened his mouth to protest, then frowned.
"You may be right, but in the end, what will you do
if you fail to get a permit?"

"Good question. I haven't even given that a
thought." Miranda scratched the softly snoring Sandy

behind his ears. "I just can't figure this out. Why would anyone want to kill her?"

Miranda paused for a moment then continued, "How long do you think it will take the authorities to find out who killed Mrs. Childers? They're not even here yet and we're assuming that the Lexington crowd will think it's an accident. Sheriff Larson didn't make any headway with suggesting that it didn't look like one. Even with the coroner supporting a further investigation, I don't think that Lexington will pay much attention."

"Don't jump the wrong way. We think it was murder, but the authorities could still prove that this was an accident."

"You don't seriously believe that, do you? If this incident goes like most things around these parts, it will get sidetracked, shoved under the rug, relegated to a cold case, and remain unsolved. That's a thousand times worse."

"Worse than her death?"

"Yes, it will spread doubt about my business and I'll lose the farm. It's my first event. Everyone is watching to see how things go. No one will trust me to hold events or drink my moonshine. Without community support, I'll lose the farm and have to go back to Dayton to live with my mom."

Austin was quiet for a moment. "I didn't look at it like that."

Miranda stood. "I think my best decision is to do a little investigating on my own."

Chapter 11

Saturday Afternoon

The sound of heavy car doors slamming alerted Miranda to the arrival of the Lexington law officials. She rushed outside and saw three uniformed officers exit a Ford Interceptor. Then from a second Ford, out came a detective in a suit and tie, along with two technicians carrying large black cases.

Deputy Spenser followed her and grabbed her arm. "Hey, you're supposed to stay inside. Remember what the sheriff said?"

"Don't you want to know who's coming to see us?"

Deputy Spenser noticed the cars and froze on the spot. His eye widened and he swallowed before he yelled, "Sheriff Larson! Lexington is here."

Miranda slipped her arm out of his grasp unnoticed and he ran into the house.

The first blue-and-black Fayette County vehicle had found a parking space by the outhouse. The man in the suit stretched his back like he had driven from California instead of the sixty-five miles from Lexington's Main Street station. She thought that it would probably have taken them more time to assemble this large a team than it would to make the drive.

Why such a large force?

The man in the suit reached into the back seat and pulled out a black Stetson, which he seated and ran a finger around the brim. When he turned, she saw that he had a pitch-black handlebar mustache. He carried off a swaggering walk with unconscious grace. He approached the house to look up at Miranda, who moved to stand at the edge of the porch.

Miranda stared. She thought he looked like Hugh O'Brian from the old Wyatt Earp TV series on the Western cable channel she was obsessed with.

"Is this the Buchanan Farmhouse?" His nasal twang exploded the Earp image.

Miranda opened her mouth to answer but standing inside the house, Sheriff Larson bellowed, "Hey, Detective Otis E. Peterson! Is that you? I thought you were too important to be called up to investigate a back-country crime." Sheriff Larson walked out the screen door and stood at the edge of the steps, effectively blocking access to the porch and deliberately holding the high ground.

Oh great, they know each other. Miranda wondered if this would make the situation better or worse.

Chapter 12

Sheriff Larson groaned in disappointment. He knew at some point in his career, he would be called upon to work with his high school rival. Wolfe County wasn't that far from Lexington in distance, but culturally it was practically another continent. A questionable case was not the ideal starting point to address their personal issues.

Detective Peterson stopped in his tracks and looked up at the sheriff. "Good afternoon, Sheriff Richard J. Larson."

Making a show of checking his watch, the sheriff replied, "Did you get lost? That can't be. You were raised up in this part of the country." He hitched his thumbs in his waistband and stood with legs wide.

"It's been a long time since I've been back to Wolfe County. The last time I can recall was for high school graduation."

"Those were some interesting times back then.

Hopefully all is forgiven if not forgotten." Sheriff Larson tilted his head as a question.

"Yesiree, the times were as you say—interesting."

Rocking back on his heels, Sheriff Larson asked, "Didn't I hear that you transferred to an out-of-state university after we both started out at the University of Kentucky? Georgia Southern, wasn't it? Last I heard, they tied for last place in football. If you follow that kind of thing, of course."

Sheriff Larson regretted that barb as soon as it left his mouth. That was a mean and petty thing to say. *What is it about this guy that brings out the absolute worst side of me?* He felt ashamed for losing focus on what was really important. Finding the killer should be his primary concern. Rivalries that interfere with duty were a waste.

Detective Peterson narrowed his eyes. "Have you been meddling in my investigation? I heard from dispatch that you think this is a murder case. A case that you're about to hand over for me to solve. Right?"

Sheriff Larson removed his thumbs from his waistband and let his arms hang relaxed by his sides. "I wouldn't jump to conclusions, myself. The body is in the kitchen. Fatal accidents happen in the kitchen. I prefer to thoroughly examine the evidence and interview the witnesses before I declare a case of murder. But then I'm just a county sheriff, not a decorated detective from the horse and bourbon capital of the world."

Damn, that didn't last long—why can't I keep my big mouth shut?

Detective Peterson displayed a thin, stingy grin and made his way up the cinder block steps to stand on the weathered porch. "We're here to investigate this incident with or without your assistance. In fact, as I think about it, it will help speed things along if you and your staff return to your little office in Campton."

"Assistance? You can't mean—" Sheriff Larson snapped his mouth shut. This was dangerous ground. In the end, the Lexington force had the proper resources and facilities to discover what had happened to Mrs. Childers.

The detective deliberately edged forward so that Sheriff Larson had to move to the side. Without a glance at the sheriff, he opened the screen door and went into the farmhouse. The Lexington team trooped after him in silence.

Sheriff Larson rolled his eyes and cringed at his juvenile behavior. *I've got to do better, but even his name raises the hairs on the back of my neck.*

"Well, that didn't go as well as I wanted. I'm off the case," Sheriff Larson told Miranda. "I'm going to take my deputy and hightail it back to the station." He opened the screen door and yelled, "Deputy Spenser, come on out here. We're going to get out of their way and leave them to it."

Deputy Spenser followed the sheriff's lead and got in the patrol car. After a three-point turn, they edged their way back onto the gravel road, then stopped in front of the farmhouse. Sherriff Larson rolled down his window to shout out to Miranda. "If things don't feel right to you about how this outfit is conducting themselves, you call me. Our

Mrs. Childers deserves the best investigation possible—the very best."

He pressed his lips together in a scowl, looked forward, and then drove away at a gentle speed, as if reluctant to leave the job in the hands of a detective he obviously didn't respect.

Chapter 13

Saturday Afternoon

Miranda waved goodbye and stepped back into the house. It was packed to the gills with almost as many people as had been there since her uncle's funeral supper. The clients had been shuttled into the front room. They looked wide-eyed and uncomfortable. Miranda felt she had failed them somehow.

The Lexington contingent was crawling all over the kitchen with cameras and measuring lasers. They were using the dining room table for sorting out the sealed evidence bags. Their open forensic cases lay around the floor wherever there was a bit of space.

One of them had been raised properly and had removed everything that had been left on the table. That was probably after they had all been photographed for future social media posts, of course. Her clients had already stacked their dirty dishes and pizza boxes on the wide sideboard along the wall.

The newlyweds approached Miranda. Laura had been crying and Brian spoke in a hoarse whisper. "We're going to miss our special dinner unless we leave right now. Can someone please drive us up to Hemlock Lodge so we can get to our rental car?"

"You booked a reservation for tonight?" she asked then shook her head. "Oh, of course you did. This is your honeymoon. A special dinner would be the perfect way to spend this evening. Where is it?"

"Our dinner is at the Merrick Inn. Reservations have to be booked months in advance. Also, this excursion wasn't supposed to take very long. The pamphlet said that it would be over by one o'clock, which would have given us plenty of time. It's been hours and hours already."

"Absolutely right, and I am so very sorry. I had our meal scheduled for not more than forty-five minutes, an hour at most. Even accounting for the late arrival of Dan and his moonshine samples, you would have been fine."

"Well, to be fair, no one could have predicted this," said Brian. "It's not your fault."

That's not how it feels. "Did any of the officials ask you to stay here at the farmhouse?"

"No, we just assumed they would want another interview," said Laura, reaching for her husband's hand.

"Actually, our statements have already been taken by Sheriff Larson. That's official." Brian looked sternly at Miranda. "It's not your responsibility to worry about the investigation. You're an artist, not Miss Marple."

"Maybe not, but that doesn't mean that I don't have something to contribute. I'm an artist with significant observation skills. I'm a local insider from my summers here, but also an outsider from my years in New York City. These things could be useful. Let me see check in and see if they want additional statements. If they do, I'll see if I can get you an early interview from the Lexington officers so that you can scoot away to your dinner. I'll be right back."

Miranda stepped into the dining room and tapped the youngest-looking officer on the shoulder. "Sir, are you going to start interviewing my clients soon?"

He turned and cut her off. "What are you doing? You're supposed to stay out in the front room. You need to keep out of our way."

Miranda raised her eyebrows. "Certainly. Sorry to be a bother." She returned to the anxious couple. "I don't see why you can't continue with your plans. Just because they haven't got their act together, you shouldn't have to lose out. I've got your cell numbers, but do you mind telling me where you'll be after the dinner?"

"We would really appreciate it." Brian grinned at Laura. "You can absolutely contact us at dinner if you need to. We're staying at the Merrick Inn for two nights. We had hoped to be checked in by now."

Miranda peeked into the dining room. The officers were standing around. It looked like they were awaiting more instructions from the detective before doing anything. She made up her mind. "Let's get you up to the lodge before they even count how many of us there are." She tapped Dan on the shoulder and pressed her index finger to her mouth for silence. She waved him and the newlyweds out onto the porch.

"Dan, would you mind taking Laura and Brian up to the lodge so they can drive into Lexington for their fancy dinner at the Merrick Inn?"

"That's a great place." He looked at the newlyweds. "Wonderful food and atmosphere. Good choice."

"But what about—" Brian nodded towards the chaos in the house.

Miranda stood tall. "I'll take the blame. They should have accounted for everyone first. Before you leave, write down your phone numbers again so that I'm sure I have you. I know I have them on your paperwork, but mistakes happen. Anyway, they might want to follow up and you won't be at Hemlock Lodge."

The Lexington officials might get annoyed, but she was helping them by making sure that her clients could be contacted as quickly as possible.

Dan bustled them into his truck and leaned out the window. "After I drop them off, I'll just keep on going back to my distillery. I'm proofing a new flavor and need to attend to it within the next few hours or I may have to dump the whole batch and start over. As far as I'm concerned, Sheriff Larson took down everything that I had to say." He waved a hand. "Tell them it was my idea if you like. As a police force, they're not really looked on with much favor back in Lexington."

"What do you mean?"

"There have been several political shake-ups due to corruption at the highest levels of the police department. There are accusations that involve senior officers. I don't know the details, but it has tainted the whole organization."

"I may need your help in getting the insider information from Lexington. Could you help me with a contact of some sort?

"Sorry, but I just hear rumors from the other distillers on the Bourbon Trail. But, sure, if I can answer a question about Lexington politics, just call." He grinned like the disappearing cat in *Alice in Wonderland*. "You have my number."

Miranda smiled, then glanced at her watch. It was well after three o'clock and with the Lexington officials just getting started. This was going to be a very long day.

One of the young officers joined her. "Ma'am, are you the owner of this place?"

Miranda turned to face him with a rueful grin. "So far, I am." She held out her hand to shake his clammy grip. She could see the tension he was feeling in the tightness of his jaw. She glanced at his name tag, which said Officer Young.

That was certainly a fair description; he looked like a teenager. But since he had graduated from the police academy, he had to be at least twenty-five. The underlying green tone of his blotchy skin indicated that he didn't feel at all well. No wonder—anyone could get queasy after a glance at the scene in the kitchen.

"What do you mean?"

"I'm worried about the death of Mrs. Childers in my kitchen. It looks like a horrible accident, but it might be something else. She wasn't clumsy. Far from it."

He nodded but she could tell he wasn't listening to what she was saying. He plodded on anyway. "Please spell your name."

Miranda tilted her head and complied. He wrote that in a small notepad.

"Can you tell me where you were when the accident occurred?"

"I don't know when the accident occurred—if it was an accident. No one has said when they believe she was killed."

"Oh," he stuttered. "I mean, when the alarm was raised."

"I was out here on the porch yelling for everyone to come to lunch and right after that I was in the dining room when I heard Mrs. Hobb come in the back door."

He wrote down a few more lines.

"If Detective Peterson needs to talk to you, do you have a phone number where we can reach you?"

"I have a cell phone, but it doesn't get reception here." She rattled off her cell number. "I'm getting a land line hooked up early on Monday morning. Shall I call you with the new number as soon as it gets installed?"

"Fine. Yes, that would be great. Oh, Detective

Peterson wants a word, miss." He pointed his pencil towards the house. "He's going to interview everyone."

"But Sheriff Larson already did that." She figured they would want another interview but hope springs eternal—or maybe not.

"Any action taken by the Wolfe County Sheriff's Office doesn't count with us."

Hope dashed, Miranda followed him. He led her to the mustachioed detective, who was standing in the doorway to her uncle's bedroom. "Did the sheriff hold interviews in this room?"

"Yes, sir. He interviewed everyone while you were on your way out here. He said he didn't want to lose any details. He asked about everything that happened."

The detective huffed through his waxed mustache. The black color contrasted with the thin sandy wisps of hair escaping from under his black Stetson. She looked down and wasn't surprised to see black embellished cowboy boots.

He is from Lexington. Lots of people own horses and like to dress in a Western style. I wonder if he actually rides or could he be one of those "all hat, no horse" types.

His mustache twitched as if he was having great difficulty suppressing his opinion of Sheriff Larson's actions. He lost that battle. "There was no need for that. It's duplicated effort. My officers will take everyone's statements where they stand. What. A. Waste."

Miranda watched his mustache puff out with each word. She frowned. She didn't particularly like or dislike this guy, but she had counted on a competent investigation. "But, what about—"

"Thank you for your cooperation, miss." He dismissed her with a finger salute to the brim of his Stetson and stood in the kitchen doorway with his broad back to her, effectively hiding the activity going on in there.

In the dining room, everyone was being asked the same short list of questions by the two youngest officers.

She inhaled a great breath and straightened her shoulders. "Excuse me, but there are a few more witnesses you haven't interviewed." She stood calmly and waited for their reaction.

"Really?" said one of the officers. "Who are they?"

Miranda frowned. "There is a newlywed couple, Brian and Laura Hoffman. They're on their way to a fancy dinner at the Merrick Inn. I can answer your short list of questions for them. I've also got their cell numbers here for you from my client list." She rattled them off and he wrote it down in his notebook.

"Thanks, miss."

"In fact—" She waved her printout. "Would you like a copy of my client list for today? It has a good amount of information."

The officer looked doe-eyed grateful so Miranda went into her bedroom and printed off the contact list for today's cultural adventure. Since each client had given Sheriff Larson far more information than she had on the list, she was comfortable helping out the young officer.

"Also, Dan Keystone, the owner of the Keystone Distillery, was here, but he returned to Lexington to tend to some sort of time-sensitive mixture he was fermenting. I'm sure he's available to your local officers. You've questioned everyone else."

He wrote down the name of Dan's distillery and turned his back to her.

She shrugged, not really sure he meant to be rude. She had done her best to be helpful. Then she overheard one of the technicians from inside the kitchen talking to the detective. "Sir, we've completed our work."

"Fine." Detective Peterson turned to Officer Young. "I want you to oversee the arrangements for the body to be transported. Call the Campton coroner to take the body to the local morgue. When I called our morgue, they told me that they're completely overrun. Coroner Larson will have to perform the autopsy."

Officer Young nodded. "Yes, sir."

In about ten minutes, the black Shackleford hearse arrived. Miranda reckoned that the sheriff must have forewarned them to be ready to pick up Mrs. Childers.

The funeral home was a multigenerational family-run business that had handled her uncle's funeral. On rare occasions, they supplied facilities to the coroner's office. Mr. Shackleford and his son parked the heavy vehicle in the road and unloaded the gurney.

In a mere few minutes, the undertakers had smoothly maneuvered their way through the gravel driveway, over the grassy side yard, and into the awkward kitchen. They respectfully loaded the body bag that contained Mrs. Childers onto their gurney to take it to their facility in Campton.

By the time the hearse left, the Lexington officials were packing up their gear and loading the evidence bags into both vehicles. They ignored Miranda completely.

Finally, they had all gone with no goodbyes and Miranda was standing on the porch with her remaining four clients and Austin. They stood in silence, trying to process what had just happened.

Miranda finally broke the somber mood. "Get your stuff. I'm taking you guys back to Hemlock Lodge." There was a bustling of activity as they got bags, backpacks, purses, cameras, and their paintings.

"I'll shove off, too," said Austin.

"Thanks for all your help today. I don't think I could have coped without you."

He smiled. "This isn't the end of it."

She rubbed the corners of her eyes and looked up at him. "I know. It's just the beginning."

Chapter 14

The four clients chattered like excited school-children in the van on the way back to Hemlock Lodge. Miranda considered it likely that they might be in the perfect mood to reveal more information about what had happened than they had told the officials.

She was a bit concerned about how her passengers might react to seemingly casual questions from her after their experience with the local law enforcement officers. Also, addressing the issues concerning a murder while driving might interfere with her ability to navigate the twisty country roads. No matter—Miranda plunged right into her new role as amateur sleuth.

She looked into the rearview mirror at the group. They didn't seem upset. They looked excited and a bit relieved.

"Hey guys. Did any of you hear anything from

the kitchen to indicate at what time there might have been an accident?"

Her question abruptly stopped all conversation.

She rolled her eyes. So much for how easy this would be. She tried another approach. "Really, I mean, how could all that silverware dump out onto the floor without at least one of you hearing?"

In another quick glance in the rearview mirror, she saw Linda and Kelly look at each other. Linda had turned pale and Kelly was flushed up to her ears.

Kelly looked into the mirror. "We came in a little late for the lunch. I didn't hear anything from the kitchen."

Kelly turned to Linda. "What about you? Did you hear anything?"

Linda sighed heavily and pressed her lips together. Finally, she spoke up. "I heard lots of things from the kitchen. There was some banging of pots on the stove, also a good bit of dishes clattering, so I didn't think anything about someone dropping forks and spoons. I just figured that Mrs. Childers was angry about something and taking it out on her cookware."

Joe Creech piped up, "You know, there did seem to be a lot of noise coming out of the kitchen. Mrs. Childers seemed upset. I think everyone decided the best thing to do was stay well out of her way." He paused. "You were out front trying to figure out where the distillery guy was."

"You're right. I was certainly irritated with Dan for being late to my first event. Without his moon-

shine, there would be no tasting. What about you?"
Miranda looked back at Joe. "Did you hear anything?"

"Me? No, I was too interested in the birds and
squirrels. An army could have marched through
the kitchen and I wouldn't have noticed."

"What about you, Shefton?"

"I agree with the others. The noise seemed like
normal angry kitchen stuff. I just stayed away like
everyone else."

After dropping off her clients, Miranda stopped
by the lobby to talk to Doris Ann. The receptionist
was ready with an assault of questions about the incident. Miranda instinctively wanted to avoid her
nosiness, but if her business was ever going to be
successful, she needed Doris Ann on her side to
talk it up with the guests.

"Miranda, honey. Bless your heart. Is it true
what I hear? What happened at your farmhouse?
Did Mrs. Childers get murdered? Did Mrs. Hobb
break her leg when she slipped on the blood? Who
is going to clean up your kitchen?"

"That's a lot of questions." She fell silent as a
group of hikers passed them on their way to the
dining room. "Can you take a break?"

Doris Ann stood up and called out in the direction of the restaurant down the hallway, "I'm taking my break now." She reached into a desk
drawer and pulled out a steepled sign:

ON BREAK, SEE DINING ROOM STAFF

Grabbing her jacket, Doris Ann pulled Miranda
by the arm outside onto the lower deck of Hem-

lock Lodge, which faced out over the cliff with a view of the lake below. It was deserted. Apparently, folks who visited the Natural Bridge State Park for fresh mountain air didn't smoke.

Doris Ann pulled a lighter and a cigarette packet from the pocket of her jacket. She leaned against the railing with her back to the view and lit up. She drew in a deep lungful of unfiltered Camel. Noticing Miranda's open jaw, she said, "Now, don't get your panties in a twist. I only have one smoke a day. I know it's awful, but I can't stop altogether and I'm already ten years older than both of my parents when they died. So, shush up."

Miranda drew back a little distance away from the smoke. "Fine."

"What happened out at your place? Is Mrs. Childers dead? I knew that bringing in shine would bring disaster. Moonshine has always been a curse as well as a blessing around these parts. I told you that."

"Yes, you warned me, but I didn't believe you. I mean, why would I? I don't think her death has anything to do with shine. Anyway, you're right on one point. Mrs. Childers was killed. That rumor is true. Both the Wolfe County Sheriff and the Lexington Police came to try to figure out what happened."

"What did happen?"

"Well, opinions vary at the moment. Coroner Larson believes it was murder, but Sheriff Larson would like to think it was an unlucky accident. I don't know what the Lexington Police think. They didn't share their opinions with me."

"That's no help. You're all over the place."

"Sorry, it was so baffling. The local sheriff and the Lexington detective acted like sworn enemies and it wasn't a pleasant time. There was more commotion, confusion, and quarrels than I've seen on any of those British TV murder shows I enjoy so much."

Doris Ann tsk-tsked. "Oh, that's right. Those two boys have been feuding since high school. That's too bad."

"One thing I do know for sure is that Mrs. Hobb didn't break a leg. She fainted. She was taken over to her doctor's office in Campton." Miranda rubbed the back of her neck. "That reminds me, I need to call in over there and see how she's doing."

"What did the sheriff say?" Doris Ann stubbed out her cigarette in the sand-filled outdoor ashtray. "Why does he think it was an accident?"

"That's difficult to tell. We had both the Wolfe County Sheriff and the Lexington Police at the farmhouse. There was a huge difference in the way that Sheriff Larson handled the situation compared to what the Lexington detective, Peterson, did."

Doris Ann shrugged. "That's not surprising."

"Why? They're both police."

"They're both police, but those Lexington fellows may as well be from Mars. They don't care about us small communities."

"I think the Lexington group was just running through a minimal investigation with no real expectation that they would catch the culprit. I didn't see the kind of professionalism that will result in the capture of a murderer." Miranda rubbed the furrows on her forehead until she relaxed. "But then again, I don't know anything about police procedures."

"So, the rumors are true? It is a murder."

"I absolutely believe that. I think if it had been an accident, the alarm would have been raised when it happened and Mrs. Childers wouldn't have been left there for poor Mrs. Hobb to find and then faint over her friend's body."

"That makes sense."

"What doesn't make sense is why anyone would want to kill a little old church lady cooking a traditional meal in a remote farmhouse kitchen. I just don't understand what kind of situation would drive someone to do such a horrible thing."

Doris Ann reached into her jacket and lit a second cigarette. She gave Miranda a "don't mess with me" look. "We all have secrets." She pulled a long drag. "Most of us don't have the kind that could lead to violence."

"I'm bothered at the spite I saw between the local sheriff's office and the Lexington Police Department. I think an investigation will suffer because of their behavior. What if the case gets shelved and no one is caught at all? Has this feud been going on for a while? Is there a root cause?"

"There's always some tension between city and county law. This time, it's grown from a personal rivalry between the two men. They both went to the University of Kentucky on basketball scholarships based on their winning team at Wolfe County High School. Detective Peterson was team captain until a knee injury sidelined him permanently."

"He didn't look permanently injured. He didn't limp."

"It wasn't permanent, but it took a long time to heal. So long that he was dropped from his scholarship program and transferred to Georgia Southern. The injury took place on the court during a championship game, and he always claimed that Larson caused it. It became even more caustic when Larson took over as captain and led the team to four straight championships. Peterson will never forgive him no matter how much time passes."

"This isn't right. I believe that someone killed Mrs. Childers and whoever did it is running around scot-free."

Doris Ann took the last deep puff of her cigarette and stubbed it out next to her other one. They were the only stubs in the sand-filled ashtray. "I've got to get back to my desk. But before I go, have you given a thought to your safety?"

"My safety?"

"Yes, missy. Are you sure you want to stay out there by yourself?"

Miranda raised her eyebrows. "I haven't thought about it. I should be safe out there. I have my little dog for an alarm."

"Your puppy? Really?"

"Well, I heard Coroner Larson say something about a serial killer, but that appeared to be just a crazy argument she was having with the sheriff."

"Hmm. They do sometimes have some interesting discussions. I've got to go. You call me if feel frightened out there." Doris Ann returned to the lodge.

Miranda stood looking down at the view. Maybe Doris Ann had a point. What if someone was lurking in the woods nearby? She pushed the thought away. Miranda didn't really have a strong presence in the community. She was considered an outsider by most locals and an insider only by those who knew her family connection with the farmhouse.

She still felt concerned about the caustic situation between Sheriff Larson and Lieutenant Peterson. It was an awful thought that an old university rivalry could redefine what was possibly a vicious murder into a ruling of a regrettable kitchen accident.

She reckoned that Sheriff Larson was at least open to the idea that it was a murder but might be powerless to change the mind of the Lexington detective. It was a bad state of affairs for this investigation to be caught between the two forces.

She needed to do something. But, what could she do? She was just an ordinary starving artist from New York City.

She narrowed her eyes and steeled her nerve. She could do plenty.

Chapter 15

Miranda drove back to the farmhouse, her mind distracted by mulling over the fact that a woman had been murdered in her kitchen.

Austin's official ranger truck was parked next to the outhouse, leaving her plenty of room to pull in the driveway. He was sitting on the porch swing cuddling Sandy. She gently sat next to Austin and motioned for him to give up Sandy. The puppy was so deeply asleep that he didn't even wake up when Austin transferred him to Miranda.

She whispered, "What happened?"

Austin whispered as well. "I got back to my house and then turned the truck back around to tell you something important. On the way, I found Sandy in the middle of the road and headed toward Roy and Elsie's house."

Miranda sighed. "That's a long way for these little legs. It looks like he's figured out how to unlatch the crate. This is the second time he's escaped.

The first time I thought I hadn't closed the latch, but I've been extra careful so I'm sure I latched it. I think I'm just going to get a combination lock. There are so many poisonous snakes here—I can't bear to think of him running into one." Miranda nodded for Austin to follow her into the house.

She took the sleeping puppy into her bedroom and placed him on the soft blankets in the crate. She hooked the latch but just to make double sure, she got a hair ribbon from her dresser and tied that on as well. She shrugged and softly closed the bedroom door.

"Would you like a soda pop? I've—" Miranda stopped mid-sentence. The kitchen door was closed on the terrible mess that lay inside. She imagined the blood and a shudder ran up her spine.

"What's wrong?" he asked.

She looked back at Austin. If the killer could be anyone, could it be Austin? For some reason, her gut was completely calm on the topic of Austin. *If he's the killer and I'm still a threat, he's had oodles of chances to act. Nope—it's not him.*

"I can't face the kitchen." She formed a little lopsided grin. "There's still some water from the well in the dining room. Would you like a glass?"

"More to the point, would you like some help cleaning up? I'm fairly experienced, what with butchering roadkill and all."

"What do you mean?"

Austin bobbed his head in the direction of the highway. "We get a lot of deer killed or wounded out on the roads. When I get called out quick enough, I take the carcass over to the orphanage. That's after I've rough-butchered it into manageable portions for the cooks." He shifted his weight from one foot to the other. "It's a long-standing tradition in these parts."

Miranda noted that he seemed awkward talking about this kindness. She liked that. "That's a good tradition."

"For right now, I could do with a glass of water."

Miranda found two clean glasses in the dining room. The police had limited their forensic tasks to the kitchen so that room was still in reasonable order. She brought Austin his drink. After he downed the entire glass, he handed it back to her.

She sipped a bit from her glass, then she squinted at him. "I don't remember how bad it was in the kitchen, but I've never dealt with a murder scene before."

Austin raised his eyebrows. "I think that's a point in your favor. Not many people outside of the law get that chance. As a matter of fact, most people inside the law don't get that chance either."

Miranda stood a bit taller. "Listen, I'm not good with asking for help, but I'm at a loss here for dealing with that kind of mess."

"It's not like television where the camera just flips to the next scene, is it?"

"No, but if I was still in New York, there would have been a hazardous material specialist company that I could call or my landlord might have done that." She tilted her head slightly towards the closed door.

"Out here, we tend to clean up our own messes."

"I'm catching on." She looked back. "I accept your very kind offer to help me with the kitchen."

"Wise woman." Austin put his glass on the dining room table. "You go ahead and start with the dining room and I'll get going on the worst of the mess in the kitchen. I'll let you know when I've cleaned up enough so's you won't get sick."

"It's a deal."

Miranda took the serving tray that Dan had used for his moonshine cocktails and stacked the plates, cutlery, water glasses, and mason jars on it. She pulled the linens off the table and piled them in a chair. Finally, she wiped off the table and would have started sweeping the floor, except that the broom and dustpan were in the kitchen.

"Wow, that was grim." Austin opened the kitchen door and stepped inside the dining room. "It was difficult knowing how upset she would have been with the mess I was wiping up."

"That's my problem, too."

"This is as good as I can do for now." He held the kitchen door open for her.

Miranda lifted the tray of dirty dishes and walked into the kitchen. Austin was as good as his word. No sign of blood, or food, or broken glass anywhere on the floor. "Thanks so much. The kitchen is still a mess, but it's a perfectly ordinary mess. I can manage."

"I used almost a whole roll of paper towels and the dish towels that were already beyond saving to clean up everything. Then I wrapped it all up in a paper grocery bag so you can burn it with the rest of your trash, okay?"

"Thanks, I've never been good with blood. I get lightheaded with a paper cut." Miranda smiled and stood at the sink as she filled up the metal dishpan with hot soapy water.

How on earth could she investigate a murder if she reacted so badly to blood? The trick would be to avoid conflict. Investigation didn't necessarily lead to violence. She hoped so anyway.

The two of them together made quick work of washing, drying, and storing all the plates, glasses, pots, pans, and baking dishes.

Miranda folded her arms across her chest and scanned the tidy kitchen. "That looks so much better." Her shoulders dropped, releasing the tension that had found an unwelcome home. "Whew, I'm bushed. Would you like a soda pop? No? How about a cup of hot cider with cinnamon?"

"Hot cider will do for me."

"Great, I'll bring them out to the front porch."

Miranda prepared the drinks and placed them on a tray with two warmed servings of the untouched Dutch apple cobbler topped with fresh-made vanilla ice cream.

She peeked into Sandy's crate on her way out to the porch. He was fast asleep, snuffling a puppy snore. She smiled and continued out the door.

My favorite," said Austin. "I love any kind of cobbler." After the first bite he continued, "Wow, this is mighty fine. Wait. Which of the church ladies made it? Mrs. Childers or Mrs. Hobb?" He looked a little concerned that he might be eating a dead woman's cooking.

"It's mine—all mine. I used dried apples from my uncle's supply." She paused. "Church ladies? Why do you call them that?"

"That's what everyone calls them. They're steadfast members of the Campton Baptist Church. In fact, they're the backbone of the fundraising committee. It's a big loss."

"You know they were going to donate all their earnings to fix the roof?" Miranda smiled as Austin ignored her until he had wolfed down the last bit.

He made a show of displaying his empty plate. "I'll bet this is better than any of the church ladies' pies."

Miranda tilted her head and offered a tiny grin. "Thanks. I make it myself to save money. I plan to cut down on the expenses for this business by preserving my own apples and preparing the cobblers myself. Yesterday I made two and froze one. You're tasting a preview."

"Mmm," said Austin.

Miranda pointed her spoon down the gravel road towards the highway. "I keep expecting someone to come barreling down the road and haul me off for questioning. You know, in a grubby room, under a bright, bare lightbulb."

"Why would you think that?"

"I've got to be considered as a principal suspect. It was common gossip that Mrs. Childers and I disagreed over the concept for my Paint & Shine business. She threatened to petition the planning committee to reject my application to serve moonshine, and to deny my building permits for the new distillery in the barn."

"She was a well-respected member of the community. Maybe you were right to be concerned."

Miranda rubbed the furrows that had sprung

up between her eyes. She was worried. This situation seemed impossible. What set of problems could lead to an elderly cook getting murdered in her kitchen?

She told herself to straighten up and shake off these negative thoughts—not as easy as it sounded. "I guess I'd better make some calls and cancel my scheduled clients, I don't have anyone who can cook tomorrow's meal. Besides, I'm not sure anyone would want to come here to eat after there's been a murder."

"It could go either way. Folks will be curious and want to see the scene of the crime, or folks will avoid you like the plague."

"I don't know which type to wish for. It feels petty to hope for the curious type for clients. But this is advertised as a cultural adventure."

"You know, Mrs. Hobb has two granddaughters just out of high school. They are what she calls Irish twins." He noticed Miranda's confused look. "That means they were born exactly a year apart. They have the same birthday."

"Oh, I get it. They share their birthday parties."

"These sisters are so devoted to each other, the school set them in the same grade. Plus, they've been living with their grandmother since they got into high school. In such a large family, they've been helping with the cooking their whole lives. What about that for a solution?"

Miranda raised her eyebrows. "That would be fantastic. When Mrs. Hobb recovers, she could supervise, but not have to do the heavy lifting. I'm good with that."

"Perfect, I'll stop by and let them know about their grandmother and see if they're willing to fill in for a bit. You should assume yes, but if it turns out that they aren't interested, I'll come back and tell you so you can cancel tomorrow's tour. Is there someplace nearby that lets your cell phone get a good signal?"

"A bit far for convenience, really. It's over a mile down my road down past my neighbors towards the highway. There's a little turnout by a wooden gate that provides access to a field that holds about twenty yearling steers. Cell signal is decent at that tiny pinpoint. But you can always text me. That seems to work most of the time as soon as I move off this hill."

Austin stood. "Well, I'd better get on my way. Fingers crossed for the Hobb sisters."

"I'm still determined to make sure that Mrs. Childers get the justice she deserves. Plus, of course, that I'm cleared of any involvement. A big hurdle is that I really don't have any way of getting reliable information about what is happening with the Lexington detective."

"I may have the perfect solution for that—or at least an excellent start to getting more information."

"What?" Miranda stood as well and took his empty glass.

He remained silent with a furrow forming on his brow. "I'm not sure I should tell you without getting permission first."

"Spill it," Miranda demanded.

He continued to frown.

She stared into his eyes. "You can't say something like that and then stand there acting the strong, silent type on me. Spill it."

He shook off whatever reservations he was wrestling with.

"I'm not sure how helpful this will be. It could backfire, but I have a sister who works for the *Lexington Herald-Leader*. She's an investigative reporter on their crime beat. Do you want me to get in touch with her?"

"Oh my goodness, that's wonderful. A direct line to a reporter would be fantastic. I could help her with some insider details if she can keep me in the loop with what's happening to the investigation in Lexington."

"It seems you won't have any trouble keeping up with the Wolfe County part of the investigation."

"What do you mean?"

"I think both Sheriff Larson and Felicia are determined to make sure that Detective Peterson doesn't sabotage this case. He could destroy the reputation of both the Wolfe County Sheriff's Office and the coroner's office."

Miranda pulled the frayed bandage off her finger. "If that happens, my adventure business will be ruined."

Chapter 16

Saturday Evening

Miranda watched Austin's truck disappear towards his house. After the road dust died down, she went into her Uncle Gene's bedroom and loaded his shotgun. She carried it in the crook of her arm. Then she walked Sandy around the perimeter of the farmhouse, back behind the barn, and along all the outbuildings for a good bit of sniffing and piddling.

Miranda kept a sharp eye out.

There were two reasons for that. First, they could flush out a murderer, but she had no real expectation for that. There had simply been too much police activity around the farmhouse. Second, there were poisonous snakes searching out places to spend the winter. Little Sandy wasn't wise enough yet to let them go about their business.

After that they wandered all the way down the road to her cell signal turnout. Austin had texted her that the Hobb sisters would be delighted to fill in for their grandmother. She rang them up and after she discussed tomorrow's menu with them, she updated Dan on the three planned courses. He said the dishes would be easy to pair with a great moonshine.

Her last call was to the phone company over in West Liberty.

"Mountain Telephone. How may I direct your call?"

"Good afternoon. My name is Miranda Trent. I'm calling to confirm that you're installing my telephone line on Monday morning. Making business calls while standing off to the side of a dirt road is ridiculous."

"One moment please. I'll transfer you to our field installation department."

Acting as if he had been personally insulted, a nearby black steer turned in her direction, stretched his head out, and belted out a long, mournful moo. Whatever that meant in bovine, all the nearby steers began to gather behind their leader and bellowed the same sorrowful sound.

"Hello, this is—" All she could hear was static and garbled speech, ending with "today?"

"Wait. I didn't hear you. Can you repeat that?" Again, the steers seem to want to join in on the conversation and they all bawled in unison. "Can you hear me? I appear to be annoying the local beef stock. They look like they want to eat me and my phone."

It was hopeless. She had no idea what the field installation service person was telling her. All she heard was the lowing of the steers. She moved a little farther down the road to get out of earshot.

Then dialed again but immediately lost the connection.

She moved even farther down the road until she had three signal-strength bars and called the phone company again. Another customer service representative answered. This time the connection was clear and she could actually understand what the representative was saying. As usual, Miranda had to start from the very beginning to explain her situation.

After going over her phone requirements for the plenty-seventh time, she queried the representative, "Can you tell me who I'm speaking to, please? Does my installation have a work order number? I want definite confirmation that you'll install my land line on Monday."

Oddly, that series of questions seemed to light a fire under the installation representative. She gave Miranda an installation time window of Monday from 8:00 a.m. to 5:00 p.m.

"The whole day is not a time window. It's the whole doggone day. Can you schedule me for the first call of the day? I've had an emergency out here at the farm today and it was dreadful to be without phone service. I definitely need a working connection to emergency services."

There was a little gasp. "Oh, of course. You're calling from out at the Buchanan farm, aren't you? That's where the cook was murdered. Were you at home when it happened?"

"You heard about that already?"

"Well, we are the phone company and our trucks are everywhere."

"Right. Yes, I was here and it was horrible not to be able to call the emergency services."

"Have they caught the killer? Do you know who it is? Is anyone else going to be killed?"

"Um, I'm not sure I should be talking to you about any of this. But I must say it would be most helpful to the investigation of this terrible event to have a working telephone here at the farmhouse. Can you please give me your earliest appointment for the installation?"

"Absolutely right, Miss Trent. You need our best response. I'm moving you up to be the first service call of the day."

Miranda looked down at Sandy, who had plopped down with his chin on her foot while she handled her calls. "Thank you, thank you. That narrows it down quite a bit, doesn't it? I appreciate it."

She finally ended her call and slipped the phone into her back pocket. Sandy lifted his head and thumped his tail in the road dirt. She picked him up. "Good thing I don't have anyone signed up for that day. Still, most adventure tours don't have events on Mondays. There might be a good reason for that."

They wandered back to the farmhouse and she made up all eight backpacks for the Sunday tour and put them by the front door, ready to load into the van.

Taking advantage of the quiet time, she sat down in the rocking chair by the front window and made a few command decisions.

First, she would keep the dinner menu the same for the rest of the week to capitalize on quantity discount purchasing of meats, cheeses, vegetables, and dessert. It also meant that Dan could offer the same pairing of moonshine cocktails without worrying about menu changes.

Second, she would stick to hiking down the same trail, so that she would become more practiced pointing out geological features and also get more polished at teaching the painting of the scenic overlook.

Her original idea to offer a new view and new menu every day really wasn't practical. She wouldn't be having repeat clients within a week. After a few weeks, she might consider offering more variety, but everything was at risk right now and she needed to keep everything as simple and low cost as she could manage.

These tweaks would make the business more profitable and might help her survive the reduced traffic. If her mental calculations were accurate, she could break even with four or five clients.

She groaned. "Sandy, this is a great idea, but we have to go back to the turnout to call Dan and the Hobb sisters." She made her calls and they started out again.

"Ack. I didn't call Austin." Since they were a fair distance from the turnout, she texted the change-up of trails to him. Doris Ann would also be able to let him know if he stopped at the lodge before heading out on the trail.

At the farmhouse, Miranda made herself a hot cup of chamomile tea, hoping it would calm her racing mind. She sat in the comfortable rocker by the fire with a brand-new black-and-white composition notebook and smooth-flowing gel ink pen. On its cover she wrote "Murder of Mrs. Childers."

On the first page, she wrote "Possible Suspects" and listed everyone who had been at the farmhouse at the time.

> Mrs. Viola Hobb
> Joe Creech
> Shefton Adams
> Laura Hoffman
> Brian Hoffman
> Kelly Davis
> Linda Sanders
> Dan Keystone
> Ranger Austin Morgan

That's a long list of people I barely know. She felt a wave of despair sweep over her. What could she possibly do? She took a breath and thought about her skills. She was both an insider and an outsider to the area, so she would be filtering things differently.

Luckily, she felt that her New York City experience gave her confidence interacting with people and a sharp business sense. She was an artist with a fantastic memory and a trained set of observational skills.

She felt her normal level of self-confidence seep back. Not overconfidence—that would be a mistake—but she did have a long list of specialized skills. She was observant, she was a visual artist with a memory for images, she was strong and athletic, she had an analytical mind, and she was a born puzzle solver.

I can do this.

I can also learn new skills. I can talk to people in a

*way that police officials certainly can't. I have a strong
local connection and history. I want to get to the bottom
of this.*

Miranda returned to the notebook. It automatically fell open to the page she had marked for
Austin. He was mostly certainly not a suspect, and
as she was thinking about him, her sketch became
more and more detailed. It looked like he was
looking out of the page at her.

Moving on, she then gave each suspect an indi-
vidual page with their name on the first line and
she drew a quick portrait in the upper right-hand
corner. Then for the clients, she filled in the information that they told her from their introductions
out on the trail. For everyone else, she filled in ad-
dresses, phone numbers, how they were known to
her. Basically, it was a brain dump for each possible
suspect.

Flipping through the pages, Miranda realized
that she really didn't know much about anyone on
the list. She needed to figure out who was where at
the time of the violence so some on her list could
be eliminated.

She turned over to the next blank page and
sketched a plan view of the farmhouse, barn, outhouse, and all the outbuildings. She labeled that
page "Buchanan Farmhouse." As an afterthought
she added the tobacco patch that was leased out,
the little creek that ran behind her property, and
the location of the family cave that she had played
in as a child.

Saying she was going to investigate a murder
and physically marshalling the proper skills and
tools to accomplish that was going to stretch her.

She would need skills that reached way beyond those she used for painting, hiking, and distilling.

She rubbed her eyes and stretched the tension from the back of her neck.

I'm totally unprepared for this.

But then a complete lack of experience has never stopped me from succeeding when tackling something new. I taught myself how to create graphics for my artwork when it became vital to have business cards, brochures, and postcards. It saved a ton of money and still does.

I can run this business.

I think.

Chapter 17

Sunday Morning, Hemlock Lodge

The lobby was bustling with activity. Whole families dressed up in their Sunday-go-to-meeting finest were gathering together to wait for straggling members before making their way up to the cramped dining room entryway. A long line had formed that threatened to reach out the main lodge door.

Enjoying the Sunday buffet in the Sandstone Arches restaurant was a multi-generational tradition with some folks. It was a chance to catch up with family news as most of their tiny local churches only gathered for a service once a month.

The cook staff was well prepared with traditional dishes that drew on the comfort foods of both young and old alike. The smell of bacon made Miranda regret the cold cereal she had gobbled down in her rush to be on time. Next Sunday she would get here early.

Today's registration list had suffered five cancellations. Miranda was definitely losing money, but she didn't want to cancel the tour. That would give the wrong signal. She led her three remaining clients up the trail and they began to paint the view. She was surprised that with only one day of experience, she was relaxed and felt confident in her teaching.

As expected, Austin met them at the lookout and told her clients the history of the rock formations. It seemed to her that he spent a little more time explaining the romantic background of Lover's Leap. He also seemed casual and relaxed in giving his talk. Since the group was small, the questions were lively and felt like a conversation rather than a lecture.

Afterwards, he thanked Miranda and followed her to stand on the trail behind the clients, watching their progress. This class had some artistic talent and didn't need step-by-step instruction.

He folded his arms on his chest and noticed her worried expression. "This is not going to make you a rich woman."

Miranda laughed softly. "No, this will make me a homeless woman in pretty short order."

"If you don't mind my asking, how long can you last?"

"Not long. I have a little cash from the estate, but if this doesn't turn around quickly, I'll eat through that in a few weeks." Miranda chewed on the nail of her index finger. She despised herself for this childhood habit. She had it mostly defeated. It returned during times of acute discomfort. "If I can get this murder cleared up to show that I'm not an omen of bad luck, my little business could boost the economic level of the entire area. It would definitely add to the cultural land-scape."

"Are you getting positive support from Doris Ann?"

"I simply can't tell from her mixed messages. She appears to be supportive, but she also feels strongly about not having any moonshine at the farmhouse dinner. I misread the symbolic signifi-cance of having painful issues brought back into the light. Unfortunately, her support is a key strat-egy for encouraging guests to sign up for my tour."

"How's your marketing plan?"

"Ha! That's a glorious label for what little I've done." She thought for a moment. "No, that's not really a true statement. I have done just about everything I can to launch this business. It's part of the new wave of agritourist events throughout east-ern Kentucky.

Austin frowned. "I'm a luddite. What do you mean?"

"I've posted on all the usual websites, but I'm crippled right now by not having high-speed inter-net at the farmhouse." She pulled a sad face. "I completely underestimated the amount of time they would take to install. Meantime, I've been using the guest Wi-Fi at the lodge, but it only works in the lobby and that's unreliable. It's enough to keep me going, but it will be great to be able to check the online bookings at home."

Austin kicked at the trail dirt with his well-worn hiking boots, staring at the scuffed ground. "I don't want to sound like a tattletale, but—"

"Too late." Miranda laughed at his discomfort. Then she turned thoughtful. "I'm sorry. This is serious and I shouldn't be kidding around. What is it?"

Austin took off his ranger hat, rubbed his hand through his hair and jammed it back on. "I know a little background about your uncle and Dan. It's not pleasant and it's probable that it could be just gossip."

"Not likely if you know about it." She looked up into his stressed eyes. "Please, just tell it straight out. You know, like it was one of your lectures."

He nodded his head. "That will make it easier. Listen, I need to tell you—"

"Miss! I need some more orange," said one of her clients.

Miranda rushed over to refill the client's palette and gave out a few dollops to the other two as they were running low as well. She demonstrated the next few steps to be painted then returned to Austin.

"What a nice group," she whispered. "I could get spoiled. You were saying?"

"Your uncle Gene had multiple visits from Dan. It was easy to spot his panel van with that huge Keystone Distillery overwrap. It stood out a mile. You could almost see it from the highway." Then he fell silent. His lips were pressed closed.

Miranda recognized that he was overexplaining himself, but why? Was he nervous? She waited, mentally telling him, *Come on. Get to the point. You're stalling again.*

Austin took a deep breath. "It was rumored that your uncle was a silent investor in Keystone Distillery. Silent partner in the traditional sense of a cash loan with nothing behind it but a handshake kind of investor."

Miranda stepped back. "What?"

"That's what I heard."

"But Uncle Gene would have documented that somewhere. He was pretty good about keeping financial records. A loan should have been written down somewhere."

Austin looked down at his boots. "There are a lot of folks around here who still don't trust banks. Your uncle was one of them. Then, to make things worse for his type, we had that recession not too long ago. I think your uncle kept his extra cash hidden."

"Hidden?" Miranda slapped her forehead with a fresh realization of how many places around the farmhouse could be used for hiding cash. "He could have hidden thousands with no trouble at all." She thought for a moment. "Does anyone else know about this?"

"Most everyone would assume that he'd have an emergency stash. But one person absolutely knew because she told me."

"Who?"

"Doris Ann."

"Oh great. Another reason for her to hate me."

"You haven't found any cash?"

"A little. There was eighty dollars hidden in a coffee can in the kitchen. I found five hundred dollar bills in the toe of his dress-up go-to-meeting socks. That's normal, right?"

"Maybe normal for city folk, but not especially the way country folk behave. There should be more, a lot more."

"Why do you say that? How would he have gotten more money? He was living on Social Security."

"He was also one of the county's best small-batch moonshiners."

"What? No one told me that he was running shine. You're mistaken—that can't be true."

"Yes, it is true. His reputation was widely respected in the elite circles of rare and fine moonshine. His infrequent batches were sought after by fanatic connoisseurs of true backwoods corn whiskey."

"I can't believe that I didn't know. I spent my summer vacations down here. Sometimes we were here for Easter and Christmas. How could he have kept that a secret?"

Austin pressed his lips tight. "He didn't make shine in the summer. He claimed that it was too hot to work for the hours it takes standing over a still. I personally think he didn't want his family to know what he was up to in the fall and the spring. That's the only time he brewed and those small batches brought him a lot of money."

"I had no idea."

"None of the women in the family were let in on it."

Miranda shook her head slowly. "I wonder why Dan hasn't said anything about the loan. Would he keep it quiet, hoping he wouldn't have to pay it back?"

"I think I know," said Austin.

Just then, one of the clients knocked over her paint water and nearly toppled the easel with the wet painting, coming dangerously close to spoiling her canvas. Miranda dashed over and caught the painting by its edge. "Whoops-a-daisy! That was close." She restored the easel's position and refilled the client's water. "You guys are doing great. Keep blobbing in the fall colors for the trees and then we'll start on the chimney rock formations."

She returned to Austin. "Sorry, where were we?"

"I think I know why Dan hasn't talked to you. Doris Ann told me after your uncle died. She says it's because Mrs. Childers knew about the loan and was going to tell you. There's been a long-standing family feud between the Childers and the Keystone families for generations. No one around here would be surprised."

"Has she told the sheriff about it?"

"The sheriff knows about the feud because it's part of the local politics in this area, but the real question is whether or not he has told the Lexington detective."

"But the Lexington detective is local as well."

"Good point," said Austin.

Miranda rubbed the back of her neck. "I'll have to start looking as soon as this tour is over. If the amount is enough to murder Mrs. Childers over, then it's bound to be enough to pay my taxes and save the farmhouse."

"Good luck," said Austin. "I think you're going to need it because if the Keystones killed once for the money, they'll kill again."

Chapter 18

Sunday Afternoon, Miranda's Farmhouse

While Miranda was loading her clients into the van for the trip down to the farmhouse, her cell phone pinged a text message. It was from Dan Keystone.

SORRY, CAN'T MAKE IT TODAY—DISASTER AT DISTILLERY. YOU CAN USE SUPPLIES I LEFT BEHIND YESTERDAY. SORRY.

"Darn!" She quickly texted back:

I'M SORRY, TOO. VERY DISAPPOINTED.

He must have found out that I know about the handshake loan. The only one I told was Austin. Why would Austin tell him? Heck! Nothing is simple and nothing stays private around here for very long.

Miranda pulled into her driveway and was delighted to see the Hobb sisters standing on the porch waiting for her little group. They dressed in designer jeans like modern girls, but each was wearing a T-shirt with a ring of her namesake flowers embroidered around the border of the V-neck.

They appeared to have a foot in both camps—liking modern clothes but embracing their highlands heritage as well.

Fantastic—I adore them already.

The sisters were also wearing Miranda's branded aprons. Each apron had a large Paint & Shine logo front and center on the bib. Thinking back, Mrs. Childers and Mrs. Hobb had been too full sized to wear them, which had embarrassed her, but the grand ladies probably wouldn't have worn them anyway. They preferred their homemade floral aprons.

The aprons looked fantastic on Iris and Lily.

Iris, the older one by exactly one year, waved. "Your dinner's ready for you, Miss Trent. Come on in."

Miranda felt her shoulders relax. She had only met the girls for a few minutes before she left the farmhouse for Hemlock Lodge this morning. Her gut had been worrying about how many things could go wrong with the dinner preparation. Leaving a major part of her cultural event in the hands of two teens was bold indeed.

She reflected that it hadn't been that long since she was in her teens. She had launched off into life as a working artist in New York City. That had certainly been an adventure. Working with Lily and Iris might be just the right thing for her. She liked the idea of mentoring them, as opposed to being criticized by the church ladies over her every decision.

Then she broke out in a sweat. *What would I do if they didn't show up? I can handle the moonshine tasting, but what would I do?* She thought for a moment. *Oh, no problem. I'd just have the clients help me cook.* It would be a cooking lesson instead of a painting lesson. She smiled. *That's actually not a bad idea.*

"I set out the moonshine fixings for you on the sideboard, Miss Trent," said Lily. "The fried green tomatoes are warming in the oven and are just ready to put on the table."

"Miranda. Please call me Miranda."

"Yes, ma'am, Miss Miranda," said Lily.

Miranda felt mildly frustrated. *I'll never get comfortable with all the nuances of country manners. This is the insider-outsider dilemma all over. Lily is perfectly correct to treat her employer with respect.*

Her three clients washed up and sat around the large round table. They seemed to enjoy Miranda's chatter about the history of moonshine and her plans for her own distillery in the barn. At least they didn't seem bored.

More quickly and with more pleasure than she would have thought, the meal was done and she had driven her clients back to the lodge. By the time Miranda returned to the farmhouse, the Hobb sisters were finishing up with the task of clearing up in the kitchen.

"I hope we put everything back where you can find it," said Lily as she slipped her apron off over her head.

"We did a little rearranging to make things a bit handier for the next time," said Iris, who also took off her apron, grabbed Lily's, and hung them on a hook by the refrigerator. "We moved the pots and pans over to the shelf that's nearest the stove."

"And we put the glasses in the cupboard by the

sink so it's easier to put them up after they're washed and dried."

"The plates were just fine up in the cupboard on the other side of the sink." Lily looked at Miranda with a serious expression. "Will you have us back tomorrow? We really need the work."

Miranda bobbed her head up and down like a robin. "Yes. Definitely yes. I'm so pleased with everything you're doing—the cooking, the cleaning, and especially the fact that you have initiative. I just checked the signups. We only have four."

"That's one more than today, Miss Miranda," said Lily.

"True. I need to keep putting on the cultural adventure tours even if only one person signs up. A canceled tour at this point might kill the momentum I've built. I'm not sure, because, well, nobody knows for sure. Social media is not an exact science. I'm also not sure if Doris Ann is helping or hurting."

"No problem, Miss Miranda," said Iris. "We'll see you tomorrow."

Miranda watched the girls drive away in their battered pickup. They were adorable, but she really couldn't get a grip on who was who yet. They looked very much alike and she got the feeling that they were on company-best behavior. Hopefully, they would relax soon.

She did a quick inventory of food and art supplies and was relieved to find enough of each for the next few tours. There was enough venison from Uncle Gene's hunting successes to carry on with the current menu for a few more weeks.

Now, the next most important thing—to look for hidden treasure.

She put Sandy on his leash and after he did his business, they examined the perimeter of the house. The foundation was as plainly basic as the rest of the farmhouse. Great big blocks of rough limestone served as footers over simple hard-packed dirt. None of the dirt seemed disturbed in any way that suggested a stash of buried cash.

On the other hand, maybe he didn't access the money very often, but even every few months would leave a sign of some sort.

She and Sandy explored the outside perimeters of the coal shed, the well box, the barn, the wood-shed, and finally the outhouse. No freshly turned dirt anywhere. Not even a sign of old digging anywhere that she could see. She didn't think his hidey-hole would be too hard to get to—he was an elderly man in the end.

This wasn't going to be a walk in the park, but then again, she reasoned, if the location was obvious, she might have stumbled on it by now.

Shrugging off her disappointment, Miranda walked down the road to her second-best cell phone signal spot with Sandy in tow. It was closer than the turnout and only a little farther away from Roy and Elsie's house. Definitely worth a try. She had brought along her investigation notebook and a small quilt to sit upon.

She spread out the quilt in a soft patch of grass and sat cross-legged with the notebook in her lap. Sandy jumped in and the notebook, cell phone, and pen went flying.

"Sandy!" She cuddled and gave him snuggles, then arranged everything back in its proper order.

She updated the Dan Keystone page with the information about the rumored cash loan from her uncle.

She also noted on the Austin page that she suspected that he had told Dan that she knew about the cash loan. Why would he do that? Maybe he canceled for a perfectly good reason.

Then she flipped to the back of the notebook and titled the page "Treasure Hunt." She refined the diagram of the buildings on the property and noted the places she had searched. Her mother had told tales of a smaller cave hidden down the hill from the barn, but she had never searched it out. She had been content to play in the large one down by the pond. Maybe tomorrow she would search for it—or maybe when Austin could go with her. She wasn't that good on unbroken trails.

Shoot! I should have gotten some background information from the sisters about Mrs. Childers. That's yet another lost opportunity. What a lousy investigator I am. Then she dialed Austin's sister in Lexington.

She answered right away.

"Tyler Morgan. I'm on deadline right now. Make it quick."

"Oh." Miranda nearly hung up in response to the terse voice. She cleared her throat and used her strong teaching voice. "Yes, my name is Miranda Trent. I'm calling because your brother said you might be able to give me some information."

"Which brother?"

He has brothers? He didn't say. "Austin."

"Yeah, okay. Who are you, again?"

Miranda could hear paper rustling like she was searching for a pen.

"I'm Miranda Trent. My farmhouse was the site of the murder of Mrs. Childers."

"Perfect! He told me you might call. Look. I'm up against a time crunch here. Can I call you back in—say, thirty minutes?"

"Well, I've—"

"Perfect." The call ended.

"—got no cell reception." Miranda looked at the phone and then down at Sandy. "Whew, that's a busy woman."

Sandy tilted his adorable head to the side trying to understand. Miranda picked up the puppy, notebook, and quilt and started back to the house. She'd call Tyler when she took Sandy back out here for his after-supper potty break.

When she opened the door to the farmhouse, Sandy barked a sharp yowl that Miranda had never heard from him before. She smelled an acrid burning odor coming from the kitchen. She put Sandy down and ran. All six burners were turned all the way up under pots burning some sort of sticky goo.

She turned off the burners and, using thick kitchen towels to hold them, she took the pans outside and threw them in the grass. The grass started to catch fire. She quickly threw a bucketful of water on the pans so that they steamed a plume higher than the house.

Ruined. Her good aluminum cookware was completely ruined. From the smell she surmised that someone filled each pot with molasses, then turned on the burners.

Now that she had gotten control of the situation, she felt her legs begin to tremble. Who could it be?

Sandy yipped and pawed at her legs. She lifted him up and they both stopped shaking. She didn't see anyone when she scanned the area from the cell phone turnout. But she wasn't really paying much attention either. No one locked their doors out here, so access was no problem.

"Well, Sandy, I'm going to lock my doors from now on. I don't care if the neighbors think I'm citified." She put Sandy in his crate, locked the front and back doors, then drove down to the cell phone turnout to report the fire to Sheriff Larson.

He wanted to send someone out to investigate the arson, but she put him off. "I've destroyed every bit of evidence by putting out the fire, but if you want to investigate, it must be you and not anyone else. Specifically, I don't want Gary over here at all." He agreed to look things over when he got a chance tomorrow.

Then she called the sisters to ask if they would bring along some cookware for tomorrow's event.

As soon as she ended the call, her cell rang.

"Hi, this is Tyler Morgan of the *Lexington Herald-Leader*. I've had a little chat with my editor about your situation and he's given me approval to work up a lead story using your perspective of what happened to Mrs. Childers. Can I come out and get an interview?"

Miranda took her time to give an answer. Would this collaboration be a good idea? What if this made things worse? But things were already worse.

"Absolutely, any time. I'm anxious to get things moving."

"Fantastic. You're living in the murder house, right?"

"Yuck! That's terrible."

"But that is where the murder occurred, right?"

"Yes. I'm at the Buchanan Farmhouse up in Pine Ridge just off Highway 15. I'm about an hour away. I'll text you some directions to bring you to my place."

"Perfect. I'll be there as soon as I can."

Miranda had time to go back to the farmhouse, stow the backpacks out of the way in the van, clear out the horrible odor from the kitchen, and light a fire. She threw a couple of resin knots in for good measure to combat the lingering smell of burnt sugar.

The sun had long gone down when Miranda heard a fast car spinning into her driveway. In seconds, Tyler slammed her car door, leapt up on the porch, and knocked on the front door.

Miranda unlocked the door and let in a tawny flash of energy that wore thick black glasses and spoke at the speed of light. "Miranda? Great, thanks for agreeing to collaborate with me on this." She looked around and took one end of the couch and pulled a smartphone out of a well-worn black leather Kate Spade tote.

"You don't mind if I record this interview, do you?" said Tyler. "See, here's the app that records everything." Tyler showed it to her after she pointed it at her. "I also take a picture to help me remember who you are. Don't worry, you look gorgeous." After she put the phone on the couch, she motioned for Miranda to sit at the other end. "I hope I can get it all done so that it will run as the lead for tomorrow."

"Tomorrow?" said Miranda as she plopped down on the couch and looked at her watch. "How?"

"My editor is holding the front page for me."

"Oh."

"Above the fold."

"Oh." Miranda's heart skipped. Was this the right thing to do? Yes. It was right for Mrs. Childers.

"First, can you spell out your full name slowly and clearly?"

Miranda spelled out, "M-i-r-a-n-d-a D-o-r-o-t-h-y T-r-e-n-t."

"Perfect. This is Tyler Morgan recording this interview from the Buchanan Farmhouse in Pine Ridge, a small unincorporated community along Route 15 just northwest of the city of Campton, the county seat of Wolfe County." She looked at her watch. "The time is eight p.m. Now, Miranda, in your own words, would you please describe what happened yesterday during your cultural adventure, the Paint & Shine tour?"

Chapter 19

Monday Morning

A few minutes after eight o'clock, Miranda heard the deep frequency of an industrial engine. She hoped that it belonged to one of the gigantic telephone installation trucks. She continued to hear it long before she saw it.

As she looked through her bedroom window across the field, the truck came into view with a bucket crane mounted on the top and the telephone company's logo plastered all over the cab.

She took her mug of hot coffee out on the front porch and waited. The gigantic truck slowly made its way up the dirt road. It parked directly in front of the telephone pole on the side of the road straight across from her driveway.

Lucky that I'm not going anywhere anytime soon. I'm completely blocked in.

Two weeks ago, she had gone over to Jackson to the nearest Walmart and purchased a telephone base with three handsets. It seemed excessive for a woman living alone to have three, but one would be in the kitchen, one in her bedroom, and the remaining handset could be down in the barn for use when her micro distillery was operational.

When she first moved into the farmhouse, she hadn't considered that getting it hooked up would be anything more than a routine call to the local phone company to switch it on electronically.

Unfortunately, it had taken a long time to get approval through the only service provider to run the wire from the telephone pole to the farmhouse for a land line. She wasn't sure if it was a political problem due to the local resistance to her new distillery or, it was just possible, that it always took a long time to add a new customer.

One of her uncle's infuriating quirks was that he had an unreasonable desire for extreme privacy. She hadn't yet figured out why he felt that way. Was it something that happened to him as a child? Could it be a phobia against strangers? She didn't know and her mother wouldn't talk about it. As a result, he didn't have a phone, cell phone, computer, or television.

She thought the isolation was magic as a child when she was staying for the summer. All her city friends were away at camp or on nice vacations. Going to a farmhouse seemed exotic to her friends.

When folks needed to contact her uncle, they either stopped by to see him or they sent him a postcard, or, in dire cases, a telegram.

She desperately needed modern high-speed internet connectivity services to run her business. She also wanted it to support a decent lifestyle, but it had been a challenge. The phone company explained to her that a brand-new line would have to be installed from the telephone pole to the farmhouse.

A large, short, heavyset man in flannel shirt and clean bib overalls climbed down from the cab and walked up to the porch. He had a clipboard. "Good morning, young lady. Is your daddy at home?"

Miranda rolled her eyes; it was not the first time that she had been mistaken for a youngster. She was standing there in a T-shirt, holding a puppy, her hair quickly pulled into a ponytail, and she wasn't wearing a stitch of makeup. "Sir, I own this place."

He checked his clipboard. "Is this the Buchanan Farm?"

"Yes. I'm the new owner, Miranda Trent. I'm so happy to see you. There's no cell service out here at all. I really need my telephone line."

He handed her the clipboard. "I need your signature there at the bottom before I can start work."

Miranda scanned the work authorization form and signed it at the bottom. She handed it back.

"Yep, we've been wondering down at the office just how long this farmhouse could stay off the grid. Did you get running water? I hear the old man had electricity, but nothing else."

"I'm hooked up to city water now. I even installed a modern bathroom. I don't have a furnace yet, but I'm desperate for modern connectivity."

"What about cable? It doesn't come out this far, does it?"

Miranda shook her head. "Not yet. Apparently, the folks who live along this road haven't been interested, so the cable company passed it over. That's my next big challenge."

"That's gonna take some work. That cable company isn't interested in serving the public. They only want to make money. That's the way things work out here."

"I know, but they also appreciate a well-researched business case, so that's what I'm working on. I've got signatures from over half the residents along this road, but I think I need to get at least seventy-five percent of them willing to sign up."

"Hm. Wouldn't want to tackle that, miss. I'm going to tap on in to the phone wire from this pole, then I'll need to run it over to the house. I usually install it onto the highest peak facing the road." He pointed to the window of her second story. "That would be the best place. There would be a little protection from your roof. Then I could run the wire down from the attic into the front room. Is that okay?"

"Then I hook up my base unit there?"

"Yep." He looked down at the ground in front of the porch and kicked up a little puff of dirt. "I'll have to bring my bucket truck up to about here in the front yard. It may leave some tracks."

"No problem. It hasn't rained in a while, so the ground is pretty firm."

"If you could move your van back towards the barn, that'll give me plenty of room to maneuver."

"Sure thing, it'll just take me a minute."

"I'll just get on with the pole upgrade, then." He climbed into the cab of the bucket truck, stowed the clipboard, and powered up the stabilizing legs of the truck to extend out to each side. The road was now fully blocked.

Miranda went back into the house, drained the

rest of her coffee, put the cup in the kitchen sink, and then tucked Sandy into his cage. She moved her van and then, going back to the porch, she heard Sandy yipping from his cage. Miranda went back, put him on leash, and walked him around to the back of the house. The whirring noise of the truck hydraulics had Sandy too distracted to perform his business. She gave up and took him back into the house. She fed him breakfast in the kitchen, then put him on leash again to watch the telephone installer work on the pole.

At that moment, Austin's truck came barreling down the road and skidded to a dusty stop right behind the bucket truck. He leaned out the window and yelled up to the installer. "Hey! You can't block the whole road.

The installer yelled down from the bucket. "I'm sorry young fellow, but there's no other safe place for me to work on this pole. This monster truck weighs more than thirty tons. I can't just park it willy-nilly."

Austin got out of his truck. "How long are you gonna be?"

"Probably no more than an hour or two. I don't know what I'm up against. You'll have to go around."

Miranda tied Sandy's leash to the heavy bench on the porch. "Sorry, Austin," she said as she walked down her driveway. "Can you drive around?"

Austin put his hands on his hips. "Not the way this is blocked. I can get my truck up through your front yard, but there's a three-foot drop back down to the road. I'll have to go around by the back way."

"What back way?"

Austin tilted his head. "You know, the track that follows the creek."

Miranda still had a puzzled look on her face. "What creek?"

"Okay, it's barely a trickle, but it runs past the road that goes up to the Adams Cemetery, then it follows up the next ravine and on out to that road across this valley." He pointed to the Adams's farmhouse.

"I didn't know about that one. Uncle Gene told me to stay away from that creek. He said there were snakes."

Austin nodded. "That's true. The brush down there is hardly ever cleared so it's a haven for rattle-snakes to birth their young."

"Really?"

"Really. There's a story from a ranger in the fifties who came across a six-year-old boy fishing along the widest part of the little creek. It was probably only two foot across. The boy was holler-ing 'Ow, ow, ow,' so the ranger squatted down next to him and asked him what was wrong.

"The boy said that the worms he found were mean and wouldn't get on the hook. The ranger looked at the so-called worms the boy had cap-tured in a jelly jar with tiny holes punched in the lid. The jar was full of baby rattlers and his hands were bitten raw from trying to use them as bait."

Miranda covered her face with both hands. "Oh no. Did he live?"

"The ranger grabbed the kid and drove like a maniac to the doctor's office in Campton. The doctor tried everything, but the boy died the next day."

Feeling a shudder travel up across her shoulders, she said, "That's awful. I'll have to watch that Sandy doesn't get loose that way."

It had been awfully quiet up in the bucket and then they heard the lineman curse in a full and expansive stream of frustration "Hey down there! I'll be gone and out of here in just a couple of minutes." He proceeded to lower the bucket. Austin and Miranda waited while he stepped down into the road.

"I don't have the right part to connect to this ancient pole."

"What?" Miranda huffed her frustration. "You didn't bring the right connector?"

The installer shook his head. "I put the right connector in the bucket myself. I knew this line out here would need one of the old-timey connectors."

Miranda frowned. "But you say it's gone from the bucket?"

"I don't understand it. Who would want one? These old connectors were supposed to be phased out years ago. I'm going to have to replace everything and I don't have enough parts. I'll have to come back when we get them from the main supply office."

Miranda and Austin watched as the installer raised the stabilizer legs, backed the bucket truck into the farmhouse driveway, then trundled down the road.

"Back to the turnout to call for yet another appointment." Miranda pressed her lips together to keep from cursing like the installer.

Chapter 20

Miranda was once more pacing at Hemlock Lodge, this time in the hallway in front of Doris Ann's vacant reception desk. A sign was displayed to indicate that guests should contact the dining room staff. Of course, Doris Ann didn't work on Sundays or Mondays, but shouldn't someone be at the desk in her place? After all, this was the prime week of leaf-peeping season.

The sign-up list on the Paint & Shine website had shown her that four clients had paid for a cultural adventure this beautiful Monday morning. It was now fifteen minutes past the official starting time and not one person had arrived.

This is going to be a failure. I'm doomed.

She went outside and searched the entire perimeter of Hemlock Lodge to make doubly certain that her group hadn't gathered at the trail head or maybe at the far end of the parking lot. She returned to the lobby to check into her website with her phone. All had canceled and their refunds had been processed. At least she kept the small termination fee.

Then she poked her head into the gift shop to speak to the cashier. "I'm going to leave now. None of my clients showed up. Hopefully, they just got their days mixed up."

The cashier looked at Miranda. "Oh, wait, I know you. You're the one on the front page of the paper."

"What?"

The cashier pointed to a stack of the *Lexington Herald-Leader* newspapers on her checkout counter. "Yeah, see. Right here. That's you on the front page, isn't it?"

Miranda saw her image staring back at her. It was the phone picture that Tyler Morgan had snapped of her face last night to identify the recording. That's what she had claimed. Tyler had out-and-out lied. There was a perfectly good publicity photo on her website.

The headline across the top screamed out in monster-sized type: "Did Tour Guide Murder Her Cook?" Miranda felt the bottom of her stomach fall into a sour pit of gloom. She swallowed quickly to hold back the bile that appeared at the back of her throat. She felt the room begin to spin.

"Are you all right, miss?" The clerk scurried around from behind the counter and grabbed Miranda around her shoulders. "You need to sit down and gather yourself together." The kind clerk led her to a bench right outside the gift store.

Miranda sat down and realized that she still held the newspaper. She reached for her billfold.

"No, don't bother with that right now, sweetie. Pay me later. I'm going to grab you a bottle of cold water from the fridge. You stay right there." The clerk dashed back into her shop.

Miranda leaned against the back of the bench and took in a few slow, deep breaths. The sensational headline explained why she had no clients this morning. She was definitely in trouble now.

The clerk returned, and Miranda drank down half the bottle. "Thanks so much."

"What's wrong, miss?" said the clerk.

Miranda pointed to her picture. "I wasn't expecting this." She sat on the bench until all dizziness had gone. She thanked the clerk for helping her, then paid for the paper and water. She left a message for Dan. Then she notified both the sisters by text that they wouldn't be serving a meal at the farmhouse today.

I'm furious with Tyler. She seemed so genuine. Have I lost my ability to judge character? Disgusting! What a betrayal.

By the time she arrived back at the farmhouse, she was calm, but keenly aware of what this situation would do to her new life if it wasn't resolved quickly. After taking Sandy for a walk, Miranda took out her murder notebook and flipped to the list of people who were at the farmhouse the day Mrs. Childers died.

She looked at the list of names in the front to determine if any others could be eliminated. She had already removed Austin, but who else?

Nothing jumped out at her, so she started with the first name on the list, Mrs. Viola Hobb. She would start there. She flipped to Mrs. Hobb's page in her murder notebook and drew in more detail to the portrait sketch.

I'm doing nothing here but lollygagging. I need to start seriously investigating. Get up and get on with it.

She looked at the address she had written down for Mrs. Hobb. It was in Campton on the main street that ran through the middle of the downtown area and back out through the east end of town. It was within easy walking distance of the courthouse.

Miranda gathered up her phone and Sandy to make a call from her cell phone spot, but then grabbed her car keys as well. She was almost to the car before she turned back into the house and wrapped a portion of the Dutch apple cobbler to take to Mrs. Hobb. In this part of the country, it was bad manners when visiting the ill to show up without a dish of food, or flowers, or a gift of some sort. At the last second, she scooped up her murder notebook.

Mrs. Hobb was certain to be home. Miranda knew from chatting with the sisters that it appeared that Mrs. Hobb was very likely to take full advantage of any ailment by letting neighbors, friends, and relations cater to her every whim while she was feeling poorly.

Miranda planned to use this visit as the excuse for a very long chat. There was a wealth of history in that memory and she needed to extract some background. She drove to Campton by way of "old 15," as folks called the state road that predated the highway. She would arrive in less than fifteen minutes.

As Miranda expected, Mrs. Hobb was holding

court with a visitor on the wide porch that completely covered the length of one side of her house. It was an impeccably tidy little white cottage with black shutters and traditional gray paint on the porch boards. Miranda pulled up into the driveway and before she could get out of the car, the neighbor hustled down the steps to the sidewalk waving a cheery "'Bye."

"Hi, Miranda," said Mrs. Hobb, resting on the wooden porch swing that hung from the far side of the porch. There was a box of candy beside her that must have been the neighbor's offering. "How sweet of you to stop by to see how I'm doing. I enjoyed the venison stew the girls brought me."

Miranda clipped Sandy's lead to his harness, grabbed the wrapped dish, and made her way up onto the cozy porch. "They're great cooks. Sadly, I never got a chance to taste the batch that Mrs. Childers made. Austin and I threw everything out when we were cleaning the kitchen." She shuddered at the vision of Mrs. Childers lying on the floor.

Mrs. Hobb sucked in a breath through her teeth. "It's a downright shame about all that wasted food."

"Couldn't be helped. Just the thought of it gives me shivers. Anyway, I've brought you some dessert. I have plenty since my tour group canceled today."

"Tsk-tsk. I heard that from Lily and Iris. They were sore disappointed." She shook her head with a sad expression. "You know that Mrs. Childers had a dark premonition about your touring. She was very concerned about the evils of drink."

"Not just her. Doris Ann at the lodge is not a fan either."

"Doris Ann has good reason. It's because her baby brother was sent to prison for drunk driving. He served hard time and was never the same boy after that. He was only sixteen."

"They sent a sixteen-year-old to prison?"

"It was a long time ago. Sixteen would have been considered a pretty near growed-up man. It was one of the few ways her folks had of getting cash money, you know. You can grow your own food, but you can't grow shoes or winter coats. There's more, but she'll have to tell you."

"She already told me about her brother, but I'll try to be more kind."

Miranda placed the wriggling Sandy in the ample lap of Mrs. Hobb. He tried to jump up to lick her face and she giggled. "How's my widdle snuggly-wuggly baby puppy?" Sandy rolled over for belly rubs and whimpered with puppy pleasure. "I missed you, Sandikins." She lifted him to look into his face. Mrs. Hobb looked over at Miranda. "Don't you just love puppy breath?"

"Of course. How could you not love that?" Miranda smiled. "Can I put your presents away for you?"

"Honey, that would be a blessing." She pointed to the pile beside the swing. "Just pop the casseroles into the fridge and put the candy on the counter. I don't like cold chocolates."

Miranda complied, then returned to sit in the rocking chair, angled to see Mrs. Hobb but also with a view of the street. Every driver that passed the house either waved at Mrs. Hobb or tapped the horn. In response, she nodded her head in acknowledgment, along with a little queen-like wave.

Definitely holding court. But neighbors are more connected here. Not just acquaintances like in the big cities but linked through events that have occurred over generations.

"You look so much better now. How are you feeling?" asked Miranda, hoping a gentle opening would lead to a lengthy conversation.

Mrs. Hobb sighed deep and long. "Oh, my dear child, thanks for asking, but I'm feeling quite poorly. I'm not over the terrible shock." She patted her large chest with quick little taps.

"What did your doctor say about your condition?"

"Young Doctor Watson is such a gentle man. He takes after his dear late father. God bless his soul. It was a blessing to us all that he followed in his father's footsteps. Our little town is lucky to have a working clinic, let alone an old-fashioned family doctor." She lowered her voice to a whisper. "He even makes house calls to his longtime patients."

"Really?" said Miranda. She didn't know that anyone did that anymore. Certainly not where she was from. Malpractice insurance would have put a stop to that.

"He checked me over and said to take to my bed for a few days. He stops by on his way home every day now." She shrugged her shoulders. "He loves my sweet tea."

Miranda thought if she was up and about enough to be making tea for company, that wasn't her definition of bed rest. But Mrs. Hobb belonged to a different generation.

Mrs. Hobb leaned forward and pointed to a

white two-story house across the street. "He and his lovely bride are just two houses down."

Miranda smiled. "Did you tell him why you were so upset? I mean, finding your friend dead with a knife in her chest was shocking."

"Of course I did." Mrs. Hobb reared up on the swing. "Why wouldn't I tell my doctor everything? He needs to know."

"Yes, yes, absolutely. I don't know what I was thinking. Please, go on."

Mrs. Hobb resettled herself on the swing and re-arranged the shawl covering her shoulders. "It was such a shock to see my dearest friend violated— yes, I know that's a harsh word, but that's exactly how it felt. Violated. Violated with her best kitchen knife."

"I'm so sorry."

"That knife had been handed down to her by her mother, who had it from her mother. The handle was carved especially for the blade by her grandfather. Even though it'll never be used again, I hope the police are taking proper care of it."

I'll bet it's lumped in with the rest of the bagged evidence. It will be in terrible condition if it's ever returned. It's merely routine procedure to them—they don't know what it's like to have things handed down. "I'm sure it's safe, but it will be a long time before it will be re-turned. You know they'll need it for a trial."

"That's right. I don't know who it would go to at this point. Maybe her niece."

Miranda returned to the point of her visit. "I'm just trying to make some sense out of this. Where were you before you found her?"

"You know all about that, girl."

Miranda pulled out her murder notebook and showed it to Mrs. Hobb. "I'm trying to get myself oriented on who was where at the time, so I've made this little book to keep track of things."

Mrs. Hobb put her hand out for Miranda to give over the notebook. "Let me see that. What on earth are you up to, child?" She didn't want to let Mrs. Hobb see it, but she did. There really wasn't anything much in the book at this point. Mrs. Hobb turned it over in her hands, flipped through the portraits, and then went right back to the page she had created for Mrs. Hobb.

"Oh my goodness. These are wonderful likenesses of everyone who was there." She pursed her lips. "You should make a page for Mrs. Childers so you have a place to write down what you find out about her." She gave the notebook back.

"That's awesome!" Miranda dug out a drawing pencil and flipped over to a fresh page. In just a few seconds, she had sketched Mrs. Childers and looked back at Mrs. Hobb. "I'm trying to keep track of things by writing them down. There are so many people involved, I don't want to get the stories scrambled."

Mrs. Hobb pursed her lips and paused. She certainly seemed to see the point of Miranda's efforts. "As you know," she continued, "I was borrowing a cup of sugar from Elsie. I wanted to sweeten up your cobbler with a little sprinkling of sugar, then just pop it under the broiler for a few seconds for the sugar to scorch. It's a simple trick, but it brings out the taste of the crust something wonderful. I can't understand why you didn't have any sugar."

"I ran out right after I finished the cobbler. Back

to my point, did you see anyone while you were out?"

Mrs. Hobb wrinkled her brow. "Why are you being so forward? Is there a reason for all these questions? I don't remember you as a particularly curious child. Of course, you were only here during the summers."

Miranda sat silent for a few seconds. Should she tell Mrs. Hobb about her need to clear up this murder so that her business wouldn't fail? How much would already be gossip? Actually, it would all be gossip.

"I'm desperate to get beyond this horrible event. It's horrible in so many ways." Miranda ticked them off on her fingers. "One, I don't like the notion of being the prime suspect in a murder case. Two, I don't want to lose the business because of the murder investigation. Three, I don't want to lose the farmhouse because I can't pay the taxes. It's been in the family for such a long time. Four, the last and most important thing, Mrs. Childers deserves justice."

Mrs. Cobb nodded absently while petting Sandy, who had curled up in the folds of her calico apron. He had fallen victim to her warm lap and drifted off to sleep. "Child, that's a long list of sorry."

"Yes, and I'm going to investigate your best friend's death myself so we can both begin to sleep. Plus, there is the fact I can't keep the farm if everyone cancels my tours."

It was Mrs. Hobb's turn to sit silent. She looked at Miranda, then looked down at Sandy sleeping in her lap. She raised her head to reveal a steely look. "I'll do what little I can to help you. I'll never have a friend like that again. You can't start over with a childhood friend as close as a sister. That has real meaning around these parts."

Mrs. Hobb cleared her throat. She paused for a few seconds, then wiped the tears from her eyes. "She helped me weather a bad marriage. She helped me recover from the death of my daughter. She helped me raise my lovely granddaughters. I owe her my sanity. What else do you want to know?"

Miranda felt the tension in her neck relax. She had hoped against all odds that she could get this kind of help. Mrs. Hobb knew everybody and everything. Miranda wrote down what Mrs. Hobb had told her.

"That notebook idea of yours is very smart, young lady."

Miranda grinned and felt a flush of pride spread in her chest. It was important to her what the elders of the community thought. "Now, tell me, what did you see on your trip back from Elsie's?"

"I saw two people going to the barn when I was on my way down to Elsie's. I think that was the honeymooners, but since the images were really only shadows, it makes me doubt that. I also saw someone out behind the woodshed when I got back just before I stepped into the kitchen, but that could have been anything. I wasn't thinking about where people might be. I was hurrying as fast as I could to get the sugar on that cobbler."

Miranda continued to scribble in the notebook as fast as she could. She looked up. "How about any background information on the locals?"

"Oh, dear. You mean Shefton Adams?"

"Yes, please."

"He's been a bit of a wild child all his life. Nothing ugly or criminal, but he's a handsome one and has a lovely voice. He's a struggling singer trying to break into the big-time. That means he's always out late. He hangs around the bars and honky-tonks down in Nashville. I think he's a good boy with a powerful desire for fame."

"What about Ranger Morgan?"

"Little Austin? He was raised up near Stanton, in Powell County. His family has been there since before the Civil War. He took over your neighbor's farm when that part of their family died out without anyone to hand it down to. That doesn't mean that there might not be trouble, but I haven't heard of anything bad coming from them."

Miranda repressed a relieved breath. That didn't mean he was innocent, but if Mrs. Hobb hadn't heard anything, it was unlikely that he had ever been in trouble. "Okay, I've got that. Any else?"

"You haven't asked about Joe Creech."

"He's from out of town. I didn't think you knew him."

"That's true, but on that terrible day, he came by to see Mrs. Childers while we were preparing for your fancy Southern dinner."

Miranda frowned at the word "fancy." Her time in New York City had certainly changed her view of fancy. Afternoon tea at the Ritz—now that was fancy. Not a wholesome meal around a farmhouse table. She shook her head to stop her thoughts from wandering.

"Sorry, can you say that again?"

"Joe Creech came by and upset Mrs. Childers."

"But he was one of my clients and met me at Hemlock Lodge. He couldn't have been in two places at once. When did he come by?"

"I don't know. It was just minutes after you left."

"Okay. He must have driven really fast. He was the last one to arrive. Well, not exactly the last one. Shefton didn't even make it in time to hike up to the painting site with the rest of us. At least Joe made that."

"She burst into tears every few minutes. She had finally stopped her crying fits just before y'all showed up."

Miranda's brow wrinkled deep. "How did he know her?"

"She wouldn't tell me and I didn't think it was my place to ask."

That flies in the face of reality, thought Miranda. *You just didn't get a chance to ask.*

"Anything else?"

"That fancy-pants Officer Young came by this morning to ask me some of the very same questions you're asking, except that he was treating it as an accident."

"Really?" *So, they're finally getting serious pursuing the case.*

"He wanted to know if she had a drinking problem, or had fainting spells. He even asked if she had a family history of strokes."

"They still think it's an accident. Argh—frustrating!"

"Not only that, but he said that you were next on his list of witnesses to check. He probably shouldn't have told me that, but Officer Young is still young." She put a hand over her mouth to giggle. "Sorry, but it is funny. You probably passed him on the highway coming over here if you took the Mountain Parkway."

"Actually, no. I drove the old Highway 15 way. It's so beautiful this time of year—I automatically take that route and it's only about five minutes longer."

Mrs. Hobb smiled. "I love that about you, dear. You always see the beauty in things—even as they're dying."

Miranda wrinkled her nose. She was a little uncomfortable with that as a judgment.

Sandy woke and stretched in Mrs. Hobb's lap. Miranda knew what Sandy's next need was going to be, so she stowed the notebook then grabbed Sandy up and put him in the grass. Sure enough, he immediately squatted for a pee.

"I'd better get back to the farmhouse and perhaps avoid annoying Officer Young." She chuckled. "I do think that he has the perfect name. There were so many of them bustling about, it was hard to keep track of what was going on." She let Mrs. Hobb give Sandy one last cuddle and put him in his travel crate in the van. "Thanks for everything."

Mrs. Hobb waved at her from the swing. "Come back soon. I'll put out the word that you want information."

Putting out the word was another way of saying spreading the gossip. That is a very scary thought.

Chapter 21

Coroner Felicia Larson normally discussed cases with her husband over dinner in their new apartment. Originally built in 1942, Wolfe County High School saw over sixty years as an educational institution. Then it closed in 2005. After sitting vacant for nearly a decade, the beloved Wolfe County landmark, listed in the National Register of Historic Places, had been transformed into nineteen units of mixed-income housing for residents fifty-five and older.

Although Felicia wasn't yet fifty, Sheriff Larson had recently reached the magic number and they became eligible to move into the luxury apartments. She loved the freedom from gardening, chickens, and house maintenance.

On the downside, it meant she had to leave her precious flower beds with those ribbon-winning dahlias that she tended like children. It was also a struggle to live in only two bedrooms, using the second one as an office. But with her recent promotion, she had even been able to hire a weekly housekeeper who also handled the laundry.

Today, she marched into her husband's side of their shared office and plopped down in his guest chair. She folded her arms, crossed her legs, and bounced one foot in a quick rhythm.

"I have a bone to pick with you."

Sheriff Larson looked at his wife's face and sat straight up in his chair, all attention. "I can see that. What have I done now?"

"It's a case of what you haven't done. You simply must get more involved in the Childers murder. I don't care about jurisdiction, political issues, or old high school rivalries. This is murder. I just got off the phone with the coroner in Lexington. He's been told the case is"—she finger-quoted—"an unfortunate accident." She huffed, refolded her arms, and tilted her head awaiting his response.

"But, honey, your report is inconclusive. You've stated that the victim died of a stab wound that pierced the heart and that she bled to death."

"Yes, but I also feel that the activities in the kitchen haven't been properly taken into account."

"Felicia, you need to be clear with me. What do you mean?"

She stood and leaned over the desk and pointed her finger. "Rick, I looked at the scene and the whole forensic team took pictures of the scene, but no one seems to have come to the obvious fact that nothing was being sliced in the kitchen."

"But she had just made fried green tomatoes."

"That's right, and every tomato had been sliced,

battered, and fried already. The cutting board was in the dish drainer by the sink. I would bet my life that the knife had been washed carefully and was sitting in the drainer, too. You can't let a good knife sit around with tomato acid on the blade. This is not an accident."

"Okay, don't get in a snit. That level of detail is beyond the understanding of city officers. In fact, I doubt that I would have picked up on that, either." Rich leaned back in his chair. "I'll have to talk to Peterson."

He checked his watch. "Ah, look. It's too late."

She raised her eyebrows. "My buddy says that Detective Peterson is staying late tonight. Something about performance appraisals that are due in the morning."

He looked up at Felicia. "This is not going to be fun."

She folded her arms and began to tap her foot. "Your job is to enforce the law. It isn't meant to be fun." She softened the harsh comment with a smile. "But you love it and you always do the right thing. That's why I love you."

He stood and took her into his arms.

Sheriff Larson gave his wife a kiss, put on his hat, then started up his patrol car. He got on the highway without second-guessing the logic of trying to talk Detective Peterson into changing his mind. Larson stopped thinking about it. He was afraid that he might turn around and head back to the safety of his home office. The image of Felicia tapping her foot dispelled that doubt.

* * *

At least he had the hour drive time to dream up an approach for convincing the detective to treat the case as a violent crime. It wouldn't be easy to work around their differences, but he had to find a way. Felicia was always right. It was annoying, but if she said it was no accident, he needed to convince the investigative team to pay attention.

Sheriff Larson found a visitor's parking spot at the Lexington Police headquarters. He leaned over and locked his weapon in the glove box. He stood beside his car, patted down his pockets, and threw in his pocketknife as well. Without an appointment, he would have to wait a good amount of time for the high-and-mighty detective to see him.

He had thought about calling ahead to make an appointment, but that would probably have meant having an argument over the phone and no chance to plead his case in person. Interagency courtesy meant that if he showed up in uniform, he was very likely going to get a chance to speak to Peterson. It might be the same result, but the chances were better.

As he expected, after a lengthy interview with various gatekeepers, he was shown to a conference room to wait for Peterson to find time to see him. He had remained patient during the questioning and endured the disdain of the impatient underling clerk who had been told to escort him.

Although she didn't appear particularly annoyed, she didn't chat. Not the usual situation with visiting officers. The staff had at least treated him with enough respect to let him keep his smart phone with him in case anything happened in Wolfe County.

After nearly twenty-five minutes, the same underling opened the door. "He can see you now."

Sheriff Larson hopped up and followed the quickly disappearing clerk down the hallway. She opened the door and waved him into a corner office with an incredible view of the lighted cityscape. The enormous chrome and fake wooden designer desk made the detective look small. Peterson's eyes were red and looked stressed. Not a square inch of desk surface was visible beneath stacks of folders, reports, notepads, and priority envelopes.

On the credenza behind the detective sat a coffee maker sputtering a new full pot of dark black coffee. The smell made the sheriff's mouth water. He loved coffee—cop coffee—black coffee.

Papers were also stacked along the walls and piled to the tipping point in the three side chairs. Sheriff Larson cautiously made his way through the office and approached the only clear chair in front of the massive desk.

Detective Peterson stood and crossed his arms in front of his chest. A civil handshake wasn't going to happen. His mouth curled. "What the hell are you doing here? I thought I saw the last of you back at that miserable farmhouse," he barked in a scathing tone.

The sheriff spoke calmly. "Good afternoon, I'll be quick. I know your time is valuable." With deliberate politeness, he sat in the chair and pointedly waited until Detective Peterson sat down behind his desk. "I want to discuss the murder of Naomi Childers."

A red flush crept up Detective Peterson's face and a vein in his right temple began to twitch. "You want to what?"

"I want to—"

"I heard you. This is a complete waste of my time. The case has been analyzed and we've determined that it was an accident. Case closed." He signaled that the interview was over with a chopping motion. "Now, get out of my office. I have real work to do."

Sheriff Larson never considered the administration paperwork real work. He wondered why the detective had a different view. He tilted his head and took in a deep calming breath. "I understand that is the official status, but the examining coroner does not agree."

Detective Peterson stood, leaned forward, and gripped the inner edge of his desk so tightly that his knuckles turned white. "I don't care what Felicia thinks. Your wife isn't in charge here. I am." He jabbed his chest with a finger.

The sheriff matched his tone. "Just because we have an ugly past doesn't mean that we can't work together to solve this case."

Silence fell like a wool blanket. Detective Peterson clenched his fists and stared daggers across his desk. "This has nothing to do with the past. That's over and done with."

"I disagree. You interfere in every interaction between our departments. You petition against us at every budgetary meeting. You block promotion and staffing requests. Why would you single out Wolfe County if not for our past?"

"I said this has nothing to do with our past."

"Then it's high time for you to stand behind that statement. If our past is truly a closed issue, I expect to see measurable changes in how things happen between our organizations from now on."

Detective Peterson's face contorted with the effort of keeping his voice calm and he slowly relaxed his fists. He looked down at the stacks of paperwork on his desk and muttered barely loud enough to be heard, "Noted."

Sheriff Larson released a pent-up breath and spoke in a calming, businesslike tone. "I'm here to officially report to you, in the spirit of official cooperation, that Mrs. Childers did not die in an accident. I will follow up this courtesy call with a written report detailing the particular issues that support additional action by your organization. Is there anything else?"

"Anything else?" Irritation flashed across the detective's face. "What I want is none of your business. This case is closed. Leave before I have you thrown out of here."

"Fine," said Sheriff Larson. "I understand your position clearly and I will be reporting to our upper management that you have refused to cooperate with the Wolfe County Sheriff's Office. Not just this case, but I'm also turning in our problems from the past. I'm kicking this issue up the chain to your superiors. You'll be hearing from me after I catch the killer." Sheriff Larson left the office and slammed the door behind him.

He was out of that building and into his patrol

car in a flash. Frustrated and angry, he fumed all the way back. He felt it had been the right move to tell Detective Peterson about his wife's assessment of the case. Unfortunately, he had predicted the outcome as well.

He phoned Felicia to say he was on his way home. It was well after dark when he pulled into one of their two parking spots in the basement. It had been a big decision to sell the little truck farm her parents had given them when they first married, but with the three kids gone and living out of state, the farmhouse was too quiet for both of them.

Also, Felicia's new job meant keeping long, erratic hours. Keeping up with the daily farm chores just wasn't possible. She had struggled for too many years to back off now. They had considered hiring help, but in the end they moved into a two-bedroom unit overlooking town.

He took the elevator to the top floor.

The comforting smell of chicken and dumplings floated through the apartment. She had anticipated that he would need a suitable reward. Even better, Felicia met him at the door with a warm, delicious kiss.

"There's spiced layer cake with ice cream, too," she said as her eyes twinkled.

Yep, this was his favorite part of the day.

Chapter 22

"**G**ood grief," Miranda fussed at herself. *I hadn't thought about Doris Ann broadcasting my every move to every man, woman, or child she met. What on earth have I done? Well, it can't be helped. That may be the best way to get things moving in these parts.*

Miranda took the faster route by way of the Mountain Parkway for her return and even risked driving a bit over the speed limit. She managed to arrive just as Officer Young was coming up along the pathway around the backside of the barn.

What was he doing poking around back there? He shouldn't be out behind the barn. Not that I know of anything there for him to find. If he was looking for the hidden money, his face doesn't look like he found it.

She pulled in the driveway without blocking his patrol car and grabbed Sandy in her arms. "Officer Young. What can I do for you?" Sandy yipped a warning and struggled to get down from Miranda's arms. "Easy, easy boy. I'm not letting you go."

Officer Young smiled but there was a hard edge in his eyes. "Miss Trent, I'm here to verify the statement you gave us about the incident that occurred here. There are some details that need more illumination."

Miranda shook her head. *Illumination?* Officer Young pronounced the word as if he'd just found it in his spelling list and needed to use it in a sentence. "Illumination? So, you need more light?"

Officer Young frowned.

"Yes, er, no, ma'am. I'm sorry to bother you here at home, but we haven't been able to contact you by phone."

Ma'am. Really? I'm not that old. Why is he doing that? Anyway, that was a lie, Why was he lying? Her cell phone recorded all missed calls. Even when she was in a dead spot. "Fine. I'm fixing to make some coffee. Will you have some?"

She dug the front door key out of her handbag and unlocked the door.

"Most folks around here don't lock their doors," said Officer Young.

"I know that. But most folks around here haven't had a murder in their kitchen," replied Miranda.

"The Lexington Police Department hasn't officially declared that this was a murder. We're investigating it as a probable accident. Anyway, Detective Peterson wanted more information about the layout of the farmhouse and all the outbuildings. I've sketched it out for him." He stuttered as he said the last word. Miranda thought there might be a glimmer of hope for him. She smiled to herself. He wasn't a good liar.

"Shouldn't that have been done at the time?"

Officer Young nodded. "Yes, it should have. It was my job to do the site sketches, but—"

"But you forgot? Is that why you're poking around my property?"

"No, ma'am. I turned in my sketches of the farmhouse."

"Yeah? Then why have you come all the way from Lexington to make a second set?"

Officer Young just stared at her.

She pushed open the door and motioned for him to follow her into the front room. "Have a seat. I'll put the coffee on." She set Sandy down and went back into the kitchen.

She could hear the rocking chair creak as Officer Young sat and waited. He drummed his fingers on the flat oak arm. Peeking from the kitchen, she could see that Sandy was sitting in front of the chair tilting his head from side to side. Miranda smiled. As an eight-pound bundle of golden fluff, Sandy's protection instincts were impressive.

"How do you take your coffee?"

"Black, please."

Sandy yipped and menaced Officer Young with an adorable growl that wouldn't have scared away a butterfly.

"Stop that, Sandy," said Miranda as she handed Officer Young his coffee. "If you don't behave, you'll have to go into your crate." She sat on the couch and wrapped her hands around her warm coffee cup. "Now, I presume you've re-created your sketch, but how can I help?"

Officer Young sipped the coffee and his eyes lit

up in surprise. "Thanks, this is good." He looked around for somewhere to set the cup down, but the rocker had nothing near it for him to use.

Miranda pretended to be oblivious of his plight and replied, "Why thank you. I'm very proud of my coffee. I get the beans from our local roaster in Campton and she grinds them specially. I only use a French press for brewing. It makes the best coffee ever."

Officer Young put the coffee cup on the floor. Sandy immediately darted forward to lick at the contents. Officer Young grabbed up the cup again. He pressed his lips into a straight line. Miranda could tell that he was embarrassed and felt sorry for his predicament. He didn't seem to fit into the Lexington crowd.

Miranda hopped up and grabbed a small stool from beside the couch. "Here, use this." Then she pointed a finger at Sandy. "No, Sandy. That's not yours. No. You'll burn your tongue. Sit."

Sandy sat obediently for a few seconds, then plopped down on his belly and put his head on his paws, guarding the stool for all he was worth.

Officer Young gulped down more than half the coffee and set the cup on the little stool. "Thanks, that's really kind."

"You seem uncomfortable. You must not have had a lot of experience for this part of the job."

"I've had training, yes, but actual experience, no. All my training seems to evaporate when I'm called on to really interview someone."

"That is strange. When did you know that you wanted to be a police officer?"

"As far back as I can remember, I've always wanted to be a policeman and help people." His voice sounded shaky, even though he was sitting taller with more confidence.

"I believe you. Did you say you had some questions for me?"

Looking like a chastised third grader, he pulled out his notebook and a pen from his upper shirt pocket. He clicked the pen and put the notebook on his knee. He cleared his throat. "When did you meet Mrs. Childers?"

"When?" Miranda scowled and looked up at the ceiling and rubbed her chin. "Oh yes, I remember that very clearly." She looked at Officer Young directly in the eyes. "I guess I was about three years old and she had come to visit my grandparents. It was right here in this room and I think she sat in the very chair you're using."

Miranda took another sip of her coffee and watched Officer Young scribble in his notebook. He stopped and moved his gaze back to Miranda.

"That's not what I meant."

"That's exactly what you asked. You asked me when I met Mrs. Childers." She paused. "I was three years old."

A red flush crept up Officer Young's neck. He cleared his throat again. "Sorry. What I meant was in reference to your new business, when did you first talk to Mrs. Childers about cooking for you?" He raised his pen, ready to copy down whatever Miranda said.

Miranda nodded her head. "Yes, that's much more specific." She stared at Officer Young until he looked up. "It was about a month ago. I asked her if she wanted to be main cook for my cultural adventure tour."

The red flush on Officer Young crept up to his ears. "And then what?"

"She said she would be proud as punch to show off her family recipes to tourists. Then she negotiated a deal that we both liked."

"What do you mean?"

"She wasn't interested in money for herself. She wanted me to bypass writing checks to her and complicating her taxes. She wanted me to donate her wages directly to her church's roof replacement fund. It was a very good value for me and she was going to be able to contribute more to the fund."

"What about the moonshine?"

"What do you mean?"

"I mean," he swallowed. "I mean," he coughed. "I mean that we heard there were arguments about the serving of moonshine at your events, many arguments."

"Do you think it's unusual to have an argument with a cook?" Miranda stood up. "Of course there were arguments. She was a cook! How much experience do you have running a business?"

"None, of course."

"Well, you certainly have some experience eating in restaurants, don't you?"

He frowned. "Yes, although I don't eat out often. My mom is a great cook."

"You mean you still live at home?"

Officer Young didn't say anything. "That's beside the point."

"Well, my point is that there are always arguments between the front of the house and the back of the house. It's not the least bit unusual." She scooped up Sandy. "If that's all you have for clarification questions, I need to get back to work."

"But—"

She tipped her head down and gave him an unruly-client stare, liking the feeling of confidence that coursed through her spine. "I said that's all."

Officer Young's face drained of color again. Miranda was beginning to think Officer Young must have a medical problem of some sort with so much blood rushing up and down his face. He stowed his pen and notebook."

"Thank you very much, ma'am. That's all I have for now."

"If you think of anything else, you might want to meet me at Hemlock Lodge. It would save you quite a bit of driving time."

Officer Young silently agreed and left.

Miranda stood on the front porch watching him drive down the dirt road.

She whispered into Sandy's ear, "He'll be back with more questions. My arguments with Mrs. Childers were spectacular. Everybody knew that."

Chapter 23

Monday Afternoon

Miranda fixed herself a peanut butter and honey sandwich and poured a glass of cold milk. Although there were a million things she knew she should be doing, none of them were going to get done right now. She went out and sat on the porch swing to let her spinning mind unwind. There were so many things to think about that she felt the most important thing to do right now was to not think about anything at all.

Sandy was exploring the front yard and found a bright red maple leaf to attack. Miranda heard a vehicle on the gravel road and smiled. Austin pulled into her drive and walked up to the porch. "Howdy. You busy?"

Miranda tilted her head. "Nope. I'm not even thinking. I don't have the energy."

"I have a suggestion." Austin pointed to the front door. "Why don't you air out some of that gear of your Uncle Gene's. Let's go fishing for some trout.

I know I get my best thinking done while casting on a creek. It might work for you, too."

"That sounds like a terrific idea, but I've got so much to do."

"It doesn't look like you're in a hurry to get started."

She smirked. "Smarty-pants."

Austin smiled. "Well?"

"Bait or fly fishing?"

"Do you know how to fly fish?"

"Definitely! I've used most of the tackle that Uncle Gene has in his bedroom. He taught me how to cast a fly when I was about eight years old." She whistled. "Sandy, let's put you in your crate for a nap. I'm a-goin' fishing."

Miranda grabbed a fly rod, her own small vest, and her waders. That's when her uncle had known she was a dedicated fisherman—when she invested in a properly fitted pair of waders. She took a small selection of her uncle's flies best suited for the fall.

Austin helped her stow her gear in his truck. "I am surprised, but I guess I shouldn't be. You and your uncle had a lot in common."

She got in the passenger side and buckled up. "He tried to teach me how to tie my own flies, but I didn't have enough patience. He was so disappointed, but I just couldn't meet his exacting standards. Where do you want to try first?"

"First? Oh, you are an experienced fisherman."

Miranda smiled. It nearly always shocked grown men how much she adored fishing. It had been an informal test about any prospective boyfriend. You can't hide your true self when you're fishing. It always comes out.

"Very experienced. Where are we going?"

"I've heard from some of the local fishing guides that Mill Creek Lake is hopping right now. They've been consistently catching their brown trout limit of a single twenty-inch fish daily. That could change any minute, but we should give it a try."

"Fine by me."

They drove in peaceful silence for about fifteen minutes. The trees along the Rogers-Glencairn Road were bursting in vivid leaf. Austin pulled into the gravel parking lot and nabbed the last spot. There were several men standing along the shore staring at their float bobbers, each praying for a small-mouth bass to take the bait. The fishermen casually looked over to Austin and Miranda and gave them a welcoming nod.

They unloaded, slipped on their waders, and moved down along the lake's edge a few hundred yards. They paused at a shallow graveled spur.

"Perfect. This part of the bank is good and hard." Miranda stepped out into the lake to stand in water that was about knee deep. "This is where Uncle Gene and I fished the last time he was able." She stood in the rippling water and blinked hard. A long minute passed without either one of them moving a muscle.

"I'm sorry, I wouldn't have brought you here if I had known."

Miranda took a cleansing breath and released it slowly. "Of course, you couldn't have known. But, honestly, I think this would tickle him pink. This was his favorite spot and now I'm here carrying on with what we used to do together." She selected a black hand-tied fly called a Woolly Bugger. Miranda attached it to the leader, then made a long graceful cast out into the lake. She turned back to Austin. "I'm sure my uncle is laughing up a storm."

Austin moved about twenty yards further up the shore and followed suit. They fished for about ten minutes, casting out the line, retrieving the line in short pulls, then casting out again. Miranda relished the soothing breath of fresh air, the sound of the rippling waves, and the rustling of leaves falling and about to fall.

Something tugged her line. She had a bite! Flicking her wrist, she set the hook and felt the battle begin.

"I got one!" she shouted to Austin.

Miranda played the ageless game of alternating slack and pulling her line until the fish broke the surface of the lake in a great heaving leap. In a few more minutes, the keeper-sized brown trout lay on the bank and Miranda sat down with a plop.

Austin squatted down. "Perfect specimen."

"I had forgotten how much I love this. It really puts things into perspective. Life here is very good."

Austin wrinkled his brow. "What do you mean by that?"

"I can't just sit on the porch and wallow in a pool of self-pity. I've got to take more action to resolve this murder. I need to make a better plan for our investigation."

"Agreed, but first let's get this baby fried up for supper. I'll cook."

"No way! It's my fish and my kitchen. I'm going to use my Uncle Gene's recipe. This has been all about him."

They packed up and made their way back to the farmhouse.

Miranda pointed. "Oh no, the door is open. I know I locked it before we left."

Austin reached into the glove box and pulled out a Smith and Wesson .38 special. He checked to make sure it was loaded. "Stay back until I look through the house. It's unlikely anyone is still around, but just to be safe . . ." He mounted the porch steps shouting, "Is anyone there? Ranger Morgan here. Come on out."

Silence.

Austin went into the farmhouse and in a few minutes waved a come-here signal. "Whoever was here has gone, but they—" He stepped back from a barging-at-full-speed Miranda.

"Sandy!" she yelled at the open cage in her bedroom. "They took Sandy."

Miranda's eye caught a flash of movement outside through the kitchen window over the sink. "Out back! He's heading out back behind the barn." She bolted out the back-porch door and sprinted down the lane to the barn in time to see someone hop onto a four-wheel all-terrain vehicle parked in the shadows of the barn.

The intruder yelped through a camouflage hunting mask that covered his mouth and chin. A camo hoodie covered his hair. He yelped again and pulled a furiously growling Sandy away from his sleeve and dropped him on the ground. He floored the vehicle and sprayed gravel and dirt clods high behind him as he disappeared into the woods.

Miranda yelled, "Sandy! Sandy!" at the little blond ball of fluff that was struggling in the grass to go after the retreating vehicle.

Miranda scooped up the little trembling bundle. Sandy was still growling and shaking a scrap of fabric he had torn from the intruder.

Austin plunged down the hill and entered the woods but he was no match for the high-powered all-terrain four-wheeler. He returned to the barn huffing and panting like a steam engine.

Miranda fussed over Sandy. "Easy, easy now. You're safe with us."

"What's in his mouth?"

"Part of the guy's shirt." Miranda pulled gently at the scrap, but Sandy growled and shook it with vigor. "Now, now. You have to give it up." She put her fingers straight into Sandy's mouth and gently teased the scrap from his sharp puppy teeth. It was part of a flannel shirt. There was blood on the scrap.

"Wait. Be careful. That's evidence." Austin went into the kitchen and got a Ziploc baggie. Miranda dropped the scrap in. "I'll go into town and give this to Sheriff Larson to process. There's DNA here if we need it."

"Of course we need it," said Miranda. "We want to know who broke into my house."

"And did what?" Austin looked at her with a wry look on his face. "Played with your puppy?"

Miranda had to admit that he nailed the silliness of raising a ruckus when nothing had been taken or damaged. "But he tried to steal Sandy."

"Or Sandy attacked him. At least now we know it's a man. A man who can run like lightning and that he's from near here or he wouldn't have been on a four-wheeler."

"Either that or he hauled it here on a truck. He seemed fairly tall, but it's hard to tell from just a glance at him running full tilt. Let's see if anything was stolen. I thought I locked the door."

"You did. But did you get rid of your Uncle Gene's secret key?"

"Uncle Gene's what?"

"His secret key. Yeah, not much of a secret since everyone knew about it." Austin walked back to the front of the house and onto the porch. He reached up to the top of the corner post, felt along the ledge, and showed Miranda the key in his hand.

"Great!" Miranda sighed. "How come I didn't know about that? I've been here most summers of my life."

"He only put it out when he left the farm for a trip." Austin placed the key in her hand. "He didn't go anywhere very often. He didn't return from his last trip."

Miranda felt the sadness creep up her throat again. Uncle Gene had gone to the Lexington Hospital for a simple overnight heart procedure. He never woke up.

"He did visit family. He came up to Dayton at Christmas every other year." Miranda looked Sandy over from tail to nose. "I don't think Sandy's hurt, but maybe I should take him over to the vet just to make sure."

"First, make sure that nothing is missing."

Miranda nodded. "Right."

Still holding Sandy against her check, Miranda looked in her room. Not only was the cage door open, but everything in her room had been opened, searched, rifled, and examined. She looked in her uncle's bedroom and found things in the same state. Nothing appeared to be missing, but she really wasn't sure. The dining room was unchanged and nothing was disturbed in the kitchen.

"Nothing obvious is missing. We must have interrupted him." Miranda walked through the house one more time and stopped in the living room. "Wait. A picture is gone."

"A picture? Which one?"

"It's been there so long, it is almost invisible. I can barely see it in my mind." Miranda closed her eyes. "I got it. It was a family lineup of one of the big reunions at Natural Bridge. More than fifty people were in it. Why would anyone want to steal an old photograph?"

"No matter, we've got to report the break-in to Sheriff Larson. He may have a different view of what's been going on out here."

"What do you mean?" Miranda could hear the high pitch of frustration in her voice.

"This is possibly the third time someone has tried to either scare you out of here or deliberately burn the house down. I'm going to ask the sheriff to put someone on patrol duty out here."

"But . . ." Miranda started to speak.

"No buts from you." Austin frowned. "This is getting out of hand."

"I have a suggestion that I think will satisfy both you and Sheriff Larson."

"What?"

"You can sleep in my Uncle Gene's bedroom until we get this mess figured out." She stood straighter and placed her hands on her hips awaiting his answer.

After a staring match, he shrugged his shoulders. "Fine. I'll grab some stuff over at my place and call the sheriff."

"Fine," said Miranda. Then she smiled. "I need to call the sheriff, too."

"Why?" Austin wrinkled his brow in confusion.

"I need to tell him that you are definitely not a suspect."

"*Pffft.* He knows that. I told him right after he arrived."

"It won't hurt to give him more justification. Besides, I need the face-to-face time with both him and his wife. They need to know what's going on out here from me—not from a neighbor—from me."

"Who is also a trained artist and observer of human behavior."

She paused. "Well, yes."

Chapter 24

Miranda returned to Hemlock Lodge after fin- ishing her cultural tour with today's two clients. Two. Only two. Again, she had considered canceling, but thought that would be much worse than going ahead.

Her clients were a husband and wife who were avid hikers with a great sense of fun. Their paint- ings were horrendous, but they spent the entire time at Lover's Leap making fun of each other's terrible paintings. Delightful. She couldn't re- member laughing quite so much during instruc- tion. She dropped them off by their car and parked the van.

On her way to the lobby to check in with Doris Ann, she narrowly avoided a head-on collision with Shefton Adams. He had bolted out the door- way of the gift shop.

He skidded to a halt to avoid a certain collision. "Hey, Miranda. How was today's class?"

Miranda tilted her head and chuckled. "It was excellent. I only had just the two customers, but they were fantastic. So much fun. They had essentially private painting lessons and a relaxed and informal chat with Ranger Morgan." She sighed. "But it was not profitable. What are you doing here?"

Shefton cleared his throat. "I consign some of my CDs in the gift shop." He nudged his head towards a display rack. "I pick up my money and restock them at least once a week."

"That's a perfect way to publicize your music. Are you working on another CD?"

"Sure, I usually get a chance to perform here at the weekly square dance on Hoedown Island. That's where I rehearse my new tunes."

"You write your own? That's awesome. Not everyone can be a songwriter."

He automatically glanced towards the dancing venue located down near the park's camping site. "There's dancing every Saturday night during the summer. But right now, the schedule's changed to weather-permitting. It'll stop altogether at the end of October and not open up again until Memorial Day."

"I haven't been to one of those in years. Mom and I used to join in the square dancing when she dropped me off each summer."

"Yeah, I know the caller. He's so good at prompting the dance steps that even the tourists are able to join in and enjoy themselves."

"What a dunce I am. I should have been attending them to advertise my cultural tours. Oh well, at least I can do that after this current crisis. How often do you sing?"

"Once or twice a month. Really, it's on any week-end that I don't go over to Renfro Valley to per-form there."

"Holy moly, that's quite a distance to drive, isn't it?"

"It's only about an hour and a half and I'm used to it. If I get too tired, I just sleep in the truck after the performance ends, then drive back home."

Miranda paused. "Did you know Mrs. Childers?"

"My oh my, yes. Mrs. Childers was my Sunday school teacher from the time I was knee high to a grasshopper. My family's attended Campton First Baptist Church since it was started way back in the forties. Then when I got older, Mrs. Childers took over the adult Bible study that met on Wednesdays just before the evening service."

"Great. Hey, I'm curious about her but I'm struggling to find anyone that has anything bad to say about her. Do you have a few minutes to tell me more?"

"Sure, I'd be pleased."

She led him over to the lobby and they sat in front of the roaring fire. "In general, what kind of woman was she?"

"Well, she was a fine upstanding Christian woman, much admired far and wide. We'll have a traffic jam all up and down the main road for her funeral. I think Shackleford's Funeral Home is already plan-ning extra motorcade escorts from the neighbor-ing counties."

"Oh, wait, you already know where the funeral will be held?"

"Sure, her folks have always been handled by Shackleford's. That's how it goes here. Your fu-

neral will either be by Shackleford Funeral Home
or Porter & Son Funerals. I know them folks pretty
well. I still work over at Shackleford's part time
even though I'm not going to be an embalmer."

"What?"

"Yeah, that didn't work out. I did all the book
learning before I found out that I faint dead away
at the sight of blood."

"You what?"

"Yeah, mighty inconvenient if your chosen career involves quite a bit of bloodletting. I'm fine as
long as I stay out of the preparation room. Anyway,
I'm trying to make music my career." He glanced
at his watch. "Oh, sorry for rushing, but I really
gotta go now."

He practically sprinted out the door.

Miranda stood and wondered what kind of appointment he was keeping. She hadn't heard if he
had a girlfriend.

"Only two customers today?" Doris Ann re-
marked from her desk. She sounded concerned
and victorious in the same breath. "I'm convinced
that your devil brew concoctions are the reason for
such a low turnout."

Repressing a tart reply, Miranda wandered over
and stood in front of the counter. She said,
"There's more to my business than just the moonshine, you know. It's a cultural experience. The
hike up the trails to create the paintings is the
biggest part. Has anyone asked about signing up
for tomorrow?"

Doris Ann shook her head. "Nary a single one."

Miranda decided she needed to spend more focused time trying to clear things up with Doris Ann. Her business needed someone to help sell it and Doris Ann was in the perfect place to make that happen.

"You know, I was chatting with Mrs. Hobb yesterday and she told me that your younger brother had some trouble with the authorities."

"That lady hasn't ever had an unspoken thought. I wish she wouldn't do that."

"What?"

"She likes the attention that gossip brings. She stores gossip like a squirrel prepares for winter—acorn by acorn."

Miranda stepped back at the malicious tone. "Okay, but even if she hadn't told me—I didn't mean to upset you with the moonshine aspect of my cultural experience tours."

"That's sweet of you to apologize. Your momma raised you right."

Miranda smiled and waited for another lecture about the evils of drink.

"Anyways," said Doris Ann, "I know that making moonshine is legal now, but I'm still uncomfortable with the problems."

Miranda struggled to understand. "What do you mean?"

"My whole family was torn apart by what happened to Johnny."

"I'm so sorry, can you tell what happened?"

"First off, he was running shine back when it was still illegal. That wasn't the bad part, 'cause he wasn't smart enough not to drink it. He was driving drunk and he hit a car with a young mother and her two kids. They died." She sniffed and dug a handkerchief out of her purse. "He was never the same after that. He was convicted of manslaughter and served jail time."

"Oh no!"

"It gets worse. He refused to see family while he was in prison. It broke my mother's heart, rest her soul. She and my daddy would go out to the prison every month and be turned away each time."

"But he was just a kid!"

"The juvenile prison here in Kentucky was pretty rough. He was miserable and let everyone push him around. The warden finally kept him in solitary. Even after he came home, he rarely went anywhere. Even when his friends would come around to visit, he wouldn't speak. Worse, he didn't eat very much, claiming that he had no right to enjoy himself at all. We should have known that was an awful bad sign."

"Of what?"

"It was depression. We just thought he was downhearted and after a while, he would get over his mistake."

"What happened?"

"He never got over it." Her voice trailed off into a breathy whisper. "He threw himself off Lover's Leap not too long after he came home from prison."

"Oh no!" Miranda reached out and patted Doris Ann's hand. "I'm so sorry. I had no idea."

"I don't talk about it anymore and I never go out on the hiking trails out there." Her voice trailed off into an emotional sob. There was a long pause while Doris Ann got herself back under control.

Miranda stood silent and felt Doris Ann's sadness seep into her bones.

Doris Ann sniffed noisily and then sat up in her chair and straightened her shoulders. "He was only seventeen."

Chapter 25

Late Tuesday Afternoon, Campton, Kentucky

Miranda fussed at herself for being such a dolt. She had forgotten that she needed to pick up a box of art supplies that they were holding for her at the post office. She had already missed the farmhouse delivery both times. It had to have a signature. Next time she wouldn't do that.

Painting supplies were expensive, of course, but this wasn't New York City. They could have been delivered to her front porch with no risk of someone filching them. She was wasting a lot of time chasing it down.

Anyway, today was the last day to pick them up in person before the post office returned the package to her supplier. As usual, she had cut things a little too short, which meant that the post office closed in only a few minutes.

She hopped out of the van and pulled open the door, then was nearly knocked over by Joe Creech.

He was looking down at a sheaf of documents he had pulled out of a large padded envelope.

She shouted, "Watch out!"

Joe jumped a foot and looked at her like a cat that had been stealing milk. "Sorry, my fault. I wasn't looking." He looked back down at the documents.

"Be more careful. You could have broken my nose."

His head tipped up but his gaze went right through her. Then he muttered, "Sorry," again and headed for the parking lot.

"Hey, Joe. You got a second?" Miranda realized that she was the one who didn't have time. She turned around and waved a friendly hello to the clerk, hoping that would give her an extra minute. The clerk smiled and waved back. Good.

She turned back to face Joe. "Do you have a second?"

"What?" His voice sounded scratchy and he then coughed a bit. "Sorry, what did you say?"

"Joe, you're practically sleepwalking." She pointed to the papers. "Have you received some bad news?"

"What? No, definitely not." He cleared his throat and stood a fraction straighter. "I've got an appointment with a source that can provide solid documentation for my research."

"That's wonderful!"

"Absolutely, the more substantiation I get, the easier it will be to attract the major research grants." He paused for a moment as if he had lost his place in a memorized speech. "I need the money to continue. Funding is always difficult for rural projects. I can't get complacent, ever."

"Who are you meeting?"

Joe frowned and pressed his lips tight into a thin line. "Does everyone here have to know everyone's business? Keep out of this." He turned and marched to his car, mumbling all the way.

Miranda shrugged. "That was rude," she muttered, and then walked up to the counter window.

The clerk tilted her head towards the parking lot. "Hi, Miranda. Did he run you down?"

Great, someone else who knows my name, but I don't remember hers.

"Almost, but I dodged out of the way just in time." Miranda was searching her memory for a clue to the clerk's name. She looked about the same age, but life in Wolfe County could be harsh so she might be younger. "He seemed distracted by the package that he had just opened."

"Yeah, he's here almost every day with some sort of special delivery. He's the talk of all the old ladies around town."

"Why?"

"He's been interviewing them for his new book. They're thrilled to be in a book."

Miranda searched her memory yet again. "Do I know you?"

"Oh, probably not. I'm a second cousin on your dad's side." She lifted her employee badge for Miranda to see the name, Faith Trent. "I was three years behind you in school—well, four by the time I finally graduated. I got held back in the third grade for not being able to read properly."

Again, Miranda was stunned by how much personal information was given freely to a comparative stranger who had merely walked up to the window. Then she replaced that thought with the fact that she was locally known as her Uncle Gene's oldest niece. So maybe she was not a complete stranger. "I haven't been back for any longer than a weekend since I went to New York City. Anyway, I think there's a package you're holding for me, right?"

"Oh, sure. It's just in the back." She dashed through a door and came back with a box about two feet square. "Here ya' are. Just sign right here and we're good.

Miranda signed, dated the receipt, and handed it back to Faith. "Thanks for staying open for me. I know it's after closing time now."

Faith rolled her eyes. "We're pretty relaxed about time in these parts. Unless I have a date, o'course. You have a good day, now, ya' hear?"

Miranda sincerely hoped that this wouldn't be the last package of art supplies she needed. While she was in town, maybe she should drop in on Sheriff Larson. There should be news about the autopsy as well as maybe some idea about what was happening with the Lexington Police.

It was a bit late in the day, but she managed to walk into the sheriff's office before the end of the public office hours. The hours posted on the door were a little longer than the post office. That made sense, but it seemed like it was normal for businesses to stay open until their customers were served. Quaint. That certainly wasn't the case in New York City. She had experienced walking right up to a post office service window and having it slammed shut in her face.

The building had to date from at least the 1800s

and looked like it had been consistently starved of proper maintenance for the last few decades. The ceiling had at one time been lowered with acoustic tiles, but there had been roof leaks, so most of the tiles were missing. Another major clue was a few five-gallon buckets strategically placed around the office. They looked permanent.

The sheriff's desk was in the back of the room facing the window out onto Main Street. The wooden desk was old but tidy. No cluttered surfaces here. The sheriff had a large green blotter, telephone, lamp, and a coffee cup on the surface of his desk. On a nearby table sat a computer screen that had gone into sleep mode with a spiraling gizmo as screensaver. A single document lay in front of him on the surface of the blotter.

"Hi there," she offered.

Sheriff Larson smiled. "Miranda, what brings you here? Has something else happened at the farmhouse?"

"Nothing since the house was ransacked. That still doesn't make sense to me. Have there been any other cases of mischief reported in the county?"

"I see you're catching on. We have tons of unreported crimes." Sheriff Larson leaned back in his chair. "It's getting close to Halloween, and this is the time of year for teenaged trouble, all right. But, typically, it's mostly shoving over outhouses and tipping cows. We haven't had an arsonist since I've been in office. Your farmhouse seems to be the focus of something else. Like someone is looking for hidden treasure. All we have around here is lost silver mines and valuable ginseng root."

"Is there any news about Mrs. Childers?"

"Funny you should ask." He glanced down at the typed form that he had been studying. "This spells out pretty much what you saw. Fatal stab wound with the cause of death as exan- exanin- exanguine—"

"You mean exsanguination?" There was a familiar tease in her voice.

He looked up her with a sheepish grin. "You know I can't pronounce that word. Bleeding out for us simple country folk."

She raised her eyebrows. "Simple, my foot." She got serious. "Was it ruled an accident?"

Sheriff Larson's gaze flicked upwards. "No, not in the report. The report gives the cause of death, but our coroner doesn't make a conclusion. She has a personal opinion, of course."

"Well, we all thought it was an accident at the time. Have you heard anything from Lexington?"

"You are getting a little pushy now. New York City ways won't get you very far down here. Anyway, I don't have confirmation that they think it is anything but an accident as far as they are concerned."

"Officer Young was looking around the farmhouse earlier today, claiming that he had forgotten to finish his sketch of the surrounding outbuildings when they first came out to investigate. He was uncomfortable when I confronted him. Do you think they've changed their mind about it only being an accident?"

"Hmm. That's certainly possible. But that's not good news for you. You would be their first choice as prime suspect."

Miranda frowned and her shoulders drooped.

Was he trying to set her up for his own reasons? Paranoia sometimes reveals problems with other issues. In any case, this meeting wasn't going in a good direction.

"I want to help."

"You should really stay out of this. You're not trained as an officer of the law."

"Maybe not, but I am a trained professional artist. I am extremely observant and detail oriented. For instance, I can completely verify that Ranger Morgan couldn't have murdered Mrs. Childers. He was walking up from his house on the road. The newlyweds saw him from the barn. I must admit that I have my concerns about Dan. He could have killed her in the kitchen, walked back down to his parked truck and then showed up late. He was visibly upset, which he could easily pass off as annoyance for being late."

"As I said, you are not a trained officer and I already knew that from the statement that the newlyweds gave."

"That reminds me. What happened to the statements that you took at the farmhouse? Did you send them over to Detective Peterson?"

Sheriff Larson pressed his lips closed as if holding back a curse. "Miss Trent, it's really none of your business. However, he hasn't asked for them. I suspect he only trusts the statements that his people documented."

"So, you haven't sent them?"

Sheriff Larson narrowed his eyes and let a long silence build. Miranda took this as a challenge and held her gaze and just stood there.

Suddenly, the sheriff turned around in his chair and tapped on the spacebar to wake up his computer. "The detective didn't ask for them, but it's a small thing to officially submit them into their system. That could trigger a new investigation thread. Someone on his staff will have to process them." His fingers were flying on the keyboard, followed by a pronounced tap on the enter key. He turned back to face her. "I've sent them."

"Thanks."

"You need to stop interfering in this. This is not a Hallmark cozy mystery television series where everything is cupcakes and kittens. It's not even similar to your childhood Nancy Drew storybook adventures. You need to leave this to the experts. The fact is that Mrs. Childers is dead and someone killed her. Hands off. I'm serious."

He sounded angry, but Miranda would have bet anything that he was frustrated. Frustrated with himself. Annoyed for not having done the right thing at the right time. He knew he should have sent those transcripts whether they were asked for or not. At least she hoped that was the case.

Chapter 26

Early Tuesday Evening, Miranda's Farmhouse

Miranda hurried home to take care of Sandy. She had stowed her art supplies and just put his bowl of warm food on the kitchen floor when she heard the distinctive sound of crunching gravel as a vehicle pulled into her driveway.

What now? This farmhouse was becoming as busy as Grand Central Station for the morning commuter rush.

She went out onto the porch to find Austin walking up the pathway. He was carrying a casserole dish covered in a dish towel.

He stepped up onto the porch and offered up the wonderful-smelling dish. "Hey, I whipped this up thinking you might like a change from venison chili. That is all you're eating, right?"

"Yes," She smiled. "That's on the menu for as long as it will last. I'm watching every cent. How did you know?"

"Everyone knows everything here. You know

that." He nudged by her into the kitchen and put the hot casserole dish on one of the stove top burners. "Anyway, I heard down at the Kroger's earlier today that you were only buying Sandy's puppy food."

"For everyone knowing so much in this county, I'm surprised that we don't know who killed Mrs. Childers."

"That would be because everyone keeps secrets from everyone as well. Your time in New York City has dulled your country instincts."

Miranda hustled to set up the kitchen table with two plates, napkins, and cutlery. "It smells wonderful." She sniffed the aluminum foil wrapped dish. "Chicken?"

"Chicken and rice casserole with fresh peas and asparagus. My specialty." He got two wine glasses down from the cupboard and put them on the table. "It's the only thing I ever take to potluck events around here. My mamma taught me that everyone needs a specialty dish. This is mine." He opened the refrigerator. "I think I saw some white wine in here the other day. Okay for you?"

"Absolutely. This is very nice. I was just going to have a peanut butter sandwich." She paused a moment and laughed. "Followed by more chili."

"Just as I suspected. Sit. Relax a bit." He poured the wine and scooped out the chicken casserole onto their plates. They ate in friendly silence. "Well, it must be good. You haven't spoken a word."

"This is fantastic and not just because I'm starving." Miranda forked the last mouthful from her plate and then got up to serve them both seconds. "You've got a winner here."

After they finished their seconds, Miranda collected the dishes and put them to soak in the sink. "I'll take care of these later. Why don't we have one of my cocktails out on the porch? I have something I want to discuss."

Miranda expertly prepared the Shine & Soda cocktails in full-sized mason jars, then filled a small dish with walnuts, roasted pecans, and raisins. She put everything on a tray, then Austin opened the front door for her. "It's getting a little chilly, but there's a couple of quilts out there."

They sat on the swing with the tray between them. After a few moments, Miranda cleared her throat. "I want you to know that when I reported your movements to Sheriff Larson this afternoon, he confirmed that he had needed an independent testimony to eliminate you completely. The newlyweds had witnessed your walk up the road and I confirmed that with Sheriff Larson."

Austin nearly choked on his drink and stopped the swing by planting his boot on the porch. "He said what?"

"Well, not in so many words, but I told him in my statement that you didn't have a single moment to yourself at the farmhouse. I told both the sheriff and the lieutenant at that first interview. All my clients kept peppering you with questions while you were holding court in the front room. I don't think you were left alone for a minute. True?"

"But—"

"I know you told the sheriff the same thing, but he said he needed corroboration and so I gave it to him."

"Thank you, I think, but why are you telling me this?" Austin lifted his boot and they resumed gently swinging.

"I need help to clear my name and get back to working on my business. You're close by and seem as interested as I am for this to get finished. Could we join forces?"

Austin said, "Sure. I was going to do my own investigation anyway. It would go a lot faster with your help."

"Goody. Let me show you my murder workbook. I've been keeping track of everything I've discovered."

Austin lifted a single eyebrow. "Murder workbook?"

Miranda dashed into her bedroom and got the black-and-white composition notebook and handed it to Austin. He opened the notebook to see the list and quickly turned through the pages, stopping on the one with his name at the top.

He looked over at her. "You are amazing. There's only about ten lines in this sketch, but it's more like me than a photograph. You did the same with everyone?"

Miranda glanced over and realized that the sketch of Austin was quite a bit better and more emotional than the others. Why was that?

"I'm an extremely visual artist. I need to sketch what's on my mind in order to work through problems both on canvas and in real life."

"We're not used to artists around here. That kind of thinking isn't talked about."

"That I know. My mother spent a lot of time drying my tears when people told me I was wasting my time trying to draw. They called it laziness. My mom called it creativity."

"Summers here must have been rough." He turned back to the first page in her workbook.

"Eventually, I figured out that country people used their creativity in different ways. The quilts, for instance, were first made to conserve precious fabrics and wools. They were pieced together from clothing that had been ripped apart at the seams to either provide material for another garment or set aside for the quilts or rag rugs. Nothing was wasted."

"It's a common misconception that a lack of money automatically means a miserable life. We know different, don't we?"

Miranda gazed at him and spoke softly. "We do."

He cleared his throat. "So far, you've eliminated Mrs. Hobb and me, right?" He looked over her notes. "You are basing her innocence on what, exactly?"

"Her reaction to her friend's death appears genuine. They have been friends since they were in grade school." Miranda looked at the sketch in the notebook. "There's also the fact that she wouldn't be able to keep it secret. Mrs. Hobb is a well-known chatterbox. I'm convinced that she would have confessed two seconds after the murder."

"It's a good thing you're not trying to build a court case out of these notes."

"Yes, I'm an artist, not a lawyer. Anyway, that leaves all the clients and Dan Keystone. They were all here."

Austin flipped to the next page in the notebook. It was labeled "Joe Creech." "What about him?"

"I haven't gotten very far as yet. I looked him up and he's an adjunct professor at the University of Alabama. His area of expertise in the catalogue is called "rural heritage," whatever that means. Anyway, Mrs. Hobb said that he visited Mrs. Childers on the day of the murder and he appeared to upset her."

"He's a long way from home."

"I know. This is not the most tolerant county in eastern Kentucky. He could be asking questions about race, income, or even religion in connection with his research. The kind of outsider questions that rile up suppressed feelings that folk feel need to stay private."

"Sad, but accurate. Cultural changes here are painfully slow."

"Anyway, I ran into him at the post office today and he's obsessively focused on his research. According to the post office clerk, who is my newly discovered second cousin, he's interviewing all of the older folks who will talk to him."

"About what?"

"About what has happened to their children and grandchildren. You know, where they got educated, where they live, and what kind of jobs they have. I looked him up and his research credentials seem genuine. He has a ton of published papers on his specialist topic—the beginning of our nation's cultural crisis regarding the demise of the American dream."

"Where's he staying?"

"According to the signup sheet, he's staying at

the Campton Inn just outside of town, but I'm more interested in catching the newlyweds before they fly out. I have their cell phone numbers, but honestly, I want to talk to them face to face."

"At the Merrick Inn?"

"Yes."

"All the way over in Lexington?"

"You make that sound like it's a million miles away. It's only sixty-five miles. Only a little over an hour's drive." She smiled, showing all her teeth.

"It's a world-famous and upscale place." He looked down at their very casual clothes. He was still wearing his khaki slacks and she was wearing jeans. They looked like they were about to go hiking, but not to visit a renowned inn. "We look like we live in the sticks. These duds won't get us in the door, let alone an interview."

"Good point. I'll slip into my little black dress and you can borrow my uncle's white button-down shirt. We can go anywhere in those."

"Shouldn't we call them first? The management might not even let us sit in the lobby."

"I know it's a risk, but I would rather just show up and take our chances. We can make up some goofy story." She grabbed her keys, then stood still for a second. "Oh, I'm taking Sandy. I can't stand the thought of leaving him."

Austin raised his eyebrows. "Agreed."

"I'll worry less if he's with us. Now, let's go.

Chapter 27

Miranda and Austin stepped up onto the wide and welcoming veranda of the Merrick Inn. The plaque next to the doorbell indicated that the historic Ward House had been built in 1843 and was listed on the National Register of Historic Places.

Shifting her grip on Sandy, she rang the bell and they were welcomed into a hallway so opulent, the lush carpet looked like it might need to be mowed rather than swept.

A tall, slender woman dressed in an updated version of a Victorian dress led them into a reception room off to the right. The spacious parlor was over-the-top charming, with furnishings carefully staged to give the impression of casually worn old-money décor. The owner motioned for them to have a seat on the Victorian settee. "What an adorable puppy. Can I hold him? Is he a rescue?"

Miranda handed over Sandy and he tucked up under the owner's chin and settled there like a sleepy kitten. "Yes, I've only had him about a week. I think maybe there's been a mistake in his age. They said he was twelve weeks old, but I'm beginning to think he's a big boy and probably only about eight weeks."

"Aw, how adorable." She scratched Sandy behind the ears. "Oh dear. I've forgotten my manners. I'm Mrs. Welsh, the resident owner-manager. Would you like a cup of coffee or perhaps a glass of sweet tea? Although we're newly pet-friendly, I manage a completely dry establishment here."

"No, thank you," said Miranda.

"Are you here to arrange for a special occasion? A wedding perhaps?"

Miranda thought for a moment, then gushed. "Oh, not us. We're here to congratulate Laura and Brian Hoffman—the newlyweds."

"Such a sweet couple. Of course, they're here, but they haven't said that they were receiving guests."

Miranda smiled brightly as she took Austin's hand into hers. "We're friends of theirs. Don't you remember us? We enjoyed a romantic meal here this spring, just like they're doing. We recommended this place to them."

Austin flinched, but he recovered quickly and placed his hand over hers. "Yes, we want to wish them well." He gazed at Miranda with cow eyes.

She struggled to keep from bursting out in giggles. "We know they're spending part of their honeymoon here at your historical guesthouse. We're desperate to apologize personally for not making it to their wedding. An unavoidable tragedy prevented our attendance."

Mrs. Welsh pursed her lips. "I've only been here a few months. The previous managers were very strict with visitors and they didn't allow small pets." She scratched Sandy's tummy. "I'm more informal, but I don't allow spirits."

Just as Miranda thought she was going to have to spin more lies, the honeymooners came down the ornate stairway and walked hand in hand into the reception room.

Laura recovered first. "Oh, hi, Miranda. What a surprise. We didn't expect to see you here."

The owner handed the wriggling Sandy back to Miranda. "I'll just leave you to your visitors." Mrs. Welsh reached over to scratch Sandy behind the ears one last time. "If you decide to leave for a visit with your friends, I'm sure y'all remember that we strictly enforce a curfew of 11 p.m. You can't get back in after that time." She looked pointedly at the couple. "Also remember, no alcohol allowed in the house at all."

"We remember," said Brian. He watched as the owner left the room and went towards the back of the hallway, presumably into the kitchen. He dropped his voice to a low whisper. "What a ridiculous rule. I expect a smoking ban in these old places—no alcohol is something else."

"I've been running into that quite a bit," said Miranda. "This area isn't as progressive as the travel brochures claim."

"Anyway," said Brian, "this has been a harsh lesson for me. I need to read the websites very carefully when making reservations. This place doesn't give a refund if you cancel or leave early, so we're stuck here."

"I wouldn't complain if I were you." Laura looked at him with adoring eyes. "I know you're a bit disappointed, but the bedroom is so romantic and this is a wonderful neighborhood. It's perfect for long walks. We can have a cocktail at one of the little bistros nearby."

Brian moved one of the single chairs closer to the one already across from the sofa. "I'm assuming you have some questions for us about the murder." He sat on the sofa and patted the seat beside him for Laura. She sat and grabbed his hand like a life preserver. Miranda and Austin sat in the chairs.

"Have the Lexington police contacted you to collect your witness statements?" said Miranda.

Brian shook his head in the negative.

"What?" blurted Austin. "Really?"

Miranda shushed him by placing her hand over his mouth. She quickly withdrew it when she realized what she had done. "I'm sorry, but please keep quiet. We don't want to bring the manager back into the room."

"Please don't," said Laura. "I don't think I can stand another complete recital of her rules."

"We want you to tell us where you were when Mrs. Childers was killed." Miranda noticed that Sandy had fallen into a deep sleep in her lap. "Your statement isn't complete, is it?"

"How do you know?"

"Mrs. Hobb saw you going out to the barn. You stayed there until just before Dan arrived. Then you were sitting at the table when I walked in, so you must have slipped in from the barn through the kitchen. What did you see?"

"Mrs. Childers was fine when we sneaked in," bleated Laura. "Her back was turned to us. She was reaching up into the far cupboard for something, so she didn't see us."

"No mystery, really." Brian's face began to flush a soft rose. "She just didn't see us."

"You didn't want to be seen, did you?" asked Miranda. "What happened in the barn?"

"Nothing," said Laura.

"No, really. What happened?"

Brian gritted his teeth and spoke between them at Laura. "Can you please just keep quiet? It's none of anyone's business."

Laura eyed him sideways. "That was the problem. Nothing happened. He couldn't, well, you know, um, perform."

Brian flushed even pinker right up to his scalp. "The infamous roll in the hay wasn't what I was expecting. There were bugs—lots and lots of bugs."

"But that's not a problem here." Laura sounded triumphant. "This place is so romantic and so very, very indoors." Laura sounded like a gleeful cheerleader. Brian blushed an even deeper shade of pink, but he snaked his arm around his bride and drew her close.

"That was awkward," said Miranda when they returned to her van. "He's awfully young for problems like that."

"We don't know anything about him. What if he had an illness as a child or has an allergy to hay? How would he even know about it? City folk are never exposed to nature in any quantity. There's no hay in the city. Most likely he is simply terrified of bugs. He always looks nervous to me."

Miranda handed Sandy over to Austin and started up the van. "Since we're already in Lexington, what do you say about making a call on Dan at the distillery? He doesn't expect me to drop by. We could have a conversation about where he was during the murder."

"Wouldn't that seem strange?"

"He is a principal part of my cultural adventure business and he didn't show up for one of our agreed events. I have the perfect excuse."

Dan's business, the Keystone Branch Distillery, was part of the famous Bourbon Trail that wound in and around Lexington. The tours flourished right alongside the popularity of visiting racehorse farms.

In less than ten minutes, Miranda pulled up to the Keystone Branch Distillery. A tour bus pulled in right behind them. "Let's tag along. I want to know more about Dan and how he runs his business before we start trying to figure out if he's a killer."

Austin raised his eyebrows. "That's putting it bluntly. What happened to having a conversation?"

Miranda twisted her lip into a smirk. "That is a conversation."

She tucked Sandy into his travel crate and they fell in behind the busload of tourists representing every size, color, and age of whiskey fan. This was evidence that everyone loved spirits.

Dan conducted the tour personally. He explained the entire process without making anyone feel like an idiot and answered each visitor's questions patiently and with respect. Miranda was impressed with his confidence and ability to tell funny stories about his untraditional startup of this traditional business.

In the last part of the tour, Miranda and Austin tried to stay out of Dan's line of sight, but they misjudged one of the turns and Dan spied them. He frowned and clenched his jaw for a moment before continuing his spiel. As the group came to the end of the tour, everyone was led into the tasting room for their free samples and purchases.

Miranda walked right up to Dan. "That was impressive. I should have made time to visit before opening my business. You've thought things through very carefully." She waved a hand at the tourists crowded around the bar. A good number were buying multiple bottles of whiskey and also picking up the branded merchandise. "I'm going to have to rethink some of my distillery plans."

"I've seen the architectural drawings that you have pinned up on the walls of the barn." He folded his arms. "Your product line is strictly moonshine. I'm in this for a client who is a bourbon aficionado. They can be fanatical about small specialist runs—that's where I'm putting my focus."

"Isn't that a bit like trying to speculate where the next lightning bolt will strike? Is that why you missed my event?"

Dan frowned. "That's right. I've got a run that has a real chance at being outstanding. But it needs special attention. Besides, you only had a few clients."

"Not the point, but anyway our agreement only

runs for my first month—six days a week. You knew that."

"I didn't know that your clientele would drop down to absolutely nothing within the first week. Did you?"

Miranda reared back and started to reach for his throat. Austin grabbed her around the waist, lifted her up, turned his back to Dan and placed her back on her feet.

She was furious. Her eyes were bright and her face was flushed with two white spots in her cheeks. "What are you doing?" she yelled at Austin.

"What are *you* doing?" Austin yelled back.

Miranda stood tall and straightened her dress. She realized that his actions had calmed her down instantly. Why had she done that? She had never had a temper before. This reaction rose in a blinding flash, but also left as quickly as it blew up. It made her blind to her surroundings. She swallowed hard and took a deep breath.

She walked around Austin and spoke to Dan. "I'm sorry. I didn't mean anything by that. Irish tempers run in my family." She lowered her head and then looked up. "I'm sorry. Believe it or not, this is the first time it has happened to me. Now that I know, it won't happen again."

Dan took in a deep breath. "Let's try to get beyond this. We're all upset by what happened to Mrs. Childers. I know I'm still freaked out." He looked around the tasting room. The salesclerk was cashing out the last few tourists. "Things are under control here. Let's go into my office."

They followed Dan into a small office that overlooked the distillery warehouse. It was paneled with cheap plywood and he had hundreds of notes tacked to a bulletin board mounted behind his office chair. The desk was an old-fashioned rolled-top office desk with stacks of reports, invoices, bills and computer printouts stacked willy-nilly. Three plastic folding chairs faced the desk.

Dan motioned for them to use the chairs and he collapsed into his creaky metal chair. He opened the left-hand bottom drawer and pulled out three shot glasses and a flask of mahogany liquor. "This will explain my panic better than any words I might offer."

He poured a half a shot for each of them and raised his towards them. They raised theirs. He said, "This bottle is the next to the last one of my supply of my Granddaddy's bourbon. This is the bourbon I'm trying to re-create."

Miranda sipped and the warm liquid slipped down her throat with not only a bold taste but also a soothing trail of pleasure that reminded her of the warmest memories of her childhood. She glanced at Austin, who returned her astonished look. Turning back to Dan, she said, "This is absolute bliss. Where did you find this? It's magical."

"This is almost the last of my grandfather's special bourbon. He made it for himself and only rarely shared it with friends and family. I have only one more bottle left after this one is gone."

Miranda scrunched her forehead. "I'm having the same issue with my uncle's moonshine recipe. Something's missing because the small samples I've tried don't taste right. You don't know exactly how this was made, do you?"

"I have the recipe, but like most old-timers,

Grandad kept a secret ingredient to himself. He was planning to tell my dad what it was so the tradition could carry on. Sadly, Grandad died of a stroke before he could tell us what the recipe was or where it was written down. That's if he wrote it down at all."

Miranda twisted a strand of her hair. "My uncle told me last summer that everything necessary to make his brew was hidden in a safe place, a dark safe place."

Austin took another sip and involuntarily groaned his pleasure. "I'm sure this is what heaven tastes like."

She took yet another sip. "That's simply ambrosia. I've never tasted a bourbon this good."

Dan dropped his chin down to his chest. "I've come close, but I don't have it yet. I thought this last batch was going to be it, but it went in the wrong direction completely. It's undrinkable. That missing secret ingredient was one of the reasons I signed up for your cultural events."

"What do you mean?"

"Apparently, Grandad did let out the secret ingredient to one of his sweethearts when he was a young man."

"Who was it?"

"It took me a while to find out. Folks keep the strangest secrets. He had apparently found out that this girl had gotten pregnant and left for a time in disgrace. No one was willing to let me know who she was."

"How did you find out?"

"By accident. When I moved this old desk into

this office, a letter dropped out from behind a drawer." Dan's voice dropped to a whisper. "It identified his sweetheart."

Miranda and Austin leaned forward.

"And . . ." she prompted.

Dan looked sad. "It was Mrs. Childers."

Chapter 28

Miranda sat at the dining room table and let her forehead plonk onto the surface. Again, only two clients had taken her cultural adventure tour today. Two. At this rate, she wouldn't make it to the end of the month. She would run out of operating cash much sooner than her checking account could cover. She didn't want to think about adding more debt to her already maxed-out credit card.

She propped her chin up with her fists and forced the anguish to leave her. She got up and went into the kitchen to clear her mind. She thought she would make a traditional candy, Peanut Butter Potato Pinwheels. It wasn't a difficult recipe, very simple and luckily very cheap. It gave her something to do with her hands while her mind wrestled with her problems.

There's got to be a way to get some quick cash.

She packed the finished pinwheels in metal tins

lined with waxed paper and put them in the refrigerator. Then she wandered into the front room and found Sandy asleep on a corner of the handmade rug. "The rug!"

Sandy hopped up with a panicked yip, then ran to Miranda. She picked him up. "Sorry, Sandy, I didn't mean to scare you. You know, that New York City girl wanted this rug. If she still wants it, I could keep things going until this catastrophe blows over."

Miranda dug out her murder notebook, flipped to the correct page and dialed Linda's cell.

"Linda? This is Miranda." There was only silence. After a longish pause, she added, "Miranda Trent from Paint & Shine."

"Oh, hi. I didn't recognize the number and thought it might have been a robocall. Is everything okay?"

"Well, not quite. Do you remember that you asked about buying the hooked rug in my front room?"

"I remember that quite clearly. You said it wasn't for sale. You said that quite abruptly, if I may say so."

Miranda sighed. She was going to have to mind her Ps and Qs much better around her clients.

"I apologize for my abrupt answer. But maybe this is lucky for you because circumstances have changed. Are you still interested?"

"Absolutely. How much are you asking?"

That stopped Miranda in her tracks. She hadn't thought about price. "Um. How much are you offering?"

I'm flailing around in the dark here. I haven't even done an online search of the auction sites to figure out a

*good asking price. Really, girl. You need to pay more at-
tention to what's going on.*

"To be honest, I've called on the spur of the moment. I haven't given that any thought whatsoever.
Are you still interested?"

"Hang on a second." Linda apparently pressed
the phone against herself, but Miranda could hear
talking in the background. A muffled voice cut a
loud wail of protest that they hadn't yet finished
going around the antique shops to search for the
perfect rug. The disembodied voice moaned that
a promise is a promise and even if this was the perfect rug, they still needed to visit the shops.

*I wonder. That's an extreme reaction. It really is only a
rug.*

Linda came back on the phone. "I'm still interested, but not for long. We've been visiting your
local craft galleries." There was a long pause again
as the distance voice said something. "As yet, we
haven't found anything close to the originality and
quality of your rug."

"Great. Let me do a little research and get back
to you. Are you still staying up at the lodge?"

"Yeah, we're checking out early tomorrow morning. We've got a few Pennsylvania antique shops to
visit on our way home."

"Perfect, I'll be by in about an hour with the rug
and a great price. Okay?"

"Sure, that's fair."

She heard more protests from Kelly in the background as she ended the call.

Miranda dragged out her uncle's ancient vac-
uum cleaner and gave the rug a thorough clean.
She rolled up the eight-by-ten-foot rug and carried

it out to the van. She gathered up Sandy and put him in his travel crate, checked that he had water, and left for the lodge.

No way I'm leaving Sandy to get taken. Ugh!

She ran a hand through her hair. *I love this rug— there has to be another way.* She recalled the frightening balance in her checking account and the fact that her credit card was over its limit. She started up the van for a moment, then shut it off again.

No, the real truth is that I don't want to explain this to my mother. I can sympathize with Mrs. Hobb and the problem with the murder knife as a family treasure. Yikes! But again, I have to do this because I want to keep the farm. Granny will understand. She can make me another rug. I will need to beg her forgiveness. No problem, I can do that.

Miranda straightened her back and started up the van. She turned it off yet again, went into the kitchen and grabbed one of the candy tins from the refrigerator. During their last phone call, her mother had mentioned that traditional Peanut Butter Potato Pinwheels were Doris Ann's favorite treat. Hopefully, hers would be up to scratch. After all that had been happening, she really needed Doris Ann on her side. Regardless of the moonshine issue, Doris Ann had more influence with the lodge residents than anyone else.

On the way, she stopped at the cattle turnout and researched the cost of handcrafted wool rag rugs. Most were selling anywhere from $1,200 to $1,800. Some rare primitives sold for more the $5,000. She mentally set her minimum sale price at $1,200. That would get her through to the end of the month.

She drove to Hemlock Lodge and pulled around the entrance into the parking area for resident guests. She turned off the van engine and let her head fall forward onto the steering wheel.

Am I really going to sell Granny's rug?

Finally, she raised her head, got out of the van, and walked down the sidewalk that ran along the numbered doors of the lodge rooms. At the middle of the two-story building, she found the access corridor that led to the more expensive rooms with a view of the valley below. She knocked and Linda opened the door.

"Come on in." Linda smiled. "Did you bring the rug?"

Miranda said, "I sure did. It's out in the van."

The room looked like it had been hit by a bomb. The nearest queen bed looked like it hadn't been made in days. Clothes, makeup, maps, and newspapers were piled on every available flat surface and also on the end of the bed among the tangle of sheets.

Linda noticed that Miranda was surveying the room.

"Oh, don't mind Kelly's mess. She can't help herself. She doesn't like for housekeeping to service the room. Mostly because she's so messy, but I make her keep her stuff on her side of the room. At home, I just pick things up. It bothers me too much if I don't."

Sure enough, the other bed had been made up with tight corners and plumped pillows as if it had never been slept in at all.

"Why do you want the rug?" Miranda eyed the messy half and couldn't envision her prized rug finding a happy home among such clutter. She was glad to see that Linda was obsessively neat enough to tidy up.

Linda laughed. "We're going to move to a just-built luxury apartment building. I'm furnishing it because I can afford the expenses on my own. Although we're both advancing in our jobs, mine has taken off like a shot."

"Congratulations. Promotions are exciting but they can be stressful. I went from a teeny-tiny New York studio to the farmhouse. So much space still feels strange. I've also had a great deal of trouble getting used to the country quiet. I can sleep through endless emergency sirens, but not the intermittent peeping of a cricket somewhere in the house."

"We've noticed that here, too. But it's definitely time for us to get larger digs with access to parks. We're going to need that."

Do I really want Granny's rug to go to these girls?

Linda continued in a nervous chatter. "Kelly's promised to clean up her act when the—when we move."

They seem a bit distracted. It's an odd time to take a vacation. Most New Yorkers escape to the Hamptons during the hot summer—not fall. New York in the fall is the best time to live there.

"That's good. A handmade rug requires a little bit of specialized care to stay nice."

"Oh, don't worry about that—I'm the obsessive neat freak." She waved an arm at her pristine bed. "Anyway, you just caught us in time. We're about to go antique shopping as soon as Kelly gets back from the convenience store."

"I did a little research on the prices for hand-made rag rugs. What's your offer?"

Linda smiled. "Okay, me first then. How about six hundred dollars?"

Miranda gulped and swallowed hard. *That's high-way robbery is what she wanted to blurt out, but didn't.* "I can see you're after a bargain, but I was thinking a little more along the lines of fourteen hundred."

Linda sucked in a breath through her teeth. "That's a little steep."

"It's a one-of-a-kind primitive rug made to a tra-ditional design with virgin wool strips salvaged from clothes worn in the mid-century time frame. Similar rugs online go for as much as eighteen hundred dollars. Some extremely rare primitives, which is what this one is, can go for up to five thou-sand. I did my research."

Linda pulled at her hem. "Fine, I was trying to get a bargain. How about thirteen hundred and fifty?"

"I'm good with that. Did you want to use a credit card?"

"Before we close the deal, I'd like to take a closer look at the rug."

"Sure. Come on out to the van."

Miranda led her to the van, opened the back door, and unrolled the rug as much as she could in the space that was left from Sandy's crate. Sandy yipped and jumped up against the sides.

"Calm down, Sandy. You're not getting out just yet."

Linda ran her hand over the nubby surface. "Oh, it's just beautiful. The traditional element is what caught my eye from the moment I saw it.

Wherever did she come up this design? It's not something I've seen."

"It's an old-style heritage pattern that shows up in all sorts of handicrafts within our family—dish-towels, pillowcases, tablecloths. You saw the laurel leaves pattern in the linen on the table, right? It's a family favorite for embellishment. I think it goes back to our Scots-Irish heritage. The Buchanan clan arrived in the United States in the early 1700s. The laurel leaves are prominent on the crest."

"Okay." Linda handed Miranda her credit card. "I adore this rug and I'll never find anything this lovely in the city. It will look fabulous in our new apartment."

Miranda processed the sale with her phone and a Square credit card scanner. She swiped Linda's card but the transaction failed because there was no signal. She tried again but got the same result. She groaned. "No reception out here for the Wi-Fi connection. Let's go down to the lobby and I'll try again."

Miranda noticed that Linda followed her with-out uttering a word. A feeling of dread soured her stomach. They stood in front of the lobby fireplace close to one of the wireless repeaters mounted on the ceiling. This time they got a signal, but after a suspenseful pause, the transaction was rejected.

"Are you sure this card is good?"

Linda frowned. "It should be. I'm confused. I used it for gas yesterday. It was fine. Here, let me wipe off the strip. Sometimes our local deli has to do that." She took the card and buffed it on the tail of her T-shirt. "Try it again."

The transaction failed one more time and Miranda's heart sank. The message in the app indicated that the card holder needed to contact the credit card company for important information.

Planting a hopeful look on her face, she said, "Do you have another card?"

"This is the only card I have." Linda appeared stunned and slowly took the card from Miranda. She stared in space as if mentally replaying a list of all the instances in the last few days when the card had worked. Linda rubbed the back of her neck. "I don't know how to explain this. This has never happened to me before."

Sensing that Linda appeared genuinely shocked and was probably not a credit risk, Miranda said, "Could you write me a check?"

"I don't carry them with me. I hardly ever use them anymore. Anyway, it might bounce since obviously there's a problem. I'm sorry. I'll check in with the bank tomorrow morning, first thing."

"I thought you were leaving tomorrow."

"We are, but I really want that rug and more importantly, I'm on the hook for the hotel bill. Kelly usually pays for the car and airfare."

"Do you think Kelly might spot you the credit card charge so that you can have the rug today?"

Linda's face lit up. "Brilliant. I'll give her a call." She punched in the call then waited. "It's going to voice mail." She groaned and left Kelly a message to call her immediately. She looked puzzled. "She's been gone a long time just to go up to the convenience store." She looked at her watch. "She's been gone for more than an hour."

"That seems long. It's not more than a couple of

minutes down the road. Do you want me to run you up there and see if she's having car trouble?"

"It's a rental."

"That doesn't mean they don't break down." Miranda motioned for Linda to get in the van. "Let's go check it out. I know the folks who own the store."

In a few minutes, Miranda walked into the convenience store with Linda behind her. "Hi, Mable. How's business?"

A middle-aged woman with black artificially dyed hair offered up a weary smile. "It's our busiest time, so that's good—just a little tiring is all. How can I help you?"

"I'm looking for one of my clients who said she was coming up here. Her name is Kelly Davis and she's staying at the lodge. Her roommate here was expecting her back more than an hour ago. She's from New York and always wears red Converse shoes."

"She's a bit plump, right?"

Linda nodded. "Yeah, about my size, in fact."

Mable pointed to the highway. "She filled up the car—it didn't take much gas at all—got a few snacks, and tore out of here like a house afire."

All the color drained from Linda's face and her lips turned the color of chalk.

Miranda and Linda left the convenience store and drove back to Hemlock Lodge in total silence. Linda motioned for Miranda to follow and she unlocked her room.

"I thought so. Something is terribly wrong." Linda stood looking at the messy half of the room. She looked in the dresser drawers and scanned the clothes hanging on the rod. "I never look over here because it annoys me so much, but most of Kelly's personal stuff is gone."

"What?"

"Her suitcase is gone. Her clean clothes are gone. The ones that are tossed everywhere are old and worn. She's left me." Tears began to stream down Linda's face. "She left me here in the middle of back country nowhere with no car and no money."

Miranda looked around the room with a fresh perspective. Linda was right. The mess disguised the fact that the important items were gone. "I don't understand why she would leave you stranded here."

"Kelly's been out of sorts lately—moody. That's why we're getting a larger apartment. This was probably going to be our last adventure with just the two of us. I thought I was being pretty good about hiding my frustration with her, but apparently not."

"Do you think she's just angry and took off for a drive to cool off?"

Linda got a tissue from the room dispenser. "No, I think she's on the way to the airport for the next flight to New York."

"Why?"

"I don't know. I thought we had our differences pretty much worked out. But now that I look back, she hasn't been herself since she met that cook who got killed at the farmhouse."

A cold shiver ran up Miranda's spine. "That doesn't make sense. They didn't know each other, did they?"

"I'm not sure." Linda blew her nose and sniffed. "She was out by herself while I was picking flowers. She met me on the front porch right before we sat at the table. It was only a minute or two before the other cook screamed."

"Then you both lied in making your statements. You told me that you were outside together picking flowers." Miranda bit her lip. "I'm going to report this to Sheriff Larson. He'll need to know that you two don't have alibis."

"I can't do anything until I get my credit straightened out and I'm sure the news is going to be bad. I'll have to ask my folks to wire me some money to get back to New York. They are going to hold this over me and claim that they have been right all along and that they saw it coming."

"Why?"

"They had Kelly investigated and found out that she's been banned by several department stores in Manhattan."

"What do you mean by banned?"

"She was stealing small items—nothing large enough to trigger an arrest. She seemed to want the attention. She's gotten counseling and that has worked really well. I also wanted to think that the stability of our relationship had something to do with that, too."

"But how—"

"I'm afraid that Kelly has taken every bit of the money out of my debit card account." She turned to Miranda with tears beginning to flow. "She's the only other person who knew the PIN."

Chapter 29

Wednesday Evening, Hemlock Lodge

Miranda called Sheriff Larson from the front seat of her van and reported that Kelly had apparently left Linda in the lurch with no car and had also cleaned out her debit card account. She also told him that Kelly and Mrs. Childers apparently knew each other and were talking in the kitchen just before the murder. He listened to her report and thanked her but didn't give any hint of what he might do about it.

Grabbing the murder notebook, she entered the incident on both Linda and Kelly's pages. She sadly admitted to herself that she just couldn't make any sense out of Kelly's actions. More was going on, but how on earth could she find out what?

Frustrated, she grabbed two of the candy tins, and made sure Sandy was asleep in his crate and that he still had water. She walked into the lodge and planted herself in front of Doris Ann. Miranda held her arms behind her back and looked down at the receptionist until Doris Ann turned in her chair and looked up.

Miranda smiled. "Guess what I have for you?"

Doris Ann's eyebrows raised and a smile appeared that would outshine the sun. "You brought me some of your delicious pinwheels?"

Miranda brought the tin out and handed it over. Doris Ann popped open the lid and downed one of the pinwheels in a flash. After the first pinwheel vanished, Doris Ann gulped down a second and finally began to nibble politely on the third. "You found out about those city girls, didn't you? I saw you talking to them."

Miranda plopped down on Doris Ann's guest chair. "Wow! I thought I knew family drama, but this is new territory for me."

"They've stirred things up around here, that's for sure." Doris Ann started eating the fourth pinwheel.

"What do you mean?"

"You haven't a clue, do you?"

Miranda squinted and shook her head. "I've been distracted, to put it mildly. What am I missing?"

"They're married."

"They're what?"

"Yes, I saw them kissing on the balcony. In full view of anyone passing by." Doris Ann shook her head. "Where do they think they are? So, the next time they came through the lobby, I asked them if they were aware that most folks around here still believe that homosexuality is against the law. Even worse, some think it is an abomination against the will of God."

"You said that? Out loud?"

"Hold your horses," said Doris Ann. "Don't get ahead of me. I wanted them to be more careful. I thought they needed to be shocked. I know they're married, but that doesn't really protect them from discrimination here in the lodge or, even more serious, out on the trails. They need to act like just good friends around these parts. Friends, not lovers. Certainly not out in public."

"You're absolutely right. Good thinking to warn them. I've been so focused on my own problems, I forget how narrow-minded some people around here can be and actually have always been. Why on earth did Linda and Kelly come here in the first place?"

"It defies logic. There must have been a reason."

"Maybe not. The Kentucky tourist board has been doing a good job of promoting the beauty of this area. They wouldn't want to point out how harsh some of the locals can be."

"You'd think since this area has turned into a world-class tourist destination, they would have seen the good that brings to the whole community."

"That's a high road some of our Wolfe County locals will never travel."

Miranda reached into the tin for a pinwheel and let the sweet sugar and peanut butter flavors melt in her mouth. A flashback memory appeared of her first attempt to make the family treat. It had been a disaster. The base potato mixture wouldn't thicken no matter how long she stirred, and she stirred it a long time.

Her mother rescued the batch by removing a quarter cup of the failed mixture into a new bowl and folding in another box of confectioner's sugar. That did the trick and Miranda never forgot that lesson—always start out small. She smiled at Doris Ann, who was working on her fifth piece.

"Change is hard, and most families have been hit hard with the loss of jobs and also their favorite cash crop—tobacco. Which is why it just mystifies me no end why they aren't welcoming tourists with open arms. Although, I hear that the rock-climbing adventure tours are doing well in the Red River Gorge just up the road from here."

"We don't see many of them up here. They're mostly the backpacking and camping out in the grass sort." Doris Ann tapped her finger on the desk. "Some of the wealthy ones stay here. Most of them are from Europe. I hear all sorts of foreign gibberish from them."

"At some point, assuming my business survives, I need to connect with that group. They are just the sort that would enjoy a cultural adventure."

Doris Ann cleared her throat. "No one has signed up for your tour tomorrow. Someone is spreading a rumor that you're probably a murderer."

Miranda dropped her head down to her chest. "Who would do that?"

"All they had to do was read the headline in the paper. It's put the kibosh on your tours."

"Perfect, just perfect. I'll tell Dan and the Hobb sisters."

Doris Ann put the lid back on the tin and slipped it into her desk drawer. "You know that one client of yours on that first day, the professor, I think. He was here asking me a passel of questions about the old days."

"You mean Joe Creech? He said he was conducting some background research on the oldest families around here. He's got a small financial grant but needs to collect more supporting data so he can get an even larger grant. Then he's sure his book will get published. What was he asking about?"

"He was asking about what happened to unwed mothers around here in the old days."

Miranda wrinkled her brow. "Really? That's not what he told me about his research. I wonder why he didn't ask me the same question."

Doris Ann looked down her nose. "Sweetie, you're far too young to have any experience with that sort of disgrace. Those poor doomed babies."

"Why?"

"It's too upsetting and I never talk about it. If you really must know, go on down to the Wolfe County Historical Museum. There's a small exhibit about those poor children. Tragic."

"Thanks. I need to make a stop by there anyway to research more traditional recipes." Miranda stood up to leave.

"Wait, you know about the Lexington policeman, don't you?"

Miranda turned an about-face. "No. What about him?"

"He was asking all kinds of questions about you. He talked to the two girls that were in your class and he talked to the chef and the dining room staff just for good measure."

"What did he find out?"

"It doesn't look good for you. He was asking about the arguments that you had with Mrs. Childers."

"Everyone knows that we didn't agree on having moonshine as part of the cultural Kentucky experience."

"He was asking about your folks, about why you inherited your uncle's farm, and about why you want to start a distillery business."

Miranda sighed deeply. "It isn't widely known that there's a clause in the will that I need to open a moonshine distillery in order to keep the farm."

"I'd say that's a closely held secret," said Doris Ann.

Miranda nodded "Yes. One I would appreciate if you could keep." It didn't look good that there had been so many arguments with Mrs. Childers. Miranda had been positive that she would get her to change her mind eventually. Could the detective stay focused and get to the bottom of the murder?

"Does the detective believe it was murder?" asked Doris Ann.

Miranda's eyes widened. "What's the local gossip about the murder? Who do they think would have done it?"

"Right now, everyone thinks everyone else has done it. It's no help at all."

Miranda scratched the back of her neck. "Anyway, could you look out for Linda? As you say, they've been indiscreet with their relationship, and now Kelly seems to have driven off in a huff. Linda thinks she's gone back to New York, but I think she'll cool down and be back before morning."

"Doesn't she know that there aren't any flights out of Lexington this time of night? I think the last flight out is at eight p.m."

"They're not used to limited services. She might have made the last one, but there's not a direct flight, so she might be in the air to Chicago or Detroit." Miranda smiled. It was quite an adjustment to get used to stores not open 24/7. Worse, there wasn't a single Chinese restaurant takeaway closer than the twenty-minute drive into Stanton.

Doris Ann glanced at her watch. "Speaking of limited services, my shift ended a half an hour ago. I've been thinking of Mrs. Childers so much, I lost track of time."

"Me too. I need to get back to the farmhouse and give Sandy get some exercise before we settle in for the night. If Kelly returns, could you have the night manager text me a message on my cell? I sometimes get texts at the farmhouse."

Doris Ann grinned. "Oh, sweetie, how cute. There's no night manager here. We only have a night watchman. He mostly sleeps behind the desk here."

Before Miranda reached the main entrance to the lodge, she caught a glimpse of one of the Lexington officers getting out of his patrol car and adjusting his utility belt. She turned around and ran down the stairs that led to the lower floor of the lodge. Then she circled around the back way and came out to the parking lot.

She saw Officer Young talking to an obviously annoyed Doris Ann. Couldn't he tell she wanted to leave? She had her purse hanging over her shoulder and her car keys in her hand.

I wouldn't want to be in the way of Doris Ann getting home. It's not only his name that's young—he's bad at reading people.

She reflected that perhaps she had assimilated more than she thought from her summers out here in the country. A deep-seated suspicion of law enforcement was a common attitude, given the early corruption that most families had experienced during Prohibition.

Miranda sprinted down the parking lot and hopped into her van. She was glad that it was still plain white. She had researched the cost for getting it wrapped with her Paint & Shine logo, but that would have told Officer Young exactly where she was. She didn't have enough evidence to prove that she didn't kill Mrs. Childers, and as yet, she couldn't tell him who did it either.

She started up the van, slowly backed out, and drove down the steep decline at a snail's pace. She was grateful that her hybrid van was as silent as a snail too. As soon as she left the park and pulled out onto the Mountain Parkway, she floored the van to hurry home.

Saving your skin was harder than it looked.

Chapter 30

"Sandy, we need to get out of here for a while." Miranda raced into the farmhouse, letting the screen door slam. She opened a can of puppy food, filled his bowl with water, and fed a starving Sandy. She wolfed down a bowl of venison chili topped with corn chips while he ate.

Then she tucked Sandy back into his crate in the van. She went back into the house, got a quilt, made a thermos of chamomile tea, and grabbed two packets of peanut butter crackers. If they were going to stay away long enough to avoid the Lexington police, it might be a long night.

She drove back along the road. Instead of continuing straight on towards the highway, she made a right-hand turn just before she got to Roy and Elsie's house. It was a primitive single-track dirt road. She turned off her headlights and let off the gas so that the van moved slowly along at idling speed. She didn't think anyone would be able to hear her.

In a couple of minutes, she pulled over into a driveway that was once going to be the homesite for her newly married cousins. Instead, it had been abandoned after the site was graded, leveled, and even the foundation poured. The cousins set up housekeeping over on the other side of the county to be closer to the bride's family.

She parked the van to face towards the farmhouse. This site overlooked the intervening valley for a perfect sightline of her farmhouse and all the outbuildings. She took Sandy out of his crate and put him in the front seat. She snugged both of them under the quilt and sipped from her cup of tea. The night was clear and the Milky Way was just becoming visible.

In no more than ten or fifteen minutes, a Lexington patrol car came barreling down the gravel road leading to the farmhouse. It left a plume of dust that hung behind the car like a ghostly superhero cape. She watched Officer Young get out of the patrol car and knock on her front door. He pulled on the handle. It was locked.

She held her breath with her hands clenched around her thermos as Officer Young felt along with top of the door frame, lifted up the welcome mat and turned over the chair cushions on the porch furniture. He was looking for the hidden key.

"Sandy, he has no chance of finding a key. I left one with Austin and I also left one with Roy and Elsie. That's gonna stop anyone from waltzing in for a rummage of my bedroom."

The officer looked in every window with his heavy-duty flashlight and then he walked down the driveway to have a snoop around the barn.

"I wonder if he has a warrant." She snuggled Sandy, who licked her chin like it was an ice cream treat. "He would need a warrant to enter. He must not have one or he would have broken down the door."

Finally convinced that she wasn't home, he got back into the patrol car and careened down the dirt road again, stirring up another huge cloud of dust. *At least no one had laundry hanging out this time of night. That jerk would have dirtied an entire clothesline full of clean clothes.*

Miranda released the breath she didn't know she was holding. Sandy had been eerily quiet even though she knew he was curious. "Let's give him ten more minutes and I'll get out and let you have some fun, I promise."

They waited and then just as she got out of the van and placed Sandy on the ground to do his business, Miranda heard the crunch of gravel across the valley. It was the patrol car inching down the road without lights.

Miranda picked up Sandy and stood by the van. "Those city boys don't have a clue about being in the dark out in the country, do they, Sandy?"

When the moon is out, we can see almost as well as we can in daylight. Do they think they can catch me this easily? She snuggled Sandy while she watched Officer Young pull into the driveway, make another pass around the house with flashlight beams glaring all over the place. Again, after a few knocks on the door, he gave up and sped down the road, lights on, and dust trail rising.

Great, now I've gotten the Lexington Police angry. I'm not winning here.

Miranda waited another twenty minutes. She returned to the house, betting that the young officer didn't have enough patience to wait around any longer. And if he did, she would face her arrest like she did most events—straight on.

The farmhouse was chilly and felt dampish because the fire had died down. Miranda added more wood and stoked it back to life. Then she went into the kitchen and dragged out bowls, flour, eggs, cinnamon, nutmeg, and everything she would need to bake a five-layer spice cake. It was at least a three-day job to create an authentic spice cake. The longer it sat in the refrigerator, the better. It would be a fitting tribute to the funeral supper for Mrs. Childers.

Her family recipe called for ten thin layers, but she only had room in her oven for five cake pans, so she made her layers a little thicker and planned to add more homemade apple butter between the layers to make it about the right height. The whirr of the upright mixer and the warm smells coming out of the oven calmed her.

She made herself another cup of chamomile tea and sat at the kitchen table waiting for the cakes to bake.

There must be someone I can find to get more information about Mrs. Childers and her history. She must have known her killer or they couldn't have gotten so close to her with all the people around. So, who knew her?

History. That's what Doris Ann said. She looked down at Sandy, who had curled up to sleep by her feet. "Sandy, since I have the whole day off, I'm going to take you for a long walk tomorrow morning so that you'll nap for most of the day. Then, I'll check out the Campton museum. I need more information about the history of Mrs. Childers."

After she wrapped up the cake layers to cool on the counter, she set her alarm so that she could be out of the house in case they drove back in the morning. She bumped noses with Sandy and they turned in for the night.

Chapter 31

Thursday Morning, Campton

The Wolfe County Historical Museum found its home in the first merchandise stores to be built along Swift Creek. The origin of the town was in its name: camp town.

Austin was waiting on the sidewalk when she parked in front of the museum.

"What on earth are your working hours? You seem to be able to come and go as you please."

"It's more like when do I ever have any time off? I'm on call 24/7 and I'm usually working any time I'm in the truck. Good, huh?"

"Okay.

"So, good morning. What are you expecting to find in here? It's mostly full of attic relics donated by old-timers. There isn't much order to the place—basically new contributions are added wherever there's a bit of room."

Miranda was surprised at how young Austin looked in regular jeans with a white T-shirt tucked

into the slim waistband. His ranger uniform added
maturity, or maybe it was authority, to his appearance. It certainly made him look older than his
years. She realized that she liked both looks—a lot.

Austin opened the door for her and they entered to the ringing of a little bell fastened to the
door. The smell of musty, dusty papers and books
hit them as soon as the door closed. It took a few
moments for Miranda's eyes to adjust to the dim-
ness. Apparently, they only turned on the lights
when absolutely necessary. One of the challenges
of a volunteer-run museum was getting enough
cash donations to pay for ongoing utilities.

Display cases, bookcases, tables, wall-mounted
shelves, anything that could provide flat surfaces
were jam-packed into the long, narrow building.
The morning sun illuminated the dust motes that
danced in the air.

From the back of the museum, they heard,
"Who's there? Is someone there?" A white-haired
gentleman popped up from a desk piled high with
stacks and stacks of paper. "Howdy, Austin. What
brings you in here—you've never set foot in this
place."

"Good morning, Doc. I've brought you a customer. She's curious about the history of Campton."

The old man wore faded bib overalls with a
white oxford button-down shirt underneath that
had apparently seen more than a few seasons of
wear. His workman's boots were stained with the
earthy dust of farming in this area. Not what she
expected for a museum curator.

"Howdy, miss." He shook Austin's hand, then stretched out a weathered hand to shake hers. "Do I know you?"

Miranda smiled, accustomed to reciting her credentials at the first meeting with anyone. "I'm Miranda Trent, the oldest niece of the late Gene Buchanan from Pine Ridge."

"Well hello, punkin'. I knew your mother when she was just a wee lass. My condolences on the death of your uncle. He was a great gentleman." He waved a hand at the jumble of stuff stacked to the ceiling in many places. "Welcome to our museum. We've just recently started sorting things out so that it's easier to view our collection. We started over there in that corner and hope to keep adding more display cases as we go."

They looked over and sure enough, there was an open space that looked somewhat like a proper museum.

Austin started over to that section but tripped over a short stack of *Wolfe County News*. He tried to catch himself by grabbing the edge of a bookcase.

Big mistake—it was apparently only being held together by good wishes. It collapsed and took him down with it. He ended up with a pile of dusty books strewn everywhere. He started coughing up a storm interrupted by violent sneezes.

"Are you okay?" Miranda tried to pull him up by an exposed arm. She only managed to entangle him more by bumping into a bowl of cat's-eye marbles. The marbles rolled in all direction and Miranda slipped on one and crashed down on Austin, landing two inches from his face.

Laughing like naughty children, Austin and Miranda untangled themselves and finally reached a relatively sober standing position.

"What are you kids doing?" yelled Doc. "I'm gonna need help a-cleaning this up. I can't get down on the floor and expect to get up anytime soon."

"Absolutely, Doc," said Austin. "We'll set things to rights before we leave."

They carefully stepped around the clutter and reached the finished part of the museum. One of the exhibits featured the Campton High School. There were pictures of its construction and how it looked today after it had been turned into apartments. There were also yearbooks collected from every graduating class.

"Can we look at these?" Miranda asked.

"Sure, I've got a key to that case somewhere," said Doc, and he took off to his desk. "It might take me a bit to find it."

Miranda looked at one of the other finished exhibits on illegitimate children and an orphanage building at the edge of town. It explained that any out-of-wedlock child was considered to be chattel and could be traded as farm labor or sold as an indentured servant. If they were lucky, the child would be given over to an apprenticeship that included room and board. There were a few photographs from the 1950s of children working in the tobacco fields who were clearly malnourished and barefoot.

"I wonder what happened to these children?" asked Miranda.

Austin leaned over the display. "Nothing good. The disgrace of an unwed mother fell upon the whole family. Most of the children died of sickness or farm accidents or simply ran away when they got old enough. Many of the unwed mothers died in childbirth and were never spoken of again."

Doc came back with the key and opened the display case. "Who are you looking for?"

Miranda began pulling out a few yearbooks that she thought might be relevant. "We're looking for Naomi Childers and Viola Hobb."

"You won't find them under their married names, child. Naomi was one of the Spenser girls and Viola was a Tolbey. That's what you're gonna need, along with a little luck, of course."

"Thanks, Doc," said Austin. He leaned over and whispered to Miranda. "I would hope that we would've thought of that."

Miranda whispered back with a chuckle, "Maybe not at first." They started looking through the yearbooks. They found Mrs. Hobb, but Mrs. Childers wasn't pictured.

Miranda flipped through the pictures again. "That's not right. She said they had gone to school together and they were in the same grade."

"Was she misremembering? Surely she wouldn't lie about it."

"Wait a minute." Miranda grabbed the yearbook of the following year and flipped the pages to find a photograph of Naomi Childers. "She graduated a year later. Let's go back a year."

Austin grabbed that one and, sure enough, they found the friends had been in the same class in their junior year of high school.

They looked at each other. Miranda broke the silence. "What happened to Naomi?"

"Let's ask Doc."

They found Doc back at his desk, elbow deep in a box filled with hundreds of pocketknives, each one individually wrapped in newsprint. He had begun to unpack the knives and log them into a green-bound journal. He was listing the make and style of each knife, along with the date on the newspaper scrap. Doc looked up.

"Did you find anything interesting?"

Miranda cleared her throat. "We found a little mystery that I hope you can explain."

"Sure, if I can."

Miranda opened the three yearbooks to the pages she had bookmarked. "We found that Naomi and Viola were in the same grade during their junior year of high school." She pointed them out. "But something must have happened the next year because only Viola was in their senior yearbook."

Austin opened the final yearbook and showed Doc. "Naomi was pictured in the following yearbook. So, we're wondering what happened that year?"

Doc frowned and pursed his lips. "I wasn't here at that point. I had already joined the Army and didn't get back home for quite a few years. By that time, both of them were married. Viola had children but Naomi never did."

"Who would know?" Miranda kept her voice low and calm. "Please, Doc. It's important."

He switched his gaze from Miranda to Austin and back to Miranda. "You'll have to ask Viola. She's likely the only one alive who knows."

Chapter 32

Thursday Noon, Mrs. Hobb's House

Miranda and Austin walked down the few blocks to Mrs. Hobb's house. She was waiting for them on the front porch swing. Standing next to the door was a low table with a tray that contained two glasses of iced tea, a selection of cold meat sandwiches, and a plate of lemon bars. The dust of the museum seemed to be clinging in Miranda's throat, so she was glad to see the tea. Austin was eyeing his tea as well.

"I thought you might be stoppin' by here when you left the museum." Her eyes were red rimmed and she had an old-fashioned floral handkerchief crumpled in her hand. She waved for them to sit. "Help yourselves. We might be here awhile."

"You know what we're here for?" Miranda downed a good bit of her iced tea, then grabbed a turkey sandwich.

"Doc sent you over to see me, didn't he?" Mrs. Hobb dabbed at her eyes with the handkerchief.

"He's as innocent as a newborn kitten. He shouldn't have let you see those yearbooks."

Miranda grabbed a lemon bar and took a couple of quick bites. She was shocked to find that she was still starving even after the sandwich. She waited a moment, then put a hand over her mouth until she had swallowed. "Sorry, I don't mean to be a glutton. I'm not clear about why he wouldn't show us books that have clearly been put on display."

"In fact, they were in full view for anyone to see." Austin wrinkled his brow. "I don't understand."

Mrs. Hobb held the handkerchief up to her face and began to weep.

Miranda spoke as gently as she could. "Please take your time, but you might start by telling us what happened during your last year of high school."

Mrs. Hobb looked down in a silence that lasted several minutes. The only sound was the squeak of the chain that held up the swing as it swayed with the movement of Mrs. Hobb's weeping.

Miranda could feel Austin hold himself rigid in discomfort. It was awkward to sit there but they didn't have a choice. She sneaked a look up to the porch ceiling to see how the swing was attached. She was relieved to see two huge eyebolts attaching the swing to one of the support beams.

Ugh. What a horrible thought—concentrate and be compassionate, girl.

She and Austin quietly finished the plate of lemon bars.

Mrs. Hobb finally sniffed loudly and blew her nose. "I don't know why this is still so painful, but it is." She stuffed the handkerchief in one apron pocket, checked that something was resting safely in the other one, then rested her folded hands on her ample lap. "I've never told this story to anyone. Naomi made me swear on my mother's life."

"Your mother's life?" said Miranda. "I don't understand that one."

"That was Naomi's curse. If I had told her secret, I truly believed that my mother would instantly die of a stroke." She sighed deeply. "Ridiculous, I know, but we were so naive back in those days. We knew about the birds and the bees." She paused and pulled out a fresh handkerchief from her apron pocket and dabbed at her eyes. "We all grew up with farm animals and knew how babies were made. I even went along with my granny to several births. She was a midwife, you know."

"I didn't know that. My mom didn't mention it." Miranda thought that maybe things had gotten off track, but at least Mrs. Hobb was talking. She prompted, "Please go on."

"Back then, you only had a midwife and there were only the two in this whole county and they used to tend to all the mothers."

Austin shifted in his seat.

Miranda glared a "be still" look at him.

Mrs. Hobb didn't notice; she was seeing the past. "My granny had a small horse that she rode side saddle. It was an expensive saddle and she also insisted that her horse could never be used for farm labor." She looked over at Miranda. "That was unusual, but she made enough in trade for her midwifery to keep that horse for her own use."

"Who was the other midwife?" asked Miranda.

"That was the beginning of the problem. Her name was Old Black Fanny."

Miranda sat up straight. "She was called that? Really?"

"Well, that was normal. Things were very different back then."

Miranda thought differently. Since she had returned, she found the discrimination and racism better hidden, but not one bit better.

Mrs. Hobb continued, "Old Black—I mean Fanny—was so dark her skin looked blue, but she was the best at easing the pain of childbirth of anybody you ever saw. All the mothers wanted her with them during their time. The two midwives worked together as often as they could manage. They only split up if there were two mothers that needed them. It was so much safer for the mothers to have them both."

"Fanny was allowed in the houses?" Austin sat up straight. "I can't believe that was permitted. We have some folks in our county who won't even look at a person of color, much less let them deliver a baby."

Mrs. Hobb shook her head. "Some things were allowed. A woman in labor was female business and the menfolk were forbidden to be in the house. Fanny would be shuttled in the house from the back if there was family around. Once the baby was born, she would make herself a pallet on the floor next to the mother and new baby. Sometimes she would sleep in the barn. She would stay there until they were out of danger—sometimes weeks."

"I never heard about this at all," Miranda whispered to Austin.

He replied, "Black folks were experts at being invisible. Some still are."

Mrs. Hobb continued as if this story had been playing in her mind over the years and now was being freed. "Women died in childbed all the time back then. The thing about Fanny was that she knew about herbs and tonics. She would give her mothers-to-be willow bark and used shepherd's purse as a tincture to stop postpartum bleeding. That's where most mothers died. They bled to death after the birth; even more tragic, as Granny would claim, were the babes who died aborning."

Mrs. Hobb stared at the floorboards on the porch, lost in a memory that upset her.

"How does that explain why Mrs. Childers didn't graduate with your year?" Miranda spoke gently. Mrs. Hobb lifted her head and wiped her eyes.

"That's when the trouble started, all right. Fanny had a handsome hired worker along. He would work for food and board anywhere he found. He would help carry her supplies. By then, she was walking with a cane and needed help with her sack." She looked up at Miranda and Austin. "She toted everything in a big ol' potato sack. I don't know what all she brought with her, but he carried it for her, smiled at Naomi, and then left."

Miranda shook her head. "I don't understand. How is that a problem? He didn't stay."

"Not that first time. But Naomi got a good long look at him and I could tell that she liked what she saw. The next time we went along with my granny to a birthing, Naomi was particularly excited. She waited alongside the path behind the house for Fanny and her hireling to arrive. Naomi was wearing her best dress. I remember that because Granny fussed at her for wearing it when she might be called in to help. She could ruin her dress. Birthing was messy."

Mrs. Hobb stopped the movement of the swing with her foot. "It turned out to be a complicated and difficult birth. The large baby boy was the mother's first child and it had started out wrong way around. They got him turned, but he delivered with the cord around his neck. He was strangled and wasn't breathing.

"Fanny had me get a big wash pan filled with a few inches of very warm water while she gently pumped on his chest. She slipped the baby into the pan and began to massage him all over. In what seemed like hours, but was probably only a few minutes, he started breathing."

Miranda realized that she had been holding her breath. She exhaled. "That's wonderful."

They all sat still with only the squeak of the swing and birdsong for company.

Austin broke the silence. "She was a formidable woman. There are still tales of Fanny and her miracle cures that are told in my family."

"That's the day the trouble started." Mrs. Hobb started to weep again. "Naomi and Fanny's farmhand disappeared for a few hours that afternoon. I think you can figure out what happened."

Miranda palmed her forehead. "What on earth was she thinking?"

Mrs. Hobb cracked a small smile. "If you had

seen that strapping boy and you were a pretty young girl with new urges raging, you wouldn't have been thinking clearly either."

"Where did she have the baby?"

"Well, it was told by her family that she had to go nursemaid her mother's sister, who was slowly and painfully dying of a belly cancer. Naomi was gone for the rest of that school year and all that summer. When she came back, she was never the same. She never talked about it—"

"But you were best friends," interrupted Miranda.

"I heard that the baby's daddy found a better job in one of the coal mines. But he was killed in a cave-in early that summer. He never knew about the baby, or at least I don't think he did."

"Then what?"

"Naomi finished high school, then her family married her off and that was that. But something bad wrong happened to her because they were never able to have children. It was a great sorrow to Naomi, and I think that's why she appeared to be a mean old thing to some." Mrs. Hobb let her gaze fall on Miranda.

Austin looked over at Miranda as well and cocked an eyebrow. "What happened to the baby?"

"I don't know. Like I said, she never talked about that time she spent away from home. It was pretty common during those days for babies to be adopted out or worse—indentured out as farm-hands."

"We just figured that out," said Miranda. "It's tragic."

"That's what would have been done with out-of-wedlock babies. Folks would have ignored their very existence. The poor things wouldn't be educated. Naomi and her entire family would have been ruined if she chose to bring up that child. They would have been shunned. No community, no fellowship, no trading goods, no help with the harvest. Back then, it was a fate worse than death. It was the path to starvation."

Austin looked down at his boots. "There were some farmhands in my family. I never asked why they came and why they left." His eyes were wide and moist. He looked sad. "I should have asked."

"I'm free to tell you this now because Naomi left me a letter. It was delivered to me this morning from her lawyer. She had instructed him to mail it after she died. In the letter, she said she wanted to make everything known. Naomi shouldn't have kept this secret from me, but some painful things never get better with time." Viola slipped her hand into her apron pocket and drew out a folded sheet of typed paper. She looked at it, then pressed it against her heart for a few seconds. She stretched it out towards Miranda. "You need to give this to the sheriff."

Miranda stood and took the paper. "Can I read it?"

Viola snuffled a yes while wiping tears away with her handkerchief.

Sitting, Miranda eyed Austin and he watched as she unfolded the single sheet.

Miranda turned to Austin. "It's a full explanation of the birth and names Joe Creech as her son. You know who we need to talk to now, don't you?"

Austin raised his eyebrows. "Yep, we got to get this paper to Sheriff Larson. He has no way of finding out about this."

Mrs. Hobb straightened herself on the swing as if steeling herself for climbing the last emotional hurdle. "It wasn't only her best dress that Naomi ruined that day. It was her innocence, too."

Chapter 33

They drove separately back to the farmhouse. Miranda unlocked the front door and let Sandy run around the front yard. He was full of pent-up energy and pounced on every single leaf he could find. It was fall. There were a lot of leaves.

Austin sat on the porch swing, without saying a word, although a deep crease formed across his forehead.

Miranda joined him and they sat in a comfortable silence. She acknowledged that her happy childhood had been a true blessing. A blessing she had taken for granted. Her heart felt sad. Not only sad—she was angry that prejudices had allowed the innocents to endure a futureless fate.

Miranda broke the silence. "What appalls me the most is the fact that there was no thought by their adult relations that it might be wrong to deny a child a home, an education, and most importantly, love. These are basic human rights."

She huffed her anger, then fell silent.

Austin waited for her to process the shocking history about the unwanted children.

Miranda finally shook off the sadness and turned to Austin. "How are we going to prove that the killer is Joe Creech?"

"It's going to be difficult. He's smart and wary. He's a planner. He will have thought about each detail. This will be tough, if not impossible."

"After talking to Mrs. Hobb, I understand the true importance of the stolen photograph is that it shows Joe walking by in the background with his parents tugging him along. I've seen that photograph hundreds of times and it never occurred to me that the child in it was connected to anyone in the group in particular. Even worse, I didn't ask about the appearance of the little family at all—ever."

"He recognized himself in the photo. That's what he saw during your dinner."

"He wouldn't have known that he was in it at all. But it's obvious that the child is looking at Naomi with her striking lock of white hair, just like Joe's."

"We need to let Sheriff Larson know what we've found out."

"I agree. I think I'll run down to Roy and Elsie's house and use their land line. I don't want to try to get this information across with a bad cell signal." She shook her head. "We should have stopped by when we were in town."

Austin stood. "I'm not sure we would have been

able to give a sensible account of what we think has happened. Anyway, better let me use my radio. The dispatcher can connect me to the sheriff's office."

"We've discovered what no police officer would have been able to find out. A shameful family secret buried in the past. So deeply buried that not even close family and friends knew. It wasn't discovered even when the evidence was displayed in plain sight." Miranda chewed on her nail.

"I wonder what happened to Joe after Mrs. Childers returned to high school?"

"I think he's the only one who can tell us."

Sandy had tired of leaf pouncing and was trying to get up the porch steps. Austin got out of the swing, bent down, and scooped him up. Sandy's tail was wagging so hard that he nearly wobbled out of Austin's grasp. "Nothing good ever comes from secrets."

He handed Sandy over to Miranda. "I'll make that call." He walked over to his truck and sat inside to contact Sheriff Larson. The conversation lasted awhile, but when he returned, Miranda was still on the swing holding Sandy, who had fallen asleep in the crook of her arm.

Austin carefully sat next to Miranda without disturbing the puppy. "I just can't figure out how we prove it's Joe. There's no reason for him to confess to anything. Unless we can prove he is her son, he's not even a viable suspect. He can return to his university, get his funding, and complete his book. There are no consequences for him."

"Meanwhile, I lose the farmhouse."

"I don't think that was part of the plan."

"I don't think killing his mother was part of the plan."

Miranda shifted her position on the swing and Sandy woke up to try to lick Miranda's chin. "It does feel petty to be worried about a bit of property when his whole life has been filled with the knowledge that he was unwanted." She lifted Sandy up in the air. With each bounce he became more and more determined to lick her face. She cuddled him on her shoulder.

Finally, Miranda thought of something. "What if we lure him out here with the news that I've discovered a box full of old reunion pictures in the attic?"

Austin scowled. "How would we get the word out to him?"

"I could have Doris Ann tell him. She knows he's looking into the early history of Wolfe County. He's been eating at the lodge and probably speaks to her when he goes in and out. Who doesn't? That would look friendly and natural coming from her."

"How would that implicate him? Everyone knows that he does research. He could just claim that he wanted to look at them to strengthen his references."

Miranda sighed with frustration. "Let me think. There's got to be a way for us to hint that one of the photographs proves an unknown connection that shows motivation for killing Mrs. Childers."

"That sounds a bit far-fetched." Austin also sighed. "But I can't think of anything better."

She paused for a few seconds. "I want Doris Ann

to have a convincing story." She poked him in the shoulder. "Come on, put on your thinking cap. We can do this. We're clever."

"I thought Doris Ann was interfering with your business?"

"We've come to a no-fault truce on the subject of moonshine, mostly because she loves the idea of the painting lessons followed by tasting real Southern cooking."

Austin shrugged his shoulders. "She's a lynchpin in Wolfe County politics. If you win her over, things will go very smoothly."

"Here's a refinement of our story. I have Doris Ann tell him that because of the missing picture, I searched through the attic and found a small box of family reunion photographs that date way back to Mrs. Childers's high school days. I'm planning to try to identify everyone by showing them to clients and locals alike."

"And you're going to donate them to the Wolfe County Historical Museum so they can add them to the display that is already set up."

"And I want to do that before the funeral so that people can see what a lovely young woman she was back then. Also, we can say that museum is planning to put the reunion pictures alongside of the high school yearbook exhibit." She raised her eyebrows. "What do you think? Plausible?"

"Barely, but we can hope that he won't be looking into the logic very closely. He'll just want to get hold of those photographs." He paused for a few moments. "How on earth can we control the timing so that Sheriff Larson can arrest him? We're assuming that he's willing to disregard the fact that it isn't his case."

"We can tell Doris Ann that Doc is so interested that he's going to visit the farmhouse just to see if the collection in the box is as fantastic as we claim. She can say he's coming over right after he closes the museum tomorrow. That way he'll have enough time to get over here and want to have a look."

"What about your clients?"

"I don't have anyone signed up for tomorrow. I'll go up to the lodge in the morning and explain everything to Doris Ann. I'm going to ask her to claim that I'm booked up if anyone wants a class. That will at least give the impression that business is good. Do you think our plan is too far-fetched?"

"There's a slim chance that it might work."

"Then it's a plan."

Chapter 34

Thursday Afternoon, Sheriff's Office

Miranda had rummaged around up in the attic and managed to find a cardboard shoebox full of family photographs. She had spread them out on the dining room table on a plain white linen tablecloth. She sorted them in chronological order as best as she could then studied them carefully. Nothing struck her as remotely useful.

She gave up and as she started to get in the van, the phone company bucket truck rumbled down the road and stopped in front of her house. The lineman hopped out. "I've got the right connectors for your phone. Do you want me to go ahead?"

"Yes, sir! That would be wonderful." She couldn't believe her luck that she would finally have a functioning telephone. She called Doris Ann with the number as soon as it began to work.

The next step was to convince Sheriff Larson to go along with their plan. She drove into Campton and walked into the sheriff's office. There was no one around. The door was cracked open, so she quietly slipped into Sheriff Larson's office and stood just inside. He didn't see her because he was peering into a computer monitor, using his finger to draw a line along an e-mail message that he was reading aloud.

He read, "Planning committee meeting postponed due to a lack of quorum among the membership. The soonest an election can be held—"

Miranda cleared her throat and Sheriff Larson startled like a cat seeing a cucumber. His hand went to the pistol on his hip as he looked up at her. "Holy smokes! What on earth are you doing in here?"

"No one is out front. The door was open." Miranda shrugged.

Larson rose and brushed by Miranda to the outer office. He groaned in frustration, then looked back at her. "Gary is supposed to be out here." He grimaced and made his way back to sit behind the desk. He waved at her to sit down in one of the side chairs. "Sorry, I'm a little busy. What do you want?"

Miranda marshalled the diplomatic skills she had acquired while negotiating with art gallery owners. It had taken a silver tongue to convince anyone in New York City to put a single one of her paintings on display. She considered charm and persuasion two of the best blessings from her Scots-Irish heritage.

She succeeded with Sheriff Larson and he agreed to the plan. He followed her back to the farmhouse after tracking down Gary. He also notified his wife and called Lexington.

He was now safely hidden away in Uncle Gene's bedroom, his patrol car hidden in the barn. She had agreed to be wired so that anything that Joe Creech said to her would be recorded. The slight weight of the little battery pack clipped to the back of her jeans was a reminder of the seriousness of the situation. She left her shirt untucked to disguise its bulk.

Joe had called Miranda shortly after he heard the news from Doris Ann. Miranda readily agreed that he could search through the photos for his research project before she turned them over to the museum.

Not fifteen minutes later, Doris Ann had again called from the lodge to tell her Joe had left and should be arriving at the farmhouse very soon.

Miranda's van was parked outside in its normal spot in the graveled driveway. Austin had walked down from his house earlier. She was surprised that she felt so glad that he was here. Sheriff Larson had initially objected but Miranda had declared that it wasn't up for discussion.

"One thing." Sheriff Larson stepped out into the dining room and gestured at the collection of firearms hanging on pegs in her uncle's bedroom. "Are you carrying a—?"

"Nope, not a chance." She cut off his request with a chop of her hand before he continued further. "Don't even think about it."

"But, girl," he continued, "you grew up around here. You know how to shoot."

"Sheriff, I'm not a girl, I'm a grown woman. Yes, I spent my summers here. But I didn't grow up here. My mom and all her kin are from here, but I'm not. I know how to shoot a snake for protection, or a deer for food, but I'm not trained to shoot at a man. There's no way I would feel safe with a gun. I would just as likely hit you, me, Austin, or Sandy."

"I don't expect you to need it. I would just feel better if you had it."

"I've had my say." Miranda folded her arms across her chest.

Sheriff Larson shrugged his shoulders. "Since you feel that strongly, you're completely right." He returned to her uncle's bedroom and the waiting began.

The seven-day wind-up clock on the dining room buffet table ticked the time away—tick by tick by tick for each long second. Each second seemed to take an agonizing hour. The noise level in the house hushed down to only birdsong and the plaintive calls of a pair of nestling hawks calling for food.

Miranda heard a car coming up the road at a fair clip. She could hear the pinging of loose gravel hitting the underside of a vehicle. "That must be him." She went out onto the porch.

Instead it was the mail truck, which was running late. The clerk from the post office leaned out of the right-hand-drive vehicle and put the mail in Miranda's mailbox. She waved a friendly hi and sped down the road to catch Austin's house and the two more behind his. She would be coming back out on her return run in about ten minutes.

Miranda put her arm up to guard against a bright beam of light in her eyes. She looked around the farmhouse to see what could have caused the flash. Binoculars maybe? She scanned around the horizon again. Nothing.

Miranda went back inside and rearranged the photographs. They were quite old and some sported border edges cut in a wavy trim.

Right on time, the postal truck sped down the dirt road on its way to the next country lane. Then another twenty minutes passed with nothing but silence.

She continued to sort through the pictures and noticed that one of them was taken at the view of Lover's Leap. In fact, it looked very much like the exact spot where she held her painting classes. It had been printed at an 8x10 size. That was pretty expensive for those days. She took the photograph and put it in her painting backpack.

Too restless to sit another second, she went into the kitchen and opened three Ale-8 soda bottles. She tapped on her uncle's bedroom door. Austin appeared, an anxious look on his face. "Is he here?"

"No, but I think he's watching us. I saw a flash that might be binoculars across the gully near the abandoned house site."

Sheriff Larson took one of the soda bottles from Miranda and gulped half of it down in one swig. He looked back at Miranda. "Thanks. These stake-out sessions make me thirsty. I don't know if it's the anticipation or the boredom."

Miranda said. "Anticipation."

Austin said. "Boredom."

Sheriff Larson chucked. "Well, I think we're

done with both. If he's out there with binoculars, he's seen me and Austin. He may be spooked."

Austin piped in, "Or it may be a hunter trying to spot game. It's deer and turkey season."

"How can we entice him in?"

Miranda's phone rang. "Paint & Shine Cultural Adventures. This is Miranda Trent. How can I help you?"

She was silent for a few seconds. "Thanks for letting me know. I hope you aren't in trouble on my account."

Miranda turned to Austin and Sheriff Larson. "That was Doris Ann. She thought I should know that Joe Creech has checked out of his room. Doris Ann overheard the cleaner report it to the cashier. He didn't pay his balance and the manager is furious that someone would skip out on a week's fee during prime leaf-peeper season."

Sheriff Larson looked at the photograph in her hand. "Is that from the box?"

"Yes, it struck me as being familiar. It's a version of the one that was stolen off the front-room wall."

"Is it the same people?" asked Austin. He looked over her shoulder at the print.

She looked closely. "I think so, but it's funny how something you see every day can virtually disappear because it's so familiar." She held it up to catch the light coming from the dining room window. "I think it's very close. See." She pointed to a small figure in the background. "Joe is still looking towards the rest of the group."

Austin sighed. "Do we think he'll come by the farmhouse, now?"

Sheriff Larson shrugged his shoulders. "Hard to say. If he's determined to get a look at these photos before they go to the museum, then he'll be here soon. If not, he's probably on the road by now. I need to let Lexington know." He walked into the front room and started to make the call and his shoulders slumped. "No signal."

"You can use my new phone," said Miranda.

"Thanks, but this discussion will go down better if I use official channels. I'll go out and use the patrol car radio."

Sheriff Larson started to head for the front door, but they all heard several fast cars coming down the gravel road and skid to a stop in front of the farmhouse. The dust they had thrown up got caught in the breeze and blew over in a cloud of thick yellow powder that enveloped the arriving passengers.

Miranda, Austin, and Sheriff Larson ran out to stand on the front porch watching four members of the Lexington Police Department emerge from the dust cloud coughing, spitting, and slapping their hats to clear off their clothes.

"That's why you don't speed on a dirt road," whispered Austin. "The drivers must be city folk."

Miranda had clasped a hand over her mouth to keep from laughing out loud. There were two tiny laughter tears making their way down her cheeks. "You'd think they would have ventured out onto a horse farm at some point. They have a lot of dirt roads."

His face red with anger combined with embarrassment, Detective Peterson walked into the front yard. Two of his officers had sprinted around the back of the farmhouse and two more stood on either end of the porch. "I don't think you're going to find this one bit funny."

Detective Peterson motioned to the officer at the far end of the porch. Pulling out a pair of handcuffs, the officer headed for Miranda.

"Hey!" Sheriff Larson stepped between Miranda and the officer. "She's not the one you want. You already know who the killer is." He turned to glare at Detective Peterson. "What is going on with you?"

"I'm here to arrest Miranda Trent for the murder of Naomi Childers." Detective Peterson pointed at Sheriff Larson. "Stop this nonsense. You know she's the one. There's means—her fingerprints are all over the knife. There's motive from the moonshine arguments that everyone heard multiple times. And for opportunity—this is her farmhouse—perfect! If you interfere, I'll arrest you for obstruction and make sure you never work in law enforcement again."

Miranda noticed that Austin had gently turned sideways to stand next to her. Sheriff Larson and Austin had bookended her against her accusers, which gave her a bit of courage. She spoke with force but didn't shout, "You've got this all wrong. We know who killed Naomi Childers."

The officer stepped onto the porch towards Miranda, but Sheriff Larson stood his ground and held up a hand to stop the forward movement. He looked down at Detective Peterson. "Before this gets too complicated, why don't you let me tell you what's in the report I sent you. What you'll find in there is the sworn testimony of Viola Hobb, who has identified that Joe Creech is the illegitimate son of Viola Childers."

"I don't have to take anything you say into account. You've been getting in the way since this happened. Now, back away and let's get her in the cruiser." He motioned to the officer on the porch to go ahead.

"Just how long do you think it will take us to get a Lexington judge to release her? Listen to me for just one minute. As a sworn officer of the law in the Commonwealth of Kentucky, you can at least do that, can't you?"

Detective Peterson growled in frustration, and then something scratched his pants leg. He put his hand on his gun ready to draw. Then he suddenly stopped and smiled. Sandy was reaching up to him with both paws, begging to be petted. His tail was wagging and his head tilted one way and then the other, accompanied by a puppy whine. Detective Peterson backed away so quickly that Sandy tumbled into a forward summersault.

That broke the tension. There was a round of nervous chuckling and Detective Peterson laughed out loud. He scooped up the blond charmer and let Sandy lick his face. "You know buddy, you've got the best idea. Let's take a little time to get this right." He looked at Sheriff Larson. "Tell me about your evidence."

"Absolutely. Let's get comfortable. This might take a spell and you don't need to be standing out in the yard. We've got to work together or we're both going to lose our jobs."

Everyone settled down, with Miranda on the swing and Austin in the rocker. Detective Peterson sat next to Sheriff Larson on the slatted bench. The other officers either sat on the edge of the porch or leaned against one of the columns.

Detective Peterson nodded and watched while Sheriff Larson pulled out a sheet of paper from his shirt pocket. He smoothed the paper on his knee and handed it over. Detective Peterson spent a few silent minutes reading the report and his expression changed from irritation to dejection and finally to resolve.

He handed the paper back to Sheriff Larson and cleared his throat. "I've been pigheaded. You've got all the proof we need to arrest Joe Creech for the murder of Viola Childers. Thanks for being persistent. It would have been a holy nightmare if I had arrested Miranda." He paused for a long time, looking down at Sandy rolling over on his beautiful boots. "Thanks." He smiled and gave Sandy a belly scratching.

Sheriff Larson acknowledged that with a tip of his hat. "The problem we're faced with now is that he knows that we're on to him."

"I don't know what we can do to fix this. It appears that probably either one of us could have spooked him." Detective Peterson picked up Sandy and handed him over to Miranda.

"What's done is done," said Sheriff Larson. "There's no telling if we'll ever see him again."

Chapter 35

Friday Morning, View of Lover's Leap

Miranda was delighted that three clients had signed up for her cultural adventure this morning. She was dreading another total cancellation. That would have stressed her out completely. At least with small classes, she was getting a little cash and with any luck some great reviews on social media.

Good reviews brought more business. More business brought more reviews.

Her clients were three sisters from West Liberty, Kentucky, a short thirty-minute drive from Hemlock Lodge. They had heard about her experience from the clerk at the post office and looked up her few online ratings. They regularly left kids and kin home to treat themselves to what they called a Sister Retreat. It had become important to them since their parents had died in an auto accident.

They were settled in with easels and had started

to paint at the Lover's Leap overlook. Lily called to tell her that she and Iris had arrived to start cooking. Venison chili again, but those girls were great. Miranda was listening for trail sounds to indicate that Austin had arrived to give his talk.

"Miss, do you have more red paint? I've spilled some and now I don't have any more."

"Sure thing." Miranda grabbed her squirt bottle of red and resupplied the sister's pallet. She looked down the trail again, but no Austin. She went ahead and taught the next segment and refilled the water cup that one of the other sisters had tipped over. They were a clumsy lot, but good-natured about it.

She pulled out the 8x10 black-and-white picture that she had discovered in the attic and found room for it on her easel. Indeed, it was taken in the exact same spot. The grouping included the little boy and his parents walking by at the very edge on the right-hand side. They weren't meant to be in the picture, but the photographer didn't bother to crop him out.

She turned back to her class to instruct the next section and spied Austin coming down the trail. What a relief to see him, but he wasn't smiling.

Not good.

"Ladies, I'm happy to welcome our very own local forest ranger, Austin Morgan. He probably knows more about the history of this area than Daniel Boone himself."

Austin smiled at her as he took a position in front of the sisters with his back to the view. He launched into a short version of the history of the red chimney stacks. By the time he finished his talk and answered their questions, the sisters were laughing and gave him a round of applause.

As he left them, he leaned over to Miranda and whispered in her ear, "Stay safe," then gave Miranda another smile.

After the pictures were completed, Miranda and the sisters packed up their painting supplies. The cheerful, clumsy sisters dropped almost everything at least once but managed to keep their paintings safe. They were chattering like magpies on the trail back to Hemlock Lodge. They had just turned the first bend in the trail when Miranda rubbed her forehead. "I forgot my water bottle. It's my favorite, too. Stay right here until I get back. I'll only be a minute."

She ran back to the overlook. The water bottle was right where she left it.

Maybe a camo-colored bottle isn't the smartest thing if I don't want to keep losing it. She scooped it up from the patch of brush and took off her backpack to stow it away.

A corner of the vintage photograph was peeking out of the exterior pocket. She pulled it out and held up the photograph once more and compared it to the view. She lowered it and did a double take as Joe Creech now stood in the same spot as he had been when the shot was snapped.

"I need that photograph." He stepped over onto the trail and stretched out his hand towards Miranda.

She backed away from his reach—aware that the three-thousand-foot drop was beside her. "What are you doing?"

"I need that. It's the only connection left to prove that I was born here."

"But you're in the background—not even in focus." She spoke louder. "Why would you think that?"

"Don't act stupid. How many times do you see a white patch of hair on a boy?"

Miranda couldn't hear the noisy sisters, so they must have continued down the trail. They wouldn't hear her if she shouted.

Joe reached for the photograph.

Miranda pulled it back out of his reach and stepped away. It placed her another foot closer to the precipice. "I can't let you have this. What did you do with the picture you stole from my farmhouse?"

"I burned it. That's what I'm about to do with this one." He reached behind his back and pulled out a gun that had been tucked in his waistband.

Miranda felt a punch of terror strike her in the chest. She gritted her teeth and calmed her voice. "But I've seen it. I've seen them both." She paused for a second. "Austin has seen it too. I'm not the only one."

"I know, I know. But the only way this is going to go away is for you both to suffer a tragic hiking accident. No one would believe that you and your ranger could get lost in the woods. It has to be a fall."

"But you didn't kill Mrs. Childers deliberately, did you?"

Joe dropped his gun arm down to his side. "No." He looked at the photograph in her hand. "It was the last thing I wanted to happen."

Miranda spoke in a low, calm tone. "She was your birth mother, wasn't she?"

"I knew you were about to figure everything out and any kind of scandal would destroy my future. No grants. No tenure at the University of Kentucky." He paused. "I wanted to let her know that I was fine. I wanted her to know that her decision to adopt me out was the right one. When I saw the photograph, I knew she was the one. I wanted to meet her and tell her that. I wanted to say that I understood why she had to send me away."

Miranda lowered the photograph. "That's why you've been researching this area. You knew that your birth would have caused havoc with her family. They would have lost everything—their store, the farm. It was a bad time. Things are very different now. But you know that, right?"

"Yes. And I know from the home's records that she stayed with me for six months. That was unusual. She started working there so she could stay longer. Most babies are adopted within days after delivery. She didn't want to leave me."

"What did she say when you told her who you were in the kitchen?"

"She was totally shocked, then she got angry." Tears began to glisten in his deep brown eyes. "I didn't expect that. She cursed at me in the ugliest whisper I have ever heard. She said she hated me and couldn't believe that I thought she wanted to see me."

Miranda furrowed her brows desperately trying to understand. "What happened next?"

"She had her butcher knife in her hand and she pointed it at me. I've never seen anyone so furious." He gulped and wiped the streaming tears from his eyes with one hand. "I'm not sure what happened next. It's a blur."

"But you appeared at the dining room table like nothing had happened."

"I was in shock. I couldn't rationalize the bitter woman who confronted me with what I thought was my loving mother." He shook his head in a quick motion. "Never mind that. I need that photograph." He stepped towards Miranda.

"Look." she could hear the quiver in her voice. "You don't want to make this worse. You say it was an accident. That's your chance to make things right."

He halted and moved a half step backward. "Things can't be right. I have killed my mother. Things can never be right. Ever." He stepped forward again.

"Stay away!" Miranda shouted. "Get back."

"Give me that photograph."

He reached for it but Miranda scurried to the other side of the bush. She was very close to the edge of the cliff.

Joe sighed. "You know you can't get by. Hand me the photograph."

"And then you'll push me over." Miranda moved back another step and bumped into a bolder that prevented her from getting back onto the trail. "How do you know this is the only photograph? My uncle saved everything. The negatives are probably in the attic."

"After I clean up this little mess, I'm going to burn the farmhouse down. That fixes everything."

"You would do that? Burn it down?"

"I'm sure that more evidence is there that you haven't found. I almost succeeded with the kitchen fire. I just have no choice."

"Oh yes you do!" yelled Austin as he lunged for the gun in Joe's hand.

A shot rang out. At such close quarters, it deafened Miranda. She saw the men struggling in extreme slow motion. Joe twisted his gun arm out of Austin's grasp and Miranda leaped over the bush and kicked Joe just behind his knee.

As his leg buckled, Joe tumbled backward over the cliff with his hand still clenched in Austin's shirt. Austin grabbed Joe around the waist. Before they slipped over the edge, Miranda grabbed Austin's belt with both hands and pulled back with all her weight. She strained every muscle in her body to pull harder than she knew she could. Then Joe found a footing and they rebounded forward into her.

They all lay there in the brush panting heavily. Miranda untangled herself, got on all fours, then crawled over to Austin. "Are you all right?"

Austin rubbed a hand over his face, sat up and looked into Miranda's eyes.

"You saved me from going over." He quickly gathered her into his arms.

"You saved me from getting shot." She buried her head in his chest. "We saved each other."

Chapter 36

The fire in the stove was overheating the room, but there were still cold spots in the corners. Austin, Mrs. Hobb, Lily, Iris, Dan, Sheriff Larson, Coroner Larson, and Doris Ann had all stopped by after the largest funeral Wolfe County had seen in a decade. Mrs. Childers had been well respected and beloved. Miranda had invited everyone over for spiced layer cake and coffee.

Sandy was begging for treats by sitting in front of each guest and tilting his head. The puppy eyes usually won over his chosen victim and Sandy would then move to his next quarry.

Mrs. Hobb sat in the most comfortable rocker in the front room with a fork on an empty china plate in her hand. She wore a black crepe de chine dress that was probably older than her granddaughters. "What's happened to Joe? I don't want to lose track of him."

Sheriff Larson cleared his throat and looked at

his wife. She smiled and tilted her head a fraction. "He's in psychiatric evaluation over in Lexington. There'll be charges, of course, and probably prison time, but I'm sure he'll find a new career in counseling his fellow inmates."

There was a sad silence, then Mrs. Hobb spoke up. "That cake was as good as I ever tasted. Whose recipe did you use?"

Miranda grinned from ear to ear. "That's my version of both my grandmother's and her sister's recipe. It was always served at Thanksgiving and Christmas. Mom never had the patience for it."

Austin downed the last of his coffee and stood stiffly, releasing a small groan. "When do you have time?"

"I get my best ideas when I'm sipping shine in the swing on the front porch. That still is the most valuable thing I own, except for the farmhouse, of course—and the van—and Sandy." She laughed.

Austin limped into the dining room and returned to place another plate of spice cake in Mrs. Hobb's hand. He transferred her fork and then whisked away the empty plate. "I thought you might like to try another sample, just to make sure Miranda's got the recipe just right."

"Young man, you need to give that gimpy leg a little rest. You want to get back to work, don't you?"

"I'm lucky that I only pulled a muscle and didn't break my neck. I need to keep moving so it will loosen up. If I sit, it tightens up." He looked over at Miranda. "I still can't believe you got away with only a few scratches."

"Hey, they were deep scratches!"

"Not even stitches. Lucky." He hobbled towards the kitchen with the empty plate.

Mrs. Hobb looked at Miranda with a twinkle in her eye. "I have a feeling you're gonna get a chance to get a lot of things just right."

"I feel very lucky that things have turned out so well. I had ten clients yesterday. Both Lily and Iris are working out very well in the kitchen. With your health issues, it might be wise to let them continue while you recover."

Mrs. Hobb smiled around her next bite of spice cake. "Did you hear from that New York City girl that took off with her girlfriend's money?"

"I called Linda last night and she said that Kelly had returned to the hotel and they reckoned that her hormones were causing some emotional problems. She's a few weeks pregnant and they weren't prepared for the emotional roller-coaster of a first-term pregnancy."

"So, that's why they were moving. They need more room for the baby."

"And everything that a baby needs—an actual kitchen, an actual bedroom, an actual backyard, and also good schools." Miranda smiled. "They're on their way back to New York with my grandmother's rug as the decorating inspiration for their new place."

Sheriff Larson came up to Miranda. "I'm not sure how this will play out, but I want you to know that Felicia and I will go to bat for you with the Lexington Police. It's doubly unfortunate that the photograph went over the cliff."

"They sure are taking an odd stance with this case." Miranda motioned for Sheriff Larson to join her on the couch. "Please sit, my neck is a bit sore."

"I heard about your acrobatics out there on Lover's Leap. What made you think you could save Austin?"

"That's the trick. I didn't think at all. I just dove for his belt and hoped that our combined weight would keep him from going over the edge. It worked. Although I have a new respect for those acrobats you see in those circus acts on television."

Miranda looked through the crowd for Sandy. He had been a popular snuggle bunny for everyone. "Has anyone seen Sandy? Who's got Sandy?"

No one could see him. One of the Hobb sisters said she saw him a few minutes earlier slipping out the back porch. She thought he was just going out to do his business.

Miranda went out the back-porch door. No sign of Sandy. She yelled his name and all she heard in return was the echo of her call rolling off the distant hills. Her next stop was the big tobacco barn—hopefully soon to be the site of her fledgling distillery. Sandy seemed to end up in there anytime he was off leash.

There was no sign of him this time. She continued to call.

She went around to the front of the house and resumed calling. After the echo died, silence.

Where could he be?

She was about to ask her guests to start a search when she heard a sharp yip coming from behind the barn. She sprinted around the back and there was Sandy, struggling up the field. He was dragging something by fits and starts through the dried-up stubble of the harvested tobacco stalks.

When she reached him, he was completely focused on the scrap and wouldn't let Miranda have a look at it. He kept turning his head this way and that and hopping around her in what he thought was the best game of keep-away he had ever known.

"Sandy! Give that up, now." Her stern voice caused Sandy to immediately sit and he dropped the scrap at her feet. He looked like he had been caught stealing and would suffer a horrible punishment.

Miranda's heart melted. She made him sit another few seconds, then began shaking her index finger at him. "You scared me to death. You must never go down into the woods behind the barn. It's not safe for puppies."

She bent down and looked at the scrap that Sandy had dragged back from his adventure. It was a bit of calico feed sack that Miranda remembered being used for kitchen towels a long time ago. It was a very long time ago. An idea appeared.

"Where did you find that, Sandy?"

Sandy tilted his head and looked up. His eyes were definitely questioning her but he had no idea what she wanted. He wiggled his tail and whined.

Miranda picked up the discarded scrap and put it under Sandy's nose. "Here, Sandy. I want more. I want more. Fetch!"

Sandy tilted his head the other way and he hopped up to Miranda's knees and yipped.

"Fetch, Sandy, fetch!"

Sandy sat down again, then stood and yipped. Miranda waved the scrap towards the bottom of the corn stubbled field.

"Fetch, Sandy, fetch!"

Sandy turned towards the tobacco field and began to run at top puppy speed through the cut-off stalks down below the end of the harvested patch. Miranda followed at a comfortable trot and met him at the edge of the woods.

Delicately placing his puppy paws onto a small animal trail, he followed the side of the creek that ran through the farm. Sandy turned left and began to follow a smooth dirt path. He trotted confidently along, following it between the tree line and the rippling stream until he stopped beside a thin waterfall that pitched down an overhang to a pool about fifteen feet below.

He looked back at Miranda to confirm that she was following and then stepped onto a series of flat stones over to the wooded side.

"Do you know where you're going, Sandy?"

He yipped.

"Okay, but I haven't been here since I was a kid. This is where we cooled off in the sweltering summer afternoons. No air conditioning back then."

After pausing to sniff, Sandy plunged onto a smaller trail away from the stream. In a few yards, he stopped and sat. "Is this it?" asked Miranda. She scanned the brush and saw nothing that looked like it had been disturbed recently. Then Sandy wiggled behind a small rare bush of white-haired goldenrod. There were several clumps of the previously endangered plant along this sandstone stretch of small overhanging ledges.

Miranda got down on all fours and followed Sandy into a low but wide opening that led into a small cave about the size of her dining room. It was about seven feet high with a dry floor and a few cracks at the back, which let in a shaft of sunlight.

This was probably one of the caves her uncle had used for making moonshine. Good height, plenty of room, clear running water close by, and vents to let the smoke escape—a perfect spot for distilling his corn-based shine.

There were remnants of an old still along the right-hand side of the space. An old barrel had rotted down to a pile of wood and rings. A circle of rocks looked like where a furnace might have stood and there was a jumble of glass jars along the back wall, some broken, some whole.

Along the left-hand side was an old army-green ammunition box wrapped in another scrap of the ancient calico feed sack.

Heart racing, Miranda grabbed the box and crawled out of the cave. "Let's go, Sandy. I want to see what this is out in the light." Sandy yipped and followed her with his tail wagging like a windshield wiper.

Out on the path, Miranda removed the remaining calico material and grabbed the latch at the front of the box. It wouldn't budge. It was stuck and wouldn't give in to her grunting and straining to get the box open.

"Well, Sandy. This has been out here in the damp for a long time. It won't open easily. But there are plenty of tools in the barn." She got up and started back over the creek. "Come on, Sandy. Let's go!"

She opened the small people-sized door on the back wall of the barn and went into the last stall, which had been used as a workshop for as long as she could remember. The walls were adorned with old tools, jars of rusted nails, and ancient harnesses for farm horses that had died long ago. There was a tall, thick workbench that had a vice mounted on one side. It still smelled of sawdust.

She hefted the ammunition box onto the workbench and grabbed a short pry bar that hung on a nail. Wedging it under the latch, Miranda pressed down using all her weight. The latch moved a tiny bit, but it wouldn't release.

On a shelf above the bench, Miranda saw a can of 3-in-1 multipurpose oil and squirted multiple drops all around the latch.

"That should do it," she said to a patient Sandy. He looked up at her and tilted his head. "We need to be patient. Just a minute more and we'll know what's in this box."

She heard footsteps and Austin stood beside her. "I wondered where you went. I see you've found your little runaway." He scooped up Sandy. "What's going on?"

"Sandy led me to one of the caves where my Uncle Gene made his moonshine." She pointed to the ammunition box. "I also found this wrapped in the same cloth as the rag Sandy dragged back to the house."

His eyes spread wide. "This could be your uncle's secret stash." He reached for the pry bar.

Miranda blocked him with an arm. "No, this is

mine to open. It's on my property and it's my right to find out what he hid in here."

Austin stepped back and executed a princely bow. "Yes, your highness. Pry away."

Miranda laughed with all her heart. "Yes, that did sound officious. Sorry."

Then she stopped to look back at Austin. "I think that's the first genuine laugh I've had this whole week. Thanks for sticking with me through this." She looked at Austin with gratitude. There was great value in a man who could make you laugh.

She turned back to the bench and wedged the pry bar under the latch again. Pressing her full weight on the bar, she heard a sharp crack and the latch flew open and the box tipped over in a cloud of rusty debris. "Wow, that was really stuck."

Miranda picked up the box and sat it upright. She looked at Austin holding Sandy and crossed the fingers of both hands. "Here's wishing for good luck." She closed her eyes and imagined a future here in this lovely farmhouse, with a distillery in one half of the barn and a teaching studio for painting in the other half.

She opened her eyes and peered into the box. There was a carefully folded calico remnant at the top. She lifted that out and found small, one-inch-thick parcels wrapped in yellowed copies of the *Wolfe County News*.

Her excitement spread to Sandy, who wriggled out of Austin's arm to hop onto the top of the workbench. He instantly stuck his nose in the box then sneezed so hard he rolled over. Miranda caught him before he fell off the bench.

"Hang on, Sandy." She put him down on the floor. "We'll know in a second if this box saves the farmhouse." She lifted out the first package, which appeared to be the newest. It was wrapped in volume 73, number 9, dated Friday, November 23, 2018. "This is only a couple of years old."

Unwrapping the parcel revealed a stack of bills precisely sorted in denominations of tens and twenties. Miranda looked over to Austin. With trembling hands, she counted the stack. It came to two thousand dollars. She held her breath as she counted the number of parcels in the box. There were twenty-five parcels. Each parcel was wrapped in a newspaper of a different year.

"This is it! Sandy found his stash. He must have been saving some of his moonshine money every season."

Then she noticed a faded red envelope underneath the money parcels. She held her breath and opened it. The frayed half-sheet of notebook paper listed the complete ingredients for her uncle's famous moonshine. The secret ingredient was there.

She grabbed Austin in a dancing embrace and they spun together in the open section of the barn. After a few swirling moments, Miranda collected herself and dropped her arms. "Oh, sorry, Austin. I didn't mean to bowl you over. I'm so relieved."

"Since you found his stash, I'm assuming you'll be staying around to keep your business running?"

Miranda smiled. "Oh yes! Paint & Shine is here to stay."

CAST OF CHARACTERS

Miranda Dorothy Trent	Protagonist
Sandy	Miranda's male puppy
Doris Ann Morris	Receptionist
Gene Buchanan	Miranda's late uncle, Mom's bachelor brother
Tyler Morgan	Austin's sister
Jerry Rose	Handyman
Joe Creech	Customer from Sydney
Laura Hoffman	Bride client
Brian Hoffman	Groom client
Kelly Davis	NYC client
Linda Sanders	NYC client
Shefton Adams	Local client
Austin Morgan	Local forest ranger
Mrs. Naomi Childers	Principal cook
Mrs. Viola Hobb	Assistant cook
Dan Keystone	Distillery owner
Gary Spenser	Wolfe County deputy
Roy and Elsie Kash	Miranda's neighbors
Sheriff Richard J. Larson	Wolfe County sheriff
Felicia Larson	Coroner
Detective Otis E. Peterson	Lexington Police detective
Officer Young	Lexington Police officer
Iris Hobb	Older granddaughter of cook
Lily Hobb	Younger granddaughter of cook

Recipes for Moonshine Cocktails

Very few package stores outside of Kentucky, West Virginia, and Ohio carry Ale-8-One, but you can substitute Mountain Dew. The cocktail will be a little sweeter, but still delicious.

Paired with Fried Green Tomatoes
Ale & Shine

1-½ oz. clear unflavored moonshine
Ale-8-One Soda or Mountain Dew
Squares of candied ginger
Lemon twist

Fill an 8 oz. mason jar halfway up with ice.
Pour moonshine over ice.
Top up with Ale-8-One and stir.
Garnish with a piece of candied ginger and a lemon twist.

Paired with Venison Stew
Cranberry & Sparkle

½ tsp. cranberry sauce (either homemade or jar)
Sparkling water
1-½ oz. clear unflavored moonshine
Unsweetened cranberry juice
Fresh sprig of rosemary

Place the cranberry sauce in the bottom of an 8 oz. mason jar.

Add 2 oz. sparkling water and mix with the jam.

Fill the jar halfway up with ice.

Pour moonshine over ice.

Top up with cranberry juice and stir.

Garnish with fresh sprig of rosemary.

Paired with Dutch Apple Cobbler
Apple & Shine

1 oz. Ole Smoky Apple Pie Moonshine
½ oz. Grand Marnier
½ oz. Amaretto
Cola to taste
Orange slice
Maraschino cherry

Build the ingredients over ice in a highball glass and stir.

Garnish with an orange slice and a Maraschino cherry.

Cider & Shine

1-½ oz. clear unflavored moonshine
Apple cider to taste
Apple slice
Cinnamon stick

Pour moonshine over ice in a highball glass. Top up with apple cider.

Garnish with a slice of apple and a cinnamon stick.

Recipes for Meals

Air Fryer Fried Green Tomatoes

These fry up super crispy with very little oil. You'll love this healthy way to eat fried green tomatoes!

Course	Appetizer
Prep Time	5 minutes
Cook Time	8 minutes
Total Time	13 minutes
Servings	4

2 green tomatoes, (3 if smaller)
Salt and pepper
½ cup all-purpose flour
2 large eggs
½ cup buttermilk
1 cup Panko crumbs
1 cup yellow cornmeal
Mister filled with olive oil or vegetable oil
Hot sauce (optional)

Cut tomatoes into ¼-inch slices. Pat dry with paper towels and season well with salt and pepper.

Place flour in a shallow dish or pie plate, or for easy clean-up use a paper plate.

Whisk together eggs and buttermilk in a shallow dish or bowl.

Combine Panko crumbs and cornmeal in a shallow dish or pie plate, or for easy clean-up use a paper plate.

Preheat air fryer to 400° F.

Coat the tomato slices in the flour, dip in egg mixture, and then press panko crumb mixture into both sides. Sprinkle with a little more salt.

Mist air fryer basket with oil and place 4 tomato slices in the basket. Mist the tops with oil. Air-fry for 5 minutes.

Flip tomatoes over, mist with oil, and air-fry 3 more minutes.

Serve with hot sauce if desired.

Venison Stew

Course	Main
Prep Time	20 minutes
Slow Cooker Time	7 hours
Total Time	7 hours and 20 minutes
Servings	4

3 stalks celery, diced
½ cup chopped onion
2 cloves garlic, minced
1 tablespoon chopped fresh parsley
2 tablespoons vegetable oil
2 pounds venison stew meat
Salt and pepper to taste
Dried oregano to taste
Dried basil to taste
1 cup tomato sauce
½ cup dry red wine
½ cup water

Place the celery, onion, garlic, and parsley in the bottom of a slow cooker.

Heat the oil in a large frying pan over medium-high heat. Brown the venison well in two batches and add to the slow cooker. Season to taste with salt, pepper, oregano, and basil.

Pour in the tomato sauce, red wine, and water. Cook on Low for 7 to 10 hours.

Classic Cornbread Sticks

Course	Main
Prep Time	5 minutes
Cook Time	15 minutes
Total Time	20 minutes
Servings	14

1 tablespoon unsalted butter, melted
1 cup plain yellow cornmeal
½ cup self-rising flour
2 tablespoons sugar
1¼ teaspoons kosher salt, divided
¼ teaspoon ground black pepper
1 cup whole buttermilk
⅓ cup vegetable oil
1 large egg, lightly beaten
Softened butter, for serving

Preheat oven to 425° F.

Brush wells of two 7-stick cast-iron corn stick pans with melted butter. Place pans in oven to pre-heat for 5 minutes.

In a large bowl, mix together cornmeal, flour, sugar, ¾ teaspoon salt, and pepper.

In a small bowl, stir up buttermilk, oil, and egg.

Make a well in the center of the dry ingredients; stir in buttermilk mixture just until combined.

Carefully remove hot pans from oven. Sprinkle wells with remaining ½ teaspoon salt. Divide batter among prepared wells.

Bake until golden brown and crisp, about 15 minutes. Remove from pan immediately. Serve with butter, if desired.

Dutch Apple Cobbler in Cast-Iron Skillet

Course	Dessert
Hands-on Time	1 hour and 40 minutes
Total Time	1 hour and 40 minutes
Servings	8

Filling
4 tablespoons unsalted butter
1 cup light brown sugar, packed
½ cup granulated sugar
Juice of 1 lemon
1 tablespoon all-purpose flour
4 pounds Granny Smith apples (about 8–10),
    peeled, cored, and cut into ½-inch-thick slices
1 teaspoon ground cinnamon
½ teaspoon ground nutmeg
½ teaspoon kosher salt
Topping
1 cup all-purpose flour
¼ cup granulated sugar, divided
1 teaspoon baking powder
¼ teaspoon kosher salt
1 cup heavy cream
2 teaspoons cinnamon
4 tablespoons unsalted butter, melted
Vanilla ice cream, for serving

To make the filling:
Heat the oven to 375° F. In a 12-inch cast-iron skillet, melt the butter over medium heat. Add the brown sugar, granulated sugar, lemon juice, and flour, and cook until sugars dissolve, about 5 minutes. Add apples and continue to cook, stirring oc-

casionally, until the apples have slightly softened, 7 to 10 minutes. Stir in the cinnamon, nutmeg, and salt, and remove from the heat.

To make the topping:

In a medium bowl, use a fork to mix together the flour, 2 tablespoons of the granulated sugar, the baking powder, and the salt. Gradually pour in the heavy cream, and using the fork, to bring mixture together into a sticky dough. Scatter pieces of the dough over the top of the apple mixture in the skillet.

In a small bowl, stir together the remaining 2 tablespoons granulated sugar and the cinnamon. Brush the top of the dough with the melted butter and sprinkle with the cinnamon-sugar. Place the skillet on a rimmed baking sheet to catch any drips and bake until top is golden brown and both the filling and the topping are cooked through, about 40 minutes.

Serve warm, preferably with vanilla ice cream.

Peanut Butter Potato Pinwheels

Course:	Dessert
Prep Time	30 minutes
Cook Time	0 minutes
Refrigeration	2 hours
Total Time	2½ hours
Servings	4

¼ cup unseasoned mashed potatoes
2 Tbsp. milk or nondairy beverage
1 tsp vanilla extract
1 pinch salt
16 oz. pkg. confectioners' sugar
2 Tbsp. confectioners' sugar for dusting
⅓ cup peanut butter, or to taste

Combine mashed potatoes, milk, vanilla extract, and salt in a bowl. Reserving two tablespoons of confectioners' sugar for later, stir confectioners' sugar into potato mixture until a dough consistency is reached. Refrigerate dough until chilled, at least an hour.

Sprinkle reserved confectioners' sugar on a cutting board or waxed paper. Roll dough into a large rectangle on prepared surface. Spread enough peanut butter on top layer of dough to cover. Roll up dough into a jelly roll shape; refrigerate roll for another hour. Slice dough into pinwheels to serve. They taste even better the next day after refrigeration overnight.

Cheesy Bits

1 cup chopped white onion
1 cup grated cheddar cheese or use a cheese mix
1 cup mayonnaise
6 slices of sourdough bread (or any sliced bread on hand)

Preheat the oven to 375° F. Line a cookie sheet with parchment paper.

Mix chopped onions, grated cheese, and mayonnaise in a bowl until thoroughly blended. Cut bread slices into fourths and heap about a tablespoon of the mixture onto each piece, covering the slice from edge to edge. Place on the cookie sheet with about a half an inch separation.

Bake for about 8–10 minutes until topping is melty and browned around the edges.

Let cool for about two minutes. Serve immediately.

Makes 24.

Also from Cheryl Hollon: the final installment of the Webb's Glass Shop Mystery series

Down in Flames

A fatal hit-and-run in front of Savannah Webb's glass shop proves to be no accident. . . .

A highlight of Savannah's new glass bead workshop is a technique called flame-working, which requires the careful wielding of acetylene torches. Understandably, safety is a top priority. But as Savannah is ensuring her students' safety inside, a hit-and-run driver strikes down a pedestrian outside her shop.

The victim is Nicole Borawski, the bartender-manager at the Queen's Head Pub, owned by Savannah's boyfriend, Edward. It quickly becomes clear that this was no random act of vehicular manslaughter. Now the glass shop owner is all fired up to get a bead on the driver—before someone else meets a dead end. . . .

On sale now

Enjoy the following excerpt from *Down in Flames*.

Chapter 1

"Fire!" screamed Rachel Rosenberg. She pointed at her twin sister. "Faith started a fire."

Savannah Webb sniffed the distinctive odor of burning hair. She ran over to Faith's student bench, grabbing the fire extinguisher on the way. She quickly scanned each twin's short white hair, which appeared untouched. Faith was near tears but pointed to a pink cashmere sweater that lay in a smoldering heap on the floor behind the metal work stool.

Faith snuffled like a toddler. "I tossed it over there."

As normal, the twins had been the first students to arrive. Also, as usual, they dressed alike and wore head-to-toe vibrant pink. From pink ballet flats and slacks embroidered with flamingoes, to cotton sweater-sets with flamingos screen-printed on the front. All topped by large flamingo earrings and pink polished nails.

Using two rapid spurts from the extinguisher, Savannah sprayed the burning sweater. Then she stomped on the remains for good measure. She turned to her perennial students, her throat still pulsing from the surge of adrenalin. "Are you all right? Did you get burned?"

"No." Faith sat very still with her eyes wide, staring at the sodden lump of pink char. "I forgot about the rule banning loose clothing. I got a chill and drew the sweater over my shoulders. My sleeve must have dangled across the flame." Faith's eyes began to fill with tears. "I'm sorry."

The twins were typically aloof, tightly controlled, but friendly. Emotion at this level felt awkward.

Savannah heard the pitch of her voice rise. "What possessed you to turn on the torch? We haven't started class."

Faith's eyes grew even wider. "I just don't know. It seemed to call to me to turn it on. I couldn't resist. I've never had that happen before."

Savannah covered her mouth with a hand and pressed her lips together. *I'm so relieved they're okay!*

Rachel huffed a great breath and put both hands on her hips. "You've always been clumsy. You should have waited for Savannah to tell us exactly how to light the torch. Perhaps this class isn't such a good idea."

Savannah put an arm around each twin and drew them into a warm side hug. "Ladies, you know that at Webb's Glass Shop, a class wouldn't be complete without you two. You've attended every class offered for the last—how many years?"

The twins looked at each other and Rachel shrugged. "It's been at least five years, don't you think?"

"Yes," said Faith. "We were walking by and noticed the poster in the window offering beginning stained-glass classes and we went right in. You know, of course, that your dad was a wonderful instructor."

Savannah smiled. "Yes, he was." She paused for just a second. His loss was still a raw spot. "Now that he's gone, you've been my security blanket and my dear friends. I need you. Don't decide about the class right now."

Faith wrung her hands. "But I could have burned the shop down. You might have lost the whole building." She put her hands over her eyes and began to cry.

"Stop that. I'm well prepared for any little accident. My friend over at Zen Glass Studio says that if there's not at least one fire a day, he's not making money. He runs a lot of students through his shop. Close calls are part of the deal."

Savannah felt her heart pounding and she huffed out a breath. Near accidents caused an aftereffect, but they were far better than a real accident. She felt her confidence drop as she thought of her six beginner students wielding molten glass inches in front of their faces.

Rachel gently pushed Savannah back and folded Faith into her arms. "Don't fret, sister. It wasn't a problem. You saw how quickly Savannah put out the fire."

Faith lowered her hands and gulped a shuddering breath. "I'm so sorry."

Savannah put a hand on each twin's shoulder. "You both enjoyed the sand-etching class, didn't you?"

The twins stepped apart, looked at each other and then glanced away.

"Remember that and give flameworking a chance. I won't hear a word about quitting until you've gotten to the end of today's class."

"But—" chirped Faith.

Savannah pointed like a teacher. "Back to your workstations."

Rachel and Faith returned to their work stools. They folded their hands and raised their chins. They looked ready to pay attention to the first lesson in making a glass bead.

Savannah sighed deeply. Her relief that no one had been injured was both personal and calculating. An accident could tarnish the reputation of the family-owned glass shop that she had inherited from her father. Even though her small business was doing well, it would all collapse in the wake of burning the whole building down.

She turned to the other three new students. "This might have been the best unplanned lesson ever. This is not a risk-free art form." They were wide-eyed and solemn with nodding heads. "I'll expect your full attention during the safety briefing."

She scooped up the sodden lump of burned sweater with a dust pan and dumped it into the trash bin. It stood next to the fifty-gallon drum that contained their unusable glass. It was nearly full and would need dumping into the bright blue city recyclables bin in the next day or so.

Today was her first afternoon teaching a workshop in glass-bead creation. The method called flameworking, or sometimes lamp-working, utilized acetylene torches fastened to the front of each table, facing away from the students. The beads were formed by manipulating colored glass rods through the flame.

Safety for the students was always Savannah's primary worry when working with an open flame, so she had been testing the torches one by one when Faith let the sleeve of her sweater catch fire.

To accommodate her growing student clientele, Savannah had installed all the student workstations in the newly acquired expansion space of Webb's Glass Shop. She owned the entire building, so when one of her long-term tenants retired and closed their art-supply retail business, she took the opportunity to expand. Luckily, the expanded classroom was adjacent to her current location. Savannah hired contractors to remove the adjoining wall and created a larger student space.

That left two more businesses in her building that still held on to their leases. One was a nail salon and the other a consignment shop. She rarely raised her rent more than two percent a year because loyalty meant so much more to her than risking an empty rental.

Because the flameworking torches needed powerful exhaust fans to remove noxious fumes and expel clouds of glass dust, she had placed the workstations on the back wall facing the alley and had a contractor knock small holes into the outside wall for the fans. The construction work on the six-station teaching space was finished mere minutes before the class began at one o'clock this afternoon.

There was a little space for her personal station, but students brought money in the door, so that work would be finished later. All but one student had shown up early to learn bead-making. They had also gotten an unplanned show and prime example of the dangers of working with an open flame.

The bell over the entry door jangled. "Am I too late?" asked a thirty-something tall woman dressed in muscle-hugging black athletic wear. "Have I missed something important?" Her pale face flushed and a sheen of sweat formed on her brow.

Savannah walked into the display room and led her into the new classroom. "A little, but you're in good time." Savannah shook her head. "We've had a bit of delay getting started. Anyway, you're the last one to arrive, so our class is complete. If you could take a seat at the end workstation, we can all make our introductions. After that I'll make some important safety and housekeeping announcements, and then we'll begin."

Savannah pointed to the late-arriving student. "Welcome. We'll start introductions with you. Give us your name, where you live, and what you want to get out of this class."

The pale lady looked extremely uncomfortable at the notion of speaking. She cleared her throat not once, but three times. "I'm Myla Katherine Nedra, but everyone calls me Myla Kay. I'm a seasonal resident from Ann Arbor, Michigan. I'm recently widowed, and I couldn't stomach the idea of a cold winter in our big house all alone, so I

rented one of the tiny bungalow cottages in a
courtyard within a few blocks of here. This class
should be a great distraction and will hopefully be
a way to get to know the neighborhood."

Savannah raised her eyebrows. *That's an unusual
way to introduce yourself—recently widowed.* Most women
would be reluctant to admit that so quickly. She's
confident.

"Thank you, Myla Kay. You must be in that street
of tiny houses near my house. I live right down the
block from you. I find the tiny-house zone in the
Kenwood Historic Neighborhood fascinating, although I could never live in one. Which one did
you rent?"

"I chose the converted Blue Bird school bus."

Savannah bobbed her head. "I walked through
that one while I was at the Tiny Home Festival last
year. The bus has a very colorful history. Remind
me to tell you about it."

She's awfully young to be a widow.

Savannah looked toward the next student. He
adjusted the collar of his green Columbia fishing
shirt and stood in front of his work stool. He said
in a booming voice, "My name is Lonnie Mc-
Carthy. I'm from Pittsburgh. My wife and I are staying downtown with friends for a few weeks and I
have some basic experience with making stained
glass. I want to present my wife with some handmade beads for her fancy Pandora bracelet." He
gave everyone a politician's wide-toothed smile
and sat.

The third student, with brown hair framing soft
brown-eyes, looked as gawky as her sixteen years of
age. She popped up before Savannah could signal

her turn. "Hi, I'm Patricia Karn." Her voice was high and thin, exactly like her teenage figure. "I'm here from Indian Rocks Beach. I'm a native Floridian but my parents are from Akron, Ohio. I want to make beads as Christmas gifts to send up to my six cousins up North. I'm home schooled and this class will fulfill my art elective credits for the year."

"Thanks, Patricia. Did you bring your signed release?"

"Yes, ma'am." Patricia pulled a folded slip of paper from her back pocket and handed it over.

The next student sat until Savannah nodded toward him. He was white-haired with a close-clipped beard and mustache. He gripped the back of the chair and stood, favoring one knee. Even at his full height, he was a little stooped. "I'm Herbert Klug." He gave a sheepish shrug of his shoulders. "I'm here because my wife wants me out of the house."

Everyone laughed. His timing and stage presence reminded Savannah of a stand-up comedian.

He smiled at the reaction. "No, I'm kidding. That's not exactly true. I'm a retired research professor. My lab was downtown at the Bayboro Campus of the University of South Florida." His well-modulated voice had everyone's attention. "Although I haven't created anything in glass as an artist, I have certainly made plenty of glass pipettes for my lab. This is my chance to explore flameworking as an artist." He maneuvered cautiously back onto his work stool.

He must have been an excellent instructor. Edward had been prodding Savannah to hire more staff. Edward was still coming to grips with his new role as her fiancé. He was cautious about giving her advice about her business, but felt compelled to solve her tendency to overcommit, quickly followed by overworking. *However, just because he's a research professor doesn't mean he'll have an affinity for teaching civilians. I'll see how he survives the chaos of the class.*

Next were Faith and Rachel. Savannah knew they were more than eighty years old, but their looks and actions declared middle-sixties. The twins deftly avoided all discussions about their age. They stood up together. "Hello, everyone. I'm Rachel Rosenberg and, obviously, this is my twin sister, Faith."

"We've been coming to all of the Webb's Glass Shop classes for years," said Faith.

Savannah stepped between them and put an arm around each twin. "Webb's Glass Shop, like any artistic enterprise, needs patrons. These two ladies have been attending classes for years and knew my father, who started this business from nothing. Without this level of support, the arts have no chance to survive." She turned her head to each twin. "I appreciate your patronage more than I can say."

"Yes." Rachel looked at Savannah. "We find the challenge of learning new skills keeps us young."

They sat down with their backs to the workstations and Savannah felt all eyes upon her.

She had taken the opportunity to brush up on her flameworking skills at the nearby Zen Glass Studio. She wasn't like her dad, in that she was open to using any resource available to make her classes the best they could be. He had been more of an "if it isn't available here, it isn't worth having" management style.

The Zen studio was less than a mile away and, like hers, was a small shop that catered to beginning glass students and offered work space and time for advanced students. The owner, Josh Poll, cheerfully advised Savannah about how to set up the student work space along with a demonstration workbench.

Josh had been turning away students and felt another teaching venue would be good for both Webb's Glass Shop and Zen Glass Studio. There were enough snowbirds and retirees seeking adult education or lifestyle classes to keep the arts-based businesses solvent. It was another example of how the business owners supported each other. They were still competitors, but all boats rise on an incoming tide.

"Thanks, everyone. First things first. I need to cover the safety issues. It is important to wear formfitting clothing, pinned-back hair and closed-toe shoes. Glass does occasionally drop onto the floor—but mostly it will stay on your work surface. If it does drop on the rubber mats, it will flame up. Let me handle it. I'll pick up the glass with pliers and stamp on the flames. It cools surprisingly quickly, but don't touch it." She lowered her head a touch and winked at Faith. "No loose sweaters on the shoulders or jackets tied around the waist. Understood?"

The students nodded their agreement.

"Okay, then. Everyone, follow me."

Savannah walked over to the back door, went outside and held the door for everyone to follow.

She pointed to the newly installed tanks that sat in a fenced-in enclosure. She pulled out a key and unlocked the gate.

"This is the butane tank—just like the ones you might use for your barbecue grill." She pointed to the controls. "Here's the knob to turn off the gas. I will probably never ask you to do this, but if I ask—turn the knob to the right. Remember this phrase: Righty tighty, lefty loosey. It's a memory trick for: Turn right for OFF and turn left for ON. That's universal. Okay, back inside."

She led everyone to a stainless-steel container not far from the end of the long workbench. There was a workstation space on the far-left side of the back wall that Savannah planned to use as her own, so it had a higher quality torch and more advanced tools.

"This is the control for the oxygen tank. The same thing applies—Righty tighty, lefty loosey."

"Question," said Herbert. "I thought we would be using those portable torches that you can get at the hardware store."

"Those don't get hot enough long enough for us to work the glass. We need our temperatures to be at least 4500 degrees. Mixing the butane with oxygen gets us there. Good question. What did you use in your lab?"

He shrugged his shoulders. "Since I was only modifying thin lab glass, I just used the Bunsen burners that were already in the lab."

"We need more heat since we're going to combine solid glass rods," said Savannah. "Now for the first aid salve you're most likely to use more than anything else. Let me introduce you to Bernie the aloe plant." On a plant stand against the right-hand wall was a moldy clay pot that contained a strange plant with ugly spikes sticking out in every direction. "If you get a slight burn, pluck off a stem, split it open, and slather the juice all over the burn. It will seal it so you can keep on working. Obviously, if you get a bad burn, we'll take further action, but for minor ones, Bernie is your friend."

Patricia stiffened. "I know this sounds silly, but I've never worked with fire before. I'm actually very nervous."

Herbert learned over and said in a low voice, "Don't let that stop you. You need practice in order to get comfortable." He quickly glanced over to Savannah and then straightened. "Oh, I'm sorry. It's not my place to answer questions. Force of habit, I'm afraid."

"But you're completely right." Savannah noted his deft handling of Patricia's fears. "It's perfectly normal to be cautious, but not to the point where you don't learn. I spent my first weeks near Seattle at Pilchuck Glass School making paperweights. I made so many I could do them in my sleep."

Patricia raised her hand. "Did you meet the famous Chihuly? I love his work! I practically haunt his museum downtown."

Savannah raised her eyebrows. "We're very lucky he decided to put a museum here. Anyway, the demand for his time was incredible, so he couldn't come near the beginning studio, but I met him later when I was one of the senior apprentices. He radiated amazing charisma—you couldn't help hanging on his every word." She paused, remembering her apprentice days.

"Gosh," said Patricia. "I've never met anyone who worked with him."

"It was the experience of a lifetime." Savannah felt a dreamy smile softening her jaw. She shook her head a bit. "Anyway, back to our class. Let's begin by becoming familiar with the tools lying on your workstation."

Each student's work area was set up with the tools they would need for the class. Savannah then described the names of the tools laid out neatly on each side of the torch. She explained how to use the tweezers, a graphite marver, a mosaic cutter, a bottle of bead release, a tungsten bead reamer, a rod rest for the glass rods, and a mandrel for holding the bead as it was formed.

She held a pair of bright blue glasses up for everyone to see. "Here's your most important safety equipment. These are didymium glasses that not only protect your eyes, but they filter out the orange sodium flare, so you can see how to manipulate the molten glass."

She walked over to her teaching workstation. "This is your primary tool for flameworking. It's called a hothead torch, which provides as big a flame as you can get with this style torch. The bigger the flame, the more BTUs and the faster you can work the glass.

"Your torch has two nozzles. Each nozzle has a dial for butane and a dial for oxygen. The small nozzle on top is for light work with the smaller rods of glass that don't require maximum temperature. The second nozzle right underneath the small one is for larger rods of glass as well as for your finishing steps—we'll talk about those later.

"To light your torch, you can use either a striker"—she held it up and made sparks by compressing the handles—"or a match." She held up a small box of wooden matches. "Most students find it easier to simply use a match or cigarette lighter." Savannah shot a glance at the Rosenberg sisters and made sure she had their full attention. She selected a match and lit one using the grit panel on the side of the box. "Turn the knob slightly to the left to start the flow of gas—remember lefty loosey— then hold the match right against the torch." The torch whooshed a bright orange flame.

Savannah blew out the match. "Now you turn on the oxygen. You want to adjust the two so that the flame is steady." Savannah turned the flame down until it was a steady pure blue. "Now go ahead and try it at your station."

Everyone except Herbert used matches. He expertly clicked the striker so that it sputtered huge sparks, lit his torch, and adjusted the oxygen and butane knobs to achieve a perfectly steady blue flame.

Not his first rodeo.

Savannah adjusted the gas-flow knobs on each student's torch so everyone had an efficient setting. Both Rachel and Faith overreacted to the sweater fire to the point that their flames were barely lit at all.

"Ladies, you couldn't toast a marshmallow on those flames." She adjusted their torches. "Can you hear the difference between a bad mix of air and butane and a good one? This is a good one." Then she increased the oxygen and the torch responded with a loud rushing sound. "This is a bad mix." She readjusted the torch so that if fell nearly silent. "Good. I want everyone to practice adjusting your torch."

After a few minutes, even the twins seemed more confident with the adjustment knobs on their torches. "Okay, now we're ready to start. The process we need to practice first is to punty up a clear glass rod with a colored rod. We will be repeating this process many times, so the more practice the better. It is not fun to be working on a piece and have the colored glass fall off the punty."

Savannah held up a rod of clear class about twelve inches long and a short three-inch rod of lime-green glass. "Punty is the name for any piece of material that is used to hold and manipulate glass. It's also used as a verb, such as 'punty this piece of glass.'" She demonstrated the steps required to join a single-color rod to a clear rod. "The trick here is to heat both glass rods to the same temperature, so they will form a good join."

Savannah explained each step in the basic process of making a glass medallion with an attached glass loop. After she showed the finished medallion to each student, she slipped the whole business into an upright kiln to keep it warm. The students caught up by selecting their medallion colors. Then they puntied each color onto clear rods.

"How hot does the glass get while in the flame?" asked Patricia.

"Good question," said Savannah. "Glass begins to melt at six- to eight-hundred degrees. It varies with thickness, of course. As you get more experienced with manipulating the hot glass, you'll be able to tell its temperature just by looking at it."

The class progressed, with Savannah working with each student on their first attempt at a medallion. Except for Herbert. He crafted a perfectly symmetrical oval with four swirls of colored glass in a pattern. "Wow. That's gorgeous. Your science-lab experience is serving you well."

He ducked his head a bit. "I have to confess. I've tried my hand at the creative side of glasswork before, but I became fascinated with all the demonstrations you can find on the internet. However, I'm delighted by how much more I retain with in-person instruction."

Myla Kay formed her first medallion using a Salvador Dali–like selection of vivid high-contrast colors—yellow, azure, lime, and royal purple.

"Well done, Myla Kay," said Savannah. "That was risky. Sometimes a high contrast selection of colors will result in a horrible muddy mixture, but yours is terrific. Beautiful!"

Myla Kay smiled broadly. "I have some experience with color. I like to paint. Actually, I like to paint a lot."

"Well, that explains your sense of color. Good job."

There were no accidents, and at the end of the class each student left behind a newly formed glass medallion annealing in the kiln. As the Rosenberg twins—always first to arrive, and last to leave—wished her a good day and walked out the door, Savannah programmed the kiln to start the cool-down cycle in four hours from now. The kiln would do its work after hours. When she first took over the glass shop, she'd felt uneasy leaving the kilns powered on. Not anymore. The kiln was absolutely safe, and it rested on fire-proof bricks, which were even safer.

Amanda Blake, office manager and instructor for Beginning Stained Glass, walked into the flame-working classroom. "So, how was the first day of bead-making class?" Amanda's voice sounded flat and toneless.

Savannah glanced up at her, concerned. "Exhausting, but exciting. I can't believe that two hours have flown by! Are you on your way to see your mother?" Savannah noted the somber outfit. A zaftig woman of size, Amanda's appearance typically displayed her bohemian side. Today she wore muted shades of beige. Her normally neon spiked hair was brushed down into a soft, wavy, fawn-like color.

"I did the Monday inventory of supplies and got everything ready for day two of the stained-glass class. The new students are great. They're attentive and calm—perfect. I'll help you clean up here and then push off for an evening of reading to Mom."

Without another word, Savannah walked over and folded Amanda into a huge hug. Amanda reacted by stiffening, then relaxed into the comforting gesture. In a flash, she was sobbing like a toddler. *Poor dear.* Savannah gave her a light squeeze and rubbed her back in small, soothing circles.

After several long moments, following a whole-body shudder, Amanda stepped back and snuffled. "Thanks for the attack hug. I'm going through an emotional roller coaster. I'm either stiff and stoic or a crying waterspout. I don't know how I would cope with the hospice visits without you, Edward, the Rosenberg twins, and even young Jacob giving me the support I need."

Savannah nodded. Jacob was her late father's final trainee in a long line of apprentices who benefited from learning to make glass art. His parents had purchased his adorable service beagle, Suzy, to let others know by a special bark if Jacob began to have an anxiety attack. She also soothed him with her calm presence. If left alone, he could escalate into a full-blown asthmatic crisis. The inhaler was stowed in the pocket of Suzy's blue service pack. "We're all here for you." Savannah continued to rub Amanda's back. "We've weathered through a few crises together."

"As your investigative posse—we have certainly made a difference."

"What are you reading to her?"

"You're not going to believe this. She *looks* like she would be the perfect candidate for listening to a cozy mystery with a magical cat who solves the murders. But, nope. She is having me read a Tim Dorsey thriller."

"Which one?"

"*The Pope of Palm Beach,* the newest installment of the Serge Storm series. When she still had good mobility, she never missed his signings down at Haslam's Book Store. I think his books keep her wondering what horrible thing he will make happen next."

Savannah shook her head and grinned. "You can't fault her logic. I didn't sleep properly for a week after I read that one. I'll stop by tomorrow night and read to her for a while."

Amanda beamed. "She would love that. Oh, I

nearly forgot. You can bring Rooney. The nurses love fur baby visits. His big, cuddly dog energy would liven up the evening for everyone."

Savannah imagined the disruption her yearling Weimaraner would bring to the peaceful facility for hospice patients who didn't have a home setup for receiving palliative care. On the other hand, the staff were experts in end-of-life experiences. They would know right away if his behavior was appropriate. "I'll think about it. If he's in a calm mood—absolutely."

"Anyway, if there's nothing else, I'm off." Amanda hiked her patchwork hobo handbag onto her shoulder and left by the back door.

The over-the-door bell sounded a single ting. Eighteen-year-old Jacob Underwood entered the front door and let his service dog, Suzy, lead the way into the shop. Jacob had a strange knack for keeping the bell practically silent when arriving. Savannah thought it was a personal challenge he was playing against himself.

He walked into the flameworking studio and handed Savannah a black journal. He didn't look her in the eye as he said, "Webb's Studio needs more supplies." Jacob's condition used to be called Asperger's syndrome, but after the recently revised medical definition, he was medically classified as a high-functioning autistic.

"Thanks, Jacob. I appreciate that you ask each artist what supplies they want for their works in progress. This is very good practice in communicating with clients."

Savannah had recently promoted Jacob to the position of journeyman in charge of Webb's Studio. It was a new venture housed in a converted warehouse with by-the-month rental work spaces for intermediate and advanced students.

"I'll just gather the requested supplies tonight and drop them off at the studio for you to pass out tomorrow." Savannah looked at Jacob to be sure that he understood.

He nodded again and picked up Suzy, then managed to get out the front door without the bell making a single sound.

She chuckled. *Looks like he won the game today. Jacob 1, doorbell 42 million.*

As Savannah entered the final key to shut down the cash register, she heard a sharp yelp directly in front of Webb's Glass Shop, followed by a sickening thud. Next, she heard squealing tires and then a roaring engine. Out the front window, she glimpsed a white car flying down the street.

Jacob! Please don't let it be Jacob. Savannah bolted out, nearly tearing the bell off the door.

Jacob stood outside on the sidewalk as stiff as the tinman from *Wizard of Oz*. He let out a keening scream, which was overlaid by a howl from Suzy.

Jacob abruptly stopped screaming. Suzy went silent as well.

As Savannah moved to stand in front of him, a yard away, a tsunami of relief rushed over her. She quietly said his name. She was careful not to touch him. A critical precaution to reduce the chances of Jacob having a panic attack.

Savannah noticed that Suzy appeared calm, so Jacob didn't need his inhaler. He stared down the street without acknowledging her presence. She made no attempt to get his attention.

Savannah followed his gaze out on the street. Crumpled faceup near the curb lay a woman dressed in khaki trousers and a white Queen's Head Pub logo shirt.

"Nicole!" Savannah shrieked. Nicole was completely unresponsive. Not even an eyelash fluttered.

Terrified, Savannah became hypersensitive to every sound around her. The murmur of onlookers, the slowing of traffic in the street, the mockingbird singing nearby.

Nicole was a good friend. She worked in the pub right next door, owned by Savannah's fiancé, Edward.

Shaking herself into action, Savannah placed two fingers on Nicole's throat. She detected an irregular heartbeat. It was barely noticeable, and her infrequent breaths were shallow.

She pulled back Nicole's thick blond hair to reveal heavy-lidded eyes. There were streaks of road filth down her face and her legs didn't line up properly. From the back of her head, a terrible wound leaked a small stream of blood, which made its way to the curb.

This is bad.

"Call 911," she yelled to the gathering crowd of bystanders, pointing at a balding man with his cell phone already in hand. "Hurry! She's still alive."

The man dialed.

A sour taste hit the back of Savannah's throat. She knew better than to try to move a victim of trauma. Instead, she gathered Nicole's limp and clammy hand in both of hers. "Nicole, can you hear me? Stay with me, girl. Help is coming."

Connect with  U(s)

Visit us online at
KensingtonBooks.com
to read more from your favorite authors, see books
by series, view reading group guides, and more.

Join us on social media

for sneak peeks, chances to win books and prize packs,
and to share your thoughts with other readers.

facebook.com/kensingtonpublishing
twitter.com/kensingtonbooks

Tell us what you think!

To share your thoughts, submit a review,
or sign up for our eNewsletters, please visit:
KensingtonBooks.com/TellUs.